FALLEN

Also by Carey Baldwin

Judgment
Confession

FALLEN

A Cassidy & Spenser Thriller

CAREY BALDWIN

WITNESS
IMPULSE

An Imprint of HarperCollinsPublishers

EPub Edition JUNE 2015 ISBN: 9780062387066

Print Edition ISBN: 9780062387073

10 9 8 7 6 5 4 3 2 1

For my husband, Bill
It's a yes from me, baby.

Prologue

IT WAS THE kind of scream that could change everything. Elwood Lawrence, known to his squad mates as Woody on account of his obvious appreciation of the hookers Vice dragged in, felt the marrow curdle inside his bones. Reaching for his preferred off-duty carry, the Glock 27 holstered at his hip, his muscles drew tight. In a heartbeat, he was spring-loaded for action, knees flexed, fingers twitching near his gun, gaze searching the crowded street.

Hollywood Boulevard to be exact.

The very personification of this town.

Here on this famous thoroughfare, out-of-work actors, tourists, and drug dealers all shared the same space, basking in the gloried California sun, sucking in air that was both heavy with the smog of despair and high on the promise of dreams come true.

A moment of tense anticipation. Then the Prince, Johnny Depp, and Cat Woman look-alikes stopped working the street for tips and went into suspended animation—the scream had been that powerful. Woody's ears pricked. Sounded like it'd come from directly above them. Tourists looked up, craning their necks, as if waiting for the show to begin. But he knew this wasn't part of the festival-o-crap put on for out-of-towners. Knifing through the pedestrians with his shoulders, he sprang in front of his charge, actor Jamie Robb, like a human shield.

What the hell?

Had the last thing he'd expected actually happened? Could there be a legit threat to Jamie Robb? Had the former child star's request for personal security at the unveiling of his refurbished Walk of Fame star been motivated by more than an inflated ego? True, his star had been vandalized—hence the replacement ceremony—but that was probably kids.

One beat followed another, passing uneventfully.

Woody flexed, then relaxed his shaky right hand, keeping it close to his pistol. It didn't figure anyone would have it out for Jamie Robb. Unlike your average everyday former child star, Jamie hadn't dropped out, coked up, or blown all his dough on whores. He was as squeaky-clean today as when he'd played the role of eight-year-old Chester in *Family Rules* some twenty-odd years ago. By all accounts, he'd never filed a lawsuit against his parents, cheated on his wife, or punched a paparazzo.

Nor was Robb the type to attract stalkers and what-have-you. He was more the type you barely noticed until he was right in front of you. Up close and personal, though, Woody had to admit he could still catch a whiff of little *Jimmy* Robb's secret sauce. But whatever remained of young Jimmy's charisma was mostly hidden by the extra pounds, balding visage, and defeated eyes of old Jamie. *Old* being a relative term. Child stars passed their prime so quick, they might as well be aging in dog years.

Jamie Robb was yesterday's headline. And Woody, on personal leave (a polite way of saying Captain Jeffers had given him thirty days to get sober) from the Hollywood division of the LAPD, wasn't the freshest slice of pizza pie himself. This bodyguard gig should've been a low-risk high-reward way to beef up Woody's underfed bank account, and hopefully that was just exactly how things would turn out.

Another empty moment passed.

Whatever that scream had been, it seemed like it would stay a mystery, and that was a-okay by him.

He eased his hand off his pistol.

At about the same time he came to the relieved conclusion that nothing other than the usual mischief was afoot, the crowd seemed to do the same. Marilyn Monroe switched on a fan beneath a full fifties-style skirt. SpiderMan motioned over a youngster in sloppy shorts, while his father pulled out a wallet and filled the tip jar. Milling, gawking, and hustling resumed per Hollywood Boulevard protocol.

"What was that?" Jamie Robb looked around almost hopefully. Woody would bet a box of Krispy Kremes that Jamie's heart had beat like an excited puppy's when he'd first heard that cry. He'd bet a year's supply of coffee for dunking those donuts that, at least for a moment, Jamie had believed he'd heard a screaming fan, like in the old days. Of course, that was impossible since there did not appear to be a single Jamie Robb fan in sight.

Woody shrugged. "Somebody screamed."

Robb's chest deflated, and his mouth screwed up like he'd just taken a shot of vinegar, then quickly relaxed into a practiced smile. You'd think his publicist would've procured a couple of fake fans, brought in a reporter, or at the very least, tipped the SLY Stars tour-bus driver to swing by the event. Speaking of which, where was the master of ceremonies? They should've had this show on the road by now. Woody hated seeing any man made into a fool in front of his offspring, so he decided to bluff concern. Looking importantly at Jamie's kid, a freckly ten-year-old slumped at his father's side and way overdressed in a long-sleeved shirt and tie, Woody bellowed, "Not to worry, Mr. Robb. My eyes are peeled for all threats."

"Thank you. My son and I feel a lot more secure with you around." Jamie made a dramatic half bow, as though playing to an audience, and the kid rolled his eyes.

Woody wondered if Jamie kept the theatrics up at home. Everyone knew celebs were quirky, but this shit was already starting to annoy him; he could only imagine what it must be like to have to live with an actor twenty-four/seven. Or maybe Woody was just edgy because the sun was beating down on the back of his neck, causing sweat to bead uncomfortably beneath his collar, or because his 6:00 A.M. shot of whiskey wasn't holding him. He was cutting back, he really was, but the eye-opener was no biggie, and he couldn't quite bring himself to let it go. The stale taste in his mouth reminded him he'd forgotten to grab his breath spray on the way out the door.

Oh well.

He scanned the area yet again, hoping to find a pair of dress shoes among the flip-flops and tennies, a hand holding a mic, *any* damn sign of someone official. Woody was just about to ask Robb if he'd maybe gotten the date wrong when he spied a kid in black slacks jogging up the boulevard with a pair of chrome posts and some twisted red rope tucked under his armpit. Woody waved at the guy like he was his long-lost friend and got a nod of acknowledgment in return. Good. They were finally setting up for the program. But he still didn't see the master of ceremonies or any invited guests—not even Tom La Grande.

La Grande, a fast friend of Jamie's ever since their *Family Rules* days, had promised to attend the program, and Woody had even offered the megastar free protection, a deluxe two-for-one bodyguard package—three-for-one if you counted Jamie's kid. But La Grande had claimed he wasn't famous enough to need a muscleman. *Yeah*, like La Grande didn't have two gold statues in his pocket and a home overlooking the surf.

The kid tugged on his father's shirtsleeve. "Can we go now, Dad?"

Humiliating. Woody tightened his belt, keeping his hands busy. He would've given Jamie a sympathetic pat on the back, but that would be overstepping. Despite the quirks, he didn't mind the guy that much. Jamie might be a washed-up has-been hanging on to the past, but he appeared to be a good dad, and a good husband, and that was a hell of a lot more than Woody could claim. Thanks to his drinking, his grown kid wouldn't speak to him, and last week, his sweet Rayleen had packed her bags and returned to Iowa. Only two creatures on the planet who still liked him were his ma and his three-legged pit bull, King . . . and sometimes his sponsor. It was his sponsor, a former Vice cop like Woody, who'd said all he needed was a break and hooked him up with Jamie Robb's people.

Another desperate scream.

This time the hairs on every inch of Woody's body lifted,

sounding the alarm. His trigger finger pulsed, ready to pull if called for. Just his lousy luck the one time a sweet gig landed in his lap, something would go and screw it up. Crouching, he drew his Glock. He jerked his gaze upward, and his brain slowed time into a molasses drip as he watched *it* fall from the sky.

From a window two stories up in the Sky Walk Hotel, a body floated backward, bounced off the awning above them, then rolled onto the ground a few feet in front of him—the head cracking sickeningly against the sidewalk and blood spraying from the neck of a half-nude blond beauty like a busted garden hose.

Woody's stomach dropped as all sound was absorbed into the uproar surrounding him. His gaze darted about so quickly, it seemed he could see everywhere at once. On every side, tourists fled, shoving, stumbling, some even falling to the ground. Beside him, Jamie Robb froze. His kid yanked on his arm, trying to drag him away, but Robb just stared ahead as though in a daze. His shoulders trembled, then the tremor turned to a full-on shake. Suddenly, Robb's eyes snapped into focus, and his lips curled away from his teeth. The guy was losing it.

Woody didn't have that luxury. He tightened his grip on his pistol. Hands steady, now that adrenaline had usurped the hold alcohol had on his nervous system, he shoved Jamie and the kid into a protected alcove to keep them from being trampled by the panicked mob. Then he lunged forward, fighting his way against the crowd until he reached the woman. Staring down at her beautiful, broken body, his breath whooshed out, shrinking his lungs into tight, airless bags. Pressure welled behind his eyes.

Holy mother of saints.

It was as if one of heaven's own angels had fallen from the sky. And landed splat on top of Jamie Robb's shiny new star.

Chapter One

Two months later: Thursday, October 3
11:00 A.M.
Hollywood, California

SPECIAL AGENT ATTICUS Spenser knew that Herby's, situated just inside the Sky Walk Hotel, which in turn stood flush with Hollywood Boulevard, was one of *the* places to be if you were either young and hip or old and rich. But while it might be all glamour and glitz after dark, in the cold light of day it looked like just another dump. He brushed sticky crumbs, no doubt left by the likes of Lohan and Bieber, from a black leather booth heavily adorned with studs and spikes, before motioning his partner, Dr. Caity Cassidy, to sit.

Caity flashed him a smile that made him forget for a moment there were others in the room: Captain Lionel Jeffers, commanding officer of the LAPD's Hollywood division, and Special Agent Jake

Felton, the National Center for the Analysis of Violent Crime's liaison from the Los Angeles FBI field office—both of whom he'd met less than five minutes ago. Sliding in next to Captain Jeffers and opposite Caity, Spense couldn't help returning her smile. Lately, she'd been having that effect on him. In fact, an entire collection of dopey expressions now queued up, ready to play across his face on a moment's notice. But he saw no reason to make apologies— not to Caity, and certainly not to Felton or Jeffers.

Spense and Caity, here at the request of the LAPD to assist in a recent high-profile case, were staying at the Sky Walk. Odd that Captain Jeffers had requested to meet at the hotel instead of at Hollywood station, unless, of course, he hadn't yet let his team know the LAPD was bringing in the Feds. Through Herby's windows, Spense had a full view of the street and surrounding area, including the latest addition to the city's collection of celebrity museums—Waxed. This teeming section of Hollywood Boulevard had quite a history. A block up, at the Roosevelt Hotel, JFK was rumored to have rendezvoused with Marilyn. And here, at the Sky Walk, the pair had dared the occasional clandestine after-dinner drink—or so the braggadocio waiter had informed their little group prior to seating them. And that, in large part, accounted for Herby's celebrity draw—if it was good enough for JFK and Marilyn, it was good enough for the C-list.

While the historic Sky Walk's lobby, main restaurant, and guest rooms had been nicely refurbished in art-deco style, Herby's interior could only be described as upscale seedy. The sheen on the tabletops was dulled from nicks and scars that Spense supposed resulted from cocaine being scraped into neat lines. Decorative air fresheners punctuated the space between the booths, but no amount of sandalwood could rid the place of the stink of ruined lives. He would've much preferred to set the meeting in the main dining room, but it was crowded with guests, whereas Herby's didn't open until 9:00 P.M., thus assuring them the privacy they required to discuss the Fallen Angel Killer case. The hotel management had been more than willing to lend its premier club to the cops, given the fact the first victim had been stabbed in an upstairs room, then tossed from a window—which didn't meet code—onto Hollywood Boulevard below. Out front, a handful of bouquets, religious ornaments, and stuffed animals still paid tribute to the first *fallen angel.*

Captain Jeffers followed Spense's gaze to the makeshift monument on the sidewalk outside. Then he wiped a hand across bushy gray brows and weary brown eyes and turned a dubious look on Caity. Spense opened his mouth and shut it again. In the past, he'd been quick to charge in to protect Caity, even though she was more than capable of speaking up for herself. But now he knew how much she hated his interference, so he settled for narrowing his eyes at Jeffers instead.

Agent Felton, however, as the official go-between for the Behavioral Analysis Unit's profiling team and local law enforcement, was quick to defend Caity's presence at the table. "May I remind you, Lionel, that Dr. Cassidy is a forensic psychiatrist specializing in the workings of deviant minds? As a contracted consultant to the FBI, she reports directly to the Special Agent in Charge at the BAU in Virginia. We've cleared her . . . so you can speak freely. And please recall she here's at the LAPD's request."

"We asked for a profiler, not a psychiatrist," Jeffers said, as though the request had come from his Hollywood division, but Spense knew the S.O.S. had actually come from the higher echelon of the LAPD.

"The chief of police put in a call personally to the SAC at the BAU. The two of them agreed that since Dr. Cassidy has recently proven herself invaluable in solving another case alongside Agent Spenser, she'd be a welcome addition to the task force. The FBI is pleased to provide you with *two* experts in criminal behavior." *So shut up and play nice,* Felton's tone seemed to say.

"Yeah okay, I know all about the Man in the Maze case in Phoenix. But I also know her history. She usually bats for the other team." Jeffers hadn't taken the hint and was reminding the others of Caity's past testimony as an expert *defense* witness. Caity was still the enemy in Jeffers's eyes.

Caity rose from her seat, the leather booth squeaking comically as she got up and leaned across the table, offering her hand to Jeffers. "I understand your concern, Captain. But I promise you, I have only one interest in this or in any other case."

"And that would be?"

"To see that the *real* perpetrator is brought to justice."

"Meaning us cops usually get it wrong."

"Meaning you asked the Bureau for help, and they think I can provide it. I'm happy to lend my expertise, but if you and your team have everything under control . . ."

Jeffers's shoulders dropped.

Caity smiled sweetly. "I'd be happy to stay and help, Captain, or happy to go. Just say the word, and I'll be on the next plane to Colorado. You see, I have pressing personal matters to attend, because, as you say, on occasion, the justice system does in fact fail. It failed my father, but I'm guessing you already know that. So if you don't need me, there are others who do. I can't afford to waste my time if my input isn't going to be utilized."

Jeffers shifted from one hip to the other, and looked at Felton, then Spense. A sigh rumbled through him. Finally, he reached his hand across the booth and shook Caity's. "If you have something of value to add, I'll be the first to listen. But don't think you can bat those baby blues at me or dazzle me with a bunch of psychobabble. Tell me something useful, something that will help me catch this mofo, though, and I'll be the first in line to pin a medal on you." His gaze went to the spot on Caity's chest just below where one would normally pin a medal.

Spense mentally counted to ten and pulled a miniature Rubik's cube, attached to his keychain, from his pocket. He scrambled it, reminding himself to hang tight to his cool.

"I'm not looking for a medal, Captain." Caity, apparently, noticing Spense's growing agitation, caught his eye and frowned.

He'd like to knock Jeffers on his tail for disrespecting Caity, but she'd be mad as hell if he did. Not to mention, at the moment, they had a much bigger problem to contend with than the captain's jerkwad behavior—the Fallen Angel Killer. Spense finished solving his cube and stuck it back in his pocket. He studied Jeffers, who, despite a sagging, deeply lined brow, managed to look commanding . . . and arrogant. Spense didn't like the guy on first take, but he reserved the right to change his mind on longer acquaintance. In his experience, assholes sometimes made good cops, and Jeffers was definitely an asshole.

Spense shaded his eyes as sunlight suddenly swept across the room, illuminating a fine mist of grime covering every surface. The tapestries, thickly woven drapes, and red-carpet walkway must stockpile dust, then release it precisely one minute after the cleaning crew finished up every day.

Jeffers blinked rapidly. "If you're not looking for recognition, Dr. Cassidy, then what *are* you looking for?"

"An open mind."

"All right." He folded his arms across his chest, contradicting his words. "An open mind it is." Then he abruptly stopped speaking as a high-heel-booted waiter swaggered over.

The young man sported a James Dean hairstyle and a T-shirt tight enough to reveal his six-pack abs. An out-of-work actor or model no doubt, since just about everyone in this town had aspirations in the entertainment industry. For example, on the cab ride over, Spense and Caity had learned all about their driver's screenplay, which had actually sounded interesting. Noting that only Felton had closed his menu, the waiter cast an exasperated glance around the group. "Are we ready to order?"

"What do you recommend?" Caity asked.

"What do you like?" he retorted, with a condescension that could not be matched—except maybe by the servers at Sardi's.

"Something filling. I'm starved."

"Cheeseburger."

"Great. I'll have a cheeseburger then, and water will be fine."

"That's *one* down." Six-Pack threw a glance behind him, suggesting he'd like to get back to the main dining room where, undoubtedly, the big tippers awaited.

Jeffers slapped his menu shut. "We'll all have the damn cheeseburgers then."

"Make mine a garden burger," Spense put in hastily. "I'll take the mayo on the side, and gimme a salad instead of fries."

Jeffers's bottom lip protruded. "You some kind of health nut?" As if that discredited Spense's acumen as an FBI profiler.

"I am. My dad died young—of a heart attack." Not that it was any of Jeffers's business, but Spense was all about good manners at the table during a first meet with local law enforcement. Especially with Caity present.

"Bring me the beer-whiskey special, will ya?" Jeffers waved his menu at the waiter, accepting Spense's explanation, but emphasizing his own *not-a-health-nut* status. Then he refocused his gaze on Caity's chest.

Too bad Spense wasn't going to get a chance to teach him better manners anytime soon. He imagined the sting of Jeffers's nose breaking beneath his fist, the satisfying crunch followed by a string of outraged curses, and smiled amiably.

Six-Pack cocked a disdainful brow at Jeffers, "This is *Herby's*, not your local grub and pub. No beer-whiskey special."

"And yet you got cheeseburgers," Jeffers fired back. "So figure one out."

"I'm going to need to see some ID."

The captain flashed a gold badge. "How's this for ID, son?"

The waiter appeared undaunted. "Just following the letter of the law . . . like I always do." Then he wheeled on his bootheels and sauntered away.

As soon as the server was out of sight, Spense turned to Jeffers. "To get back to our previous discussion—you said you asked for a profiler." Keeping to his good-manners policy, he paused, removing any unfriendliness from his tone. "Why?"

"What do you mean, why? It's obvious."

"Not so much. As I understand things, you've had two possibly connected murders in as many months. It seems early to ask for help, and specifically to ask for profiling help."

"Both the mayor and the governor are breathing down our necks on this one. The press has had a field day stirring folks up with all the different monikers for this creep. Between the papers and the TV newscasters, they've come up with at least three different names, but the one that's currently sticking is from SLY: *Fallen Angel Killer*. Emotions are running high among the locals, and tourism is already trending down. If we've got a serial on our hands, we want the BAU's input sooner rather than later."

"Yes, but isn't *if* the operative word?" Spense said. "The press intends to sell all the papers they can, and coming up with serial-killer nicknames to scare the shit out of John Q Public will undoubtedly sell a boatload. I bet SLY's ratings on their entertainment 'news' show are way up. But I don't think we can look to the media to determine whether or not a single individual is responsible for both of these murders."

"I'm not looking to the press. I'm looking to you." Jeffers brought out an accordion file and set it on the table. "I'll give you seventy-two hours. That should be plenty of time to profile this son-bitch." He laid a headshot of a smiling blonde with perfect bone structure on the table. "Selena Turner—the first victim. An aspiring actress. Her father owns some kind of bolt factory in Pennsylvania. The family isn't exactly pedigreed, but they're richer than Aunt Mabel's Rum cake."

"So, did Miss Turner have a day job? Or did she pursue acting full-time on Daddy's dime?" Caity asked.

"A few years ago, there was some kind of a falling-out over one of her boyfriends. Her parents say they hadn't heard from her since. No day job . . . so . . ."

"Neither parent was funneling her money? Did she have a trust fund?" Caity frowned.

"Nope."

"A hooker?" Spense picked up the photograph. The woman

didn't have that hard look you'd expect from a prostitute. Her expression was, in fact, aptly described as angelic. She could've been the girl next door. But somehow he didn't think that's who she'd turn out to be.

"No arrests. She rented a nice little bungalow in Encino. Paid her bills on time."

"Not every hooker is on the streets," Spense said.

"Sugar daddy?" Caity suggested.

Jeffers nodded. "We think so. But we haven't found him yet. Must be married because not even her friends claim to know who she's been seeing. They do know, though, that her mystery boyfriend takes very good care of her."

"You mean *took* very good care of her. Before she got stabbed in the neck and shoved out a window."

Caity's tone implied, and Spense agreed, that this sugar daddy might be the individual responsible for Miss Turner's demise. Spense also couldn't help wondering if the LAPD had really turned every stone in their efforts to locate him. In two months, they still hadn't uncovered the boyfriend's identity, and to him that meant either no such boyfriend existed or their focus had been elsewhere. But if they did have a person of interest already, Jeffers was right not to volunteer that information. By giving them a target suspect, he could bias the profile he was asking Spense and Caity to create.

Jeffers laid down a second photo. "This is Adrianne Simpson." Another very lovely, very blond, very innocent-appearing woman. It was easy to see why the papers would dub the victims *fallen angels*. If this was the work of a serial killer, he definitely had a type.

"Victim number two," Caity supplied. The woman's photo had

been all over the news since her murder just one week ago. "Any bookings for solicitation?"

"None. And, like Selena Turner, she'd broken off relations with her family and had no visible means of support. She was staying in a nice place out in Laurel Canyon, and you won't believe who the landlord is. The place is owned by . . ." Jeffers paused dramatically.

Spense put up his hand. "If this landlord is a person of interest, better wait to give us his name until after we've delivered a preliminary profile."

"You think Adrianne and her landlord were lovers?" Caity asked.

"We're looking into that. There was a lease, and she paid her rent regular. No reason to suspect him any more than Miss Turner's landlord, just because he's . . . a recognizable figure in this town. Besides, Simpson had an associate degree in business from a local community college."

"You're speculating what then? Maybe she had some private consulting arrangement with a company and earned a living legitimately?" Caity sounded doubtful.

"Oh, she had private arrangements all right, but I doubt they were the legitimate kind. No two-year degree is going to buy the kind of life she was living. She drove a Beemer and hung out at a celebrity gym in Beverly Hills. Buddied up to some of those *Real Housewife* types, told them she had a book deal and was living off a big advance."

Spense's mind had been wandering, but this jolted him to attention. "Should be easy enough to check. If she was writing a tell-all, that could be a motive for murder."

"We did check, and there was no book deal. At least not with any major publisher. That was just her cover story for how she got her money. It doesn't explain why her half-naked body was found on the SLY tour bus. Let's face it, there's a sicko killing women and dumping them in high-profile tourist spots for his own twisted reasons. And that means we've got to find him and stop him ASAP, before any more damage is done to the city's reputation."

Caity's back went ramrod straight. "You mean before any more innocents are murdered, don't you?"

Jeffers jabbed both elbows on the tabletop. "Sure. Yes. Only I wouldn't characterize these . . . young women . . ." He let the words sit a moment before continuing . . . "as innocents. The press has got one thing right, if they were ever angels to begin with, they're fallen now."

Chapter Two

Thursday, October 3
3:00 P.M.
Los Angeles, California

STANDING IN LINE for LAX security, Spense winced at the strain apparent in Caity's profile. It looked as though someone had smudged his grimy thumbs beneath her eyes, then sponged the color from her cheeks. But that didn't take away from her beauty. Not in Spense's view, anyway. She turned her head, as if checking to be sure he was still there, and the idea that she was keeping him close sent a warm feeling spreading through his chest . . . followed in short order by a steely cold determination to keep her safe.

Two days ago, their business in Phoenix had been concluded, but that didn't mean all was right with their world. During the Man in the Maze case, Caity had been shot, beat up, and put through an emotional ringer, and afterward all Spense had wanted to do was gather her in his arms and transport her somewhere safe and warm—like Tahiti. Miraculously, she'd agreed to go with him.

After spending years as rivals, the Man in the Maze case had forced them to work together on the same side. Unable to keep each other at arm's length any longer, they'd shared a kiss—but nothing more. Tahiti was supposed to be their chance to take a breath and figure out what was happening between them. But then the LAPD had put out a call for help, spoiling their plans, and from the moment they'd left Phoenix, Spense had sensed Caity's doubts about taking things to the next level between them. Pushing a hand through his hair, he adjusted the weight of his carry-on.

Part of him thought the Fallen Angel investigation would be good for Caity. After all, there's nothing like starting a new assignment to take your mind off the prior one. But despite her tough-girl swagger, the Man in the Maze case had gotten both personal and dangerous, and, whether or not Caity admitted it, the ordeal had to have sucked the life out of her physical reserves. He couldn't help worrying that this new assignment, in addition to costing them a tryst in paradise, might be too much too soon for her.

As the line inched forward, he eased closer to her, like they were an old married couple, perfectly accustomed to getting into each other's space. When she didn't move away, he congratulated himself on his sex appeal. Of course, there was really nowhere for her to go, unless she wanted to get intimately acquainted with the elderly gentleman in front of her. Spense took a step to the side, opening up a little more breathing room. Crowding her, either physically or emotionally, wasn't the best idea right now. After all, there was still that pressing personal matter she had to attend to in Colorado. And it was something that simply couldn't wait. That was why they'd headed straight to the airport after their meeting with Felton and Jeffers earlier that day.

"You don't have to come to Boulder with me, Spense. I can deliver my news and be back in LA first thing tomorrow morning."

Any hint that he might not be looking forward to another twenty-four-hour turnaround would have her insisting he stay behind. She had a hard time accepting help, even from him, though recently she'd gotten better about that. "We both need a break from work, Caity. Even a short one is better than nothing. Are you trying to take my one day of R and R away from me?"

"Trust me, Spense. A visit with my mother doesn't constitute R and R. Bickering isn't a spectator sport, or at least it shouldn't be. I'm only trying to spare you the headache." Her smile reeked of forced cheerfulness.

"I don't need you to spare me anything. Your headache is my headache." He wasn't buying what she was selling. Touching her shoulder with his hand, he said, "Your *heartache* is my heartache."

Caity responded with silence. She'd told him very little about her relationship with her mother, but it was obvious they weren't on the best of terms. Six weeks ago, when Caity had suffered a near-fatal gunshot wound, her first words to the trauma team had been *do not call my mother.* Later, she'd asserted she was only trying to protect her mom from the worry of seeing her daughter injured and from the pain of returning to Arizona—the place where her father had been executed for a crime he didn't commit. But Spense didn't completely trust that explanation. He didn't know exactly what had caused the rift between Caity and Arlene Cassidy, but he expected that the news Caity had for Arlene would cauterize and eventually heal old wounds. Surely, this particular visit home would go well.

"I know what you're thinking," Caity said.

He arched an eyebrow. If she really could read his mind, then she knew the effect she had on him and was choosing to ignore it, either because they were working another case together, or because . . .

"You're thinking once Mom hears what I have to tell her, it will be all *happy days are here again* at the Cassidy house, but you haven't met my mother."

"You're right. I haven't. But I'm looking forward to it."

Caity shook her head. "You don't know what you're signing up for."

Gathering his scattered thoughts, he fought the impulse to pull her into his arms right there in front of God and everybody. "I'm signing up to be part of your life—or at least I'm trying to. I thought I'd said so already, back in Phoenix." He paused, wanting to gauge Caity's response. But she kept her poker face, so he couldn't tell what she thought about his plan to become an integral part of her world, and an airport security line wasn't the place for amorous declarations. "If your mother is anything like you, she'll be wonderful."

"You're a profiler, Spense. I'd think you would do a better job picking up on the clues I'm giving you. My mother may be a wonderful woman as far as the rest of the planet is concerned, but when it's my picnic we're talking about, she makes sure to provide the ants." Caity studied her toes. "You may think I'm being unkind, but I'm just trying to prepare you. It's not too late for you to back out of this trip."

Security line or no security line, he intended to make himself clear. He grabbed her bag from her, set it on the ground along with his, and took her by the hands. "Unless you tell me straight out you don't want me by your side, I'm going to Colorado with you."

An eternity passed before she squeezed his hands, blinked away the sheen from her eyes, and said, "I want you to come with me, Spense."

That was all he needed to hear. As a smattering of applause started up in the security line, he gave the thumbs-up sign to their captive audience. Then he planted a quick kiss on the top of Caity's head and watched her cheeks flush a very sexy shade of pink.

Only a few hours later, he set down his overnight bag in Arlene Cassidy's living room. When Mrs. Cassidy hugged Caity, then welcomed him into her home, a sense of déjà vu—only all fucked up—came over him. Before him stood an older version of Caity herself, but . . . not quite. Mrs. Cassidy's glossy, dark hair, small, straight nose, and full, peaked lips, were identical to Caity's. The color of her wide, intelligent eyes was an exact, heaven blue match to her daughter's. But her mother didn't have Caity's vitality—a vitality that was even apparent when she was dog tired, like today. Instead, Arlene's eyes conjured deep pools that had been drained of water—so that only the memory of their ebb and flow remained.

Spense didn't have to ask himself what tragedy had befallen this woman. It was the same one that had befallen Caity, and he wished to God he could stop the hurt for both women. But there was no bringing back the dead.

Thursday, October 3
6:30 P.M.
Boulder, Colorado

"MOM, THIS IS Special Agent Atticus Spenser." Caitlin heard the stiffness in her voice and felt her shoulders rise into a defensive stance.

Relax. You don't have to pick up where you left off.

Spense sent her a reassuring look, but not even his easygoing vibe could change the uptight person she always became around her mother. Her gaze went to her father's photograph, displayed on the mantel above a fireplace that, without him around to build a crackling blaze, had lain cold and barren for years. Caitlin could easily imagine what he would have to say about the great divide that had developed between Mom and her: *She loves you, Caity. I know she's hard on you sometimes, but try to remember she's on your side.* Caitlin had always been a daddy's girl, and even as a child, her relationship with her mother had been distant.

"May I call you Atticus?" The smile her mother sent Spense seemed warmer than the one she'd given Caitlin, but that was no surprise. It was only Caitlin who brought out the ice queen in Arlene Cassidy. Her mother was beloved by friends, neighbors, and small children—and not just because she always had some sort of treat at the ready. She was the type of person who could be counted upon when your car broke down, or your sitter didn't show, or your husband ran off with his personal trainer. She was a good person, and Caitlin knew it.

Your mother's a giver—even after all she's been through, people would whisper the words reverently in Caitlin's ear, and she'd feel all the more guilty for the resentment she'd held toward her mom ever since her father's execution. An execution Caitlin had attended on her own, against her mother's wishes, on her eighteenth birthday. Thinking back to that day now, to how desperately alone she'd felt, how desperately alone *Daddy* must've felt without his wife there, she couldn't meet her mother's eyes. Instead, she found a spot on the wall to look at, swallowed her memories, and announced, "He doesn't like to be called Atticus. He prefers Spense."

Spense stepped forward, extending his hand. "No. No. All my favorite mothers call me Atticus. Please feel free."

Caitlin's brow shot up as her mother briefly placed her hand in his. Spense barely tolerated *Atticus* from his own mother, and Caitlin figured that was just because he really couldn't protest the woman who'd named him to begin with. But here he was giving Arlene the go-ahead to call him whatever she pleased.

"Great to meet you," Spense added quickly, then turning things around on her for once, shot Caitlin a chill-out look.

She frowned at him. It wasn't like she was trying to be difficult.

"I've laid out clean towels on the dresser in your room, Atticus." Placing her hand on the small of her swayed back, her mother turned to her. "I hope you don't mind taking the couch, Caitlin. I'm afraid my arthritis has been bothering me lately, or I'd do the honors."

"I insist on taking the couch, Mrs. Cassidy," Spense said, dropping to the sofa and patting the cushions. "Feels very comfy."

Caitlin understood that Spense wasn't just acting the gentleman. Though she managed her pain well enough most days, she'd had a minor surgical tweak only ten days ago, and she had yet to fully recover. Of course, when it came to her injuries, Caitlin had only shared the bare minimum with her mother, so she could hardly fault her for offering the guest room to Spense, who was, in fact, the actual guest in the house.

"Call me, Arlene, dear. Are you sure you're not too tall for the sofa? Caitlin's so petite, and she can always share my bed if it comes down to it."

"The couch is perfect. I insist." His grin was wide, and he waited for her mother to look away before teasing Caitlin with a knowing wink.

She smothered a grin with her hand. Really, how could she be expected to resist a man who'd just saved her from this god-awful couch, or worse—sharing a room with her mother? No way would oversized Spense be comfortable on that undersized sofa. She could just picture him, all dangly arms and legs, tossing and turning and rolling off a time or two, the confused look in his golden brown eyes as his drop to the floor woke him from a restless sleep.

A pang of guilt stabbed her in the chest.

Maybe they should just go to a hotel—but that would offend her mother, and offending her mother wasn't on her to-do list. Not this visit, anyway. Even if she couldn't forget the past, she'd decided it was time to call a truce. It was what Daddy would've wanted, and . . . it was what she wanted, too. Maybe they could make a new beginning, starting right here and now. She met her mother's eyes and was rewarded with a smile. A spark of hope set her heart beating faster.

"Well then, if you insist." Mom addressed Spense and checked her watch. "I've got a women's Bible study group coming in half an hour. You two are welcome to sit in. We don't usually allow men, but I'm sure the church ladies won't mind Atticus's presence in the least." Mom lifted a shoulder and giggled like a schoolgirl.

Good grief. Her mother was actually flirting with Spense. It was nice to see her laughing, but company . . . right now? "Can't you cancel? Remember I told you I had something important to tell you?"

"I'm sorry, sweetheart, but this was such short notice, and we'll have all the time in the world to visit tomorrow."

The reprimand in her mother's tone wasn't lost on Caitlin. The spark that had warmed her heart earlier flickered into nothingness. Since she'd last seen her mom, Caitlin had nearly been killed. She sighed. But she *hadn't* been killed, and she hadn't told her mom much of anything. It wasn't the least bit reasonable to get angry with her over a Bible study group . . . but she'd come all this way, and she'd been waiting to deliver this news for what seemed like a lifetime. It was simply too important to put off any longer. In a few days, everything would be official, and by then, the papers would get hold of it. Caitlin couldn't let her mother find out that way.

She squared her gaze with her mom's. "I think it'd be best to cancel—"

"Oh no. I can't call off Bible study. It wouldn't be right. The women have been looking forward to this all month, and Betty Jean's husband is at the top of a very long prayer list . . . I'm afraid I just can't. It'll only be for the evening, and, like I said, we'll have all the time in the world to visit."

"I'm afraid we won't, Mom. Spense and I have a 6:00 A.M. flight back to LA tomorrow."

"You what?" Her mom's eyes widened, almost, but not quite filling with emotion.

Was Caitlin imaging it, or was her mother actually hurt by her declaration? "I'm sorry. I wish we could stay longer, but we can't. You've heard of the Fallen Angel Killer?"

Suddenly the breath hissed from between her mom's teeth. "Not any more than I can help." She cowered away from Caitlin, her eyes empty once more. "I should've known you'd get yourself involved in another horrible murder case. I've begged you to turn your mind to other, more wholesome matters, but it's clear you don't care how I feel. So if you insist on making your life about these unspeakable crimes, I can't stop you. But I'm not reading about any Fallen Angel Killer, or thinking about one, and I don't intend to start now. Go back to LA in the morning and leave me alone again if you must, but please, do *not* drag me down in the gutter with the salacious details. If that's what you've come here to talk about—"

"I'm not here to drag you down with salacious details, Mother. I only brought up the case because I need you to understand why I can't stay longer." Every instinct told her to turn around and run, not walk, out that door. But she couldn't. Not this time.

"Why *are* you here then? If you're just going to leave me alone again tomorrow, why bother coming home at all?"

Caitlin glanced about the living room, walls painted bright yellow, eyelet-lace curtains in the windows, family photographs everywhere—but none since Caitlin's fourteenth birthday—the year her father had been arrested for the murder of Gail Falconer. The room was in a time warp. It was like someone had cracked a clock, and the dial had shattered one second before Thomas Cassidy's arrest. This entire house raged against the truth. Life had not been kind to the Cassidy family, but this and every other room in the house asserted it had. Life had been damn cruel, and no matter how much her mother wanted to deny it, evil did exist. Caitlin wasn't going to shut her eyes to that truth, whether her mother approved or not, because looking the other way did no one any good. It only gave evil an opportunity to flourish. Her chest grew heavy with the burden of delivering what should have been good news. She realized now, without a doubt, this wasn't going to go well.

"It's about Daddy."

Her mother wobbled backward on one foot, then lost her balance completely and crumpled onto the couch next to Spense. As the color drained from her face, she clutched at her throat. For a moment, she couldn't seem to catch her breath. "It's about Daddy? Or about his case?"

"Both. They're not exactly easy to separate," Caitlin said in a determinedly even voice.

Spense had pulled a neutral face the moment the women's voices sharpened, but now he appeared to be eyeing her mother with real concern. A twinge of irritation flickered through her. Surely, Spense could see her mother's behavior for what it was: high drama.

"Caity, I think your mother's right. This should wait until after Bible study. Then we can all sit down and discuss things without interruption."

Her mother bolted back to her feet, inexplicably regaining both her balance and her breath. "*I* can easily separate your father, the man I married, from the Gail Falconer murder case."

"Arlene, I think what Caity meant—"

"Stay out of this." Caitlin's voice shook in spite of her efforts to remain calm. It was just like Spense to try to charge in and take over at the slightest sign that things were getting tough. He was far too protective of Caitlin—he'd admitted as much to her, but he couldn't seem to change his behavior. She knew his intentions were good, but this was between her and her mother.

Her mom closed the distance between them. "Your father had nothing to do with that poor woman's death, and I will not let that abomination of a verdict become his legacy. I will not give that trial, or what came after any space in my brain . . . or my heart."

"But don't you see, Mom? That verdict, that case, *is* his legacy. And I simply could not let that stand."

"And I told you I'm done with those days. Let the past stay in the past. Your father is dead." Her mom practically spit the words at her, as if she hated her daughter for reminding her of that fact. "There's not one blessed thing you can do to bring him back home to his family. You've wasted too much time, not to mention money, on PIs and lawyers, and even if you won't admit it, it's tearing you apart. I can see what hanging on to the past has done to you. If you cared about me at all, you'd let go of your father's case. What if something terrible happens to *you* while you're off chasing these demons from the past, trying to set something right that can *never* be undone? Please, please, just let this be." Regardless of the words, her mother's voice always carried an inherent sweetness. At the moment it sounded both fragile and brittle—like burned sugar. "I simply couldn't bear it if I lost you, too."

And that type of reasoning, that *fear*, was exactly why Caitlin had kept her mother in the dark about the injuries she'd sustained while working the Man in the Maze case in Phoenix. "He didn't do it, Mom."

"I *know* he didn't do it." Her mother wrung her hands, making Caitlin's heart contract painfully.

She understood Mom wanted to live in denial, pretend her father had died of natural causes instead of having been put to death by lethal injection. Yet all these years, Caitlin had been refusing to let her forget. And yes, she had put herself in harm's way, so her mother had a point about that. "We both know he didn't do it. But can you really just go on with your life, letting that lie about Daddy stand? Because I can't."

Her mother wiped away her tears. "You think your way is so much better than mine. You think you're the only one who loved Daddy. Well, I loved him, too. Your father was my whole world."

There was a telling pause, and Caitlin wondered if her mother understood the implications of what she'd said. If her husband had been her entire world, that didn't leave much room for her daughter. Caitlin swallowed back the lump of emotion welling in her throat, waiting for Mom to finish her speech.

"And you walk around like you're the only one who cares, just because you've been trying to prove his innocence all these years. But I don't need some group of legal jackasses to tell me my husband wasn't a monster because I already know the truth. And the fact that you need that external confirmation . . ."

She willed herself to reach out to her mother, but found her limbs were paralyzed.

"I want justice for my father. And I want justice for Gail Falconer, too. I don't know anyone besides you who could turn that into a shortcoming."

"You want justice for *yourself*. You want the courts to say your father was an innocent man because *you* don't want to be known as the daughter of a sadistic killer."

"Of course I don't want to be known as the daughter of a sadistic killer." Anger bubbled up inside her, raising the decibel level of her voice, no matter how hard she tried to stop it. "Because I'm *not*."

Their gazes locked. This wasn't what she wanted—fighting with her mother like this. She hauled in a breath and made herself remember the woman her mother used to be before their world turned black, the woman who'd baked cookies and tucked her in with a sweet kiss at night.

Her mother raised her hand, then stopped it a few inches from Caitlin's cheek. Caitlin wasn't sure if it had been a thwarted gesture of anger or of comfort, but at this point, she decided to give her mother the benefit of the doubt. She grabbed her hand and squeezed tight. "You and I both know that Daddy did not kill Gail

Falconer. And now the world knows it, too. Or they will very soon. You may want to sit down for this."

Her mother stared at her uncomprehendingly, remaining rooted to the spot. Spense got up and gently guided her back to the couch. With her heart pounding in her chest, Caitlin made sure to take in a few good breaths so she could enunciate her next words clearly, "Gail Falconer's murder has been solved . . . and this time they got it right, Mom. Daddy has been exonerated."

Chapter Three

Thursday, October 3
10:00 P.M.
Hollywood, California

SUSAN SMITH NURSED her root beer and drummed her fingers on a tabletop at Perks—the coffee place that adjoined the gift shop for the new wax museum—while she awaited instructions from her madam. She'd come here to meet a john.

Three years ago, at the age of twenty-one, Susan made a conscious decision to lose her virginity. According to Madam Lucille, none of her other girls could say the same. Lucy, herself, claimed to have been twenty-one and a half when she lost hers to a Hollywood record producer—one who was now on trial for the manslaughter death of a famous actress, but that wasn't really relevant. Since Lucy was a madam rather than an actual escort, Susan thought hers was a legit claim as the longest holdout in the stable. In any case, she prided herself on the fact that she'd chosen her own path from the moment she'd first lost her virginity right up until today.

She was no man's puppet. And not Lucy's, either, though Lucy liked to think she could control all of her models.

Model was a euphemism.

Model. Actress. Escort.

No one controlled Susan. She hadn't been seduced by a pimp who'd injected her with smack until she became dependent on him, then coerced into *the life* to fund her habit. She hadn't been abused as a teen and forced to run away to make her living on the streets. She came from a comfortable, upper-middle-class family in Van Nuys. She had a bachelor's degree in poli sci, and she *chose* to sell her body for money. Though she had plenty of other options, none of them would've afforded her the lifestyle she desired.

And while it might be true that she and her mom didn't get along, and that in some small way she was getting back at her mother for paying so little attention to her, it was still her choice. There was no reason to feel sorry for her. No reason at all.

She'd first met Lucy in the student union during senior year of college. She'd gone down to the lounge to catch an episode of *Days of Our Lives*, and Lucy had bought her a Coke and told her about her modeling agency. Susan had an inkling right away that something was up because at five-foot-nothing, weighing 110 pounds, she wasn't the type of girl the Ford Agency recruited. Anyway, Lucy had been very up-front. She'd explained that she'd started out placing her models into auto shows and trade mags, but received so many requests from her clients for introductions to her girls that she'd finally wised up and made an adjustment to her business model. Over the past two years with Lucy's agency, Susan had only gotten two sitcom walk-ons and one beer commercial—but she made a good living turning tricks.

Lucy's wasn't a typical escort/modeling agency.

You couldn't find it online. The only way a client could get to Lucy was through a personal connection, friend of a friend, that kind of thing. It was all very Hollywood, in that you had to know someone to get ahead.

Ha-ha. Get a head?

Anyway, the johns were mostly minor celebs and international businessmen though Lucy claimed one girl had gone with an A-lister to the Oscars, so you never knew what might come your way. The men Susan went with loved to pamper her. In exchange, she did whatever they required to get off. Half the time, they simply wanted her company. Men like sex, but they also like to get high and talk. So she listened to them ramble on about their lives and watched them get wasted on their drugs of choice.

Her one unbreakable rule was that she didn't partake in mind-altering substances. The exception being alcohol, and only when she poured her own from a bottle that she'd opened herself, or if she was served at a club, and the drink had remained within her control at all times. She sometimes acted as a safety monitor for her clients, calling the guy's best friend if he got too wack on the dope. Occasionally, she got to go home with a wad of cash without ever having taken off her clothes. It wasn't a bad life, as long as you knew what you were doing. As long as you were careful. It was important to have safety rules . . . and to follow them.

After all, nobody wanted to become the next *fallen angel.*

With the fallen angels in mind, she was feeling more cautious than usual tonight. Besides which, this was by far the creepiest place she'd ever been asked to meet a john. While part of her thought a rendezvous like this might be fun, her guard was up. If she didn't like the vibe the guy gave her, she'd bounce. She checked her phone, reviewing the text Lucy had sent earlier. When Lucy gave her the signal, she was to proceed to the alley behind Waxed and wait at the employee entrance. Her cell phone beeped:

Go.

She gulped a final sip of root beer, stuffed her napkin in the empty cup, and headed out. In less than five minutes, she'd reached the back door of the museum. Some people probably think whores are used to dark alleys, but she wasn't that kind of whore. Normally, she'd refuse a meet like this one, but this particular john was offering $5,000, and Lucy was giving her a fifty-fifty split instead of the usual forty-sixty. She could really use that $2,500 since she was planning to get her boobs done at the first opportunity. Small, natural boobs like hers appealed to a niche group of men—that's part of how she got her place in Lucy's agency—but a nice pair of double D's would mean more clients. Then Lucy would have to find another girl to fill her niche requests. Of course, Susan didn't only get the specialty guys. Some men . . . or women . . . didn't care about the rack, as long as the girl was beautiful. Not being conceited or anything, she knew she fit the bill. Her hair was I-was-born-with-it blond, brightened by the Cali sunshine, and her eyes were ocean blue—at least that's what her bio said. She'd gotten lucky, with good skin and full, pouty lips, too. Her only real handicap was her height. She couldn't please the ones who went for long legs, so that was another reason she needed the implants.

She sucked in a deep breath and noticed the goose bumps on her arms. It was a warm night, but the wind and the spooky alley were giving her the shivers. She was wearing an expensive, white gauze blouse, and a butt-hugging, short, Lycra skirt. Stilettos, of course. Her Michael Kors shoulder bag contained her keys, ID, and $100 in cash in the zipper pouch. There was also the brass, four-leaf clover her grandma gave her and pepper spray in the main compartment. She let out a choppy breath. Somewhere on the street, a car backfired. Startled, she turned her ankle on a stupid alley rock.

Take it easy. Stick with your rules. It's all good.

She told herself there was nothing to be afraid of. Lucy knew exactly where she was and who she was meeting, even if she didn't. She'd vetted this john just like all the others. He would be high-class, because Lucy's accounts always were, and when they had spoken earlier, Lucy hinted this might be one of her bigger celebs. Not to mention a scream from Susan would bring the whole of Hollywood Boulevard running back here to check things out.

You. Are. Fine.

Twenty-five hundred for a couple hours of work, she reminded herself. She waited, and she waited some more. The breeze in the alley was bringing her smells from the coffee shop and a pizza joint, and it made her stomach growl. The sting in her ankle was subsiding, though, so that was good. She checked her phone again and noticed it was after ten. Maybe this guy was full of shit. How was he going to get into Waxed after hours anyway? He might work there, but that didn't add up. It was mostly kids making minimum wage manning the desk and counting the tickets. Of course he might own the place. Or maybe . . . he was one of the artists who made the wax figures. She'd heard each statue cost over 150 grand to create, so the sculptors could definitely afford a girl like her. Her phone beeped again:

Are you in yet? Lucy asked.

No, she typed back. But just then, she heard creaking, and the back door to the museum swung open.

"Hang on a minute. I gotta check in with my boss." She raised one finger in the sticky night air, making a point that she was texting on her phone. Then she typed *I'm in* and hit SEND. Her phone made the reassuring blurp of a message sent. She dumped her cell in her bag and focused on the positive: They were sneaking into the wax museum. One of the perks of working for Madam Lucille was that the clientele were not only connected, they were often creative. This guy right here was wearing what looked like a custom silk suit . . . in addition to a Charlie Chaplin mask. Tonight could make for a good story, like that Oscar extravaganza.

The john was playacting at being someone he wasn't, and she was doing that, too. After all, she'd been pretending to be Gina since she went to work for Lucy. Her real name, Susan Smith, wasn't nearly as catchy as Gina Lola. She'd renamed herself after Gina Lollobrigida because if she was going to be someone else, she figured it might as well be someone she wished she could be—like an exotic Italian movie star with long legs. Life was so much easier when you pretended.

You got this.

Her shoulders relaxed.

Charlie Chaplin motioned her inside, and the door slammed shut behind her, sending a cool wind across the backs of her knees. Compared to outside, the air in the narrow stairwell felt heavy and oppressive in her lungs. It was creepy dark here, but she could see light seeping around the edges of a door on the landing. It was that light, and the draw of $2,500, that kept her from calling things off right there and then.

"I'm Gina," she said, blinking hard, waiting for her eyes to adjust to the low light. Until she walked up those stairs, she hadn't fully committed.

Wordlessly, Charlie turned his back to her and headed toward the landing, which was somewhat reassuring, as she thought this was his way of showing her that she could stay or leave as she pleased.

Damn straight.

But, apparently, he's wasn't the talkie type—probably why he was wearing a silent film star's mask and wig—and this was not good news for her. The talkers were the ones who didn't require much out of a girl, and since Charlie didn't seem to want to bend her ear, her guess was he'd have plenty of other stuff he'd want her to do for him.

Likely things he wasn't proud of. But the mask would also keep his secrets . . . She'd never be able to identify him.

Thinking again of the fallen angels, she hesitated.

He was halfway up the stairs, and she could turn around and go if she wanted. Lucy had a no-repercussions policy. Anytime a girl felt like it, she was free to shut things down, no questions asked.

Twenty-five hundred dollars.

She followed Charlie upstairs, her high heels clicking on the industrial metal steps, her hand trailing reluctantly along the cold railing. When she reached the top, he flung open the door, and they stepped into the A-List party room at Waxed.

Her breath caught. She couldn't help it.

Wow.

This was probably as close to being invited to a Hollywood bash as she'd ever get. To her right, Fred Astaire, dressed in black tie and tails, was dancing cheek to cheek with a lovely, and very lifelike Ginger Rogers. Ginger was wearing a beaded brocade gown that was simply too beautiful to be true. Susan walked over, reached out her hand, and let her palm slide over the heavily textured fabric. She wondered if it was a real costume from one of Ginger's movies.

Throughout the museum, rope lights, like those used to guide your path in a dark theater, lined the perimeters of the walls. The overhead lights were off, but there was moonlight sifting in through breaks in the drapes, imparting an eerie glow to the hordes of wax figures. They looked so real, she got the feeling they might come to life and start following her with zombie arms any minute.

Her stomach flipped over.

She really wished he'd turn the lights on, but they were not supposed to be in here, so it made sense he'd keep them off. Anyway, there was plenty of ambient light for them to move around without bumping into furniture or statues or anything, so she decided to immerse herself in the experience and enjoy her private tour of Waxed. She really did want to please her customers. Especially one like Charlie, who'd be paying well for her time. "This is cool."

Moving forward, she all but tripped over George Clooney and Matt Damon, who were laughing and clinking champagne glasses. Closing her eyes, she sniffed. She thought she could smell their aftershave. She wasn't sure if it was her imagination, or the statues, or Charlie Chaplin over there, but she liked the scent. No, it couldn't have been aftershave. The smell seemed too sweet for a man's cologne. In her head, soft music played. Enchanted, she swung around, wishing she had on a full skirt that would fly out as she twirled, but then . . . she remembered why she was there. She clapped her arms down to her side.

With a tilt of his head, Charlie motioned to her, and she followed him into another statue-filled room, then another and another. At least ten minutes passed, and he still hadn't spoken. She was starting to feel like she needed to take charge, or they might be here forever. She noticed Charlie wasn't that tall for a man, and that gave her a mental advantage, made it easier for her, someone who bought her clothes in the Junior Petites department, to assume control of the situation. "Tell me what you want," she commanded in her sultriest voice.

He shook his head.

"Show me then."

Still, he said nothing.

Maybe he wanted her to guess. But the clock was ticking. She still might have time to squeeze in another client if this one didn't keep her tied up all night. "Charlie, baby," she whispered, then licked her lips and slowly unbuttoned her blouse, just enough to reveal the tops of her breasts and her lacey red push-up bra. Even if the john didn't specifically request it, it was a good idea to wear sexy lingerie. Lucy had a big walk-in closet, filled with specialty and designer items for the girls to borrow. Looking down at her small tits, she thought about the $2,500 that, along with Lucy's plastic-surgery discount, would all but pay for her implants. It wouldn't be long until she could broaden her customer base and start making real money, like Lucy said some of her other girls did. Smiling, Susan gave Charlie a come-hither finger.

At last, an obedient Charlie closed the distance between them. *Finally!*

"That's a good boy. Now, don't worry about a thing, baby. Just tell me what you like, and we can get started."

He stared at her, and above the silence she thought she heard the wax figures breathing. Charlie raised an arm and gently swept soft fingertips over her eyelids. She'd just bet he was one of those guys who got manicures.

"You want me to close my eyes," she guessed.

He nodded, and she did what he wanted. In the next few seconds, she heard a faint rustling of fabric followed by a tearing noise. A spasm of unease closed her throat. What was that? Did he open a condom? Whatever he was doing, he was taking his time, so she let her lids flutter slightly open and peeked out from beneath her lashes. First, her heart stopped beating entirely, then it began to jackhammer in her chest.

Charlie was wearing latex gloves.

Unable to fully process what was happening, she froze. He raised both gloved hands toward her neck as if to strangle her

Now you panic?

Adrenaline jetted through her blood, unlocking her paralyzed limbs. She thrust her knee into his groin. Grunting, he doubled over with pain. She didn't miss her chance. She barreled past him, racing for the door. Behind her, she heard him panting. She ran faster.

Faster.

She passed a statue and from instinct, threw out her arm and knocked Richard Gere to the floor. A loud thunk was followed by a muffled cry. Daring a look over her shoulder, she saw Charlie sprawled on the ground over the statue.

Where are those stairs?

She flew to another room and realized she was going the wrong way. The stairs were in the party room. Then she heard them. Slow, deliberate footfalls coming toward her. Trapped, she spun around, desperately searching for a weapon. Anything she could use to defend herself. A few feet to her right, moonlight bounced off a shiny object.

A sword!

She grabbed it from a statue's hand.

But when she touched the tip, her heart sank. It was square and dull. Still, the sword was heavy, and it was all she had, so she hung on to it anyway. Wait, she had her pepper spray!

Thank God!

She reached for her shoulder bag and hot tears filled her eyes. Somewhere, somehow she'd lost her purse. With each passing moment, the footfalls grew louder, more menacing. Slow, taunting steps told her he was in no rush—promised her there was no escape.

Hide.

Edging around the room, she mashed her back against the wall, trying to find the darkest corner. That's when she felt cold steel pressing against her spine. Too scared to breathe, she found and turned the knob, then eased through the doorway behind her before closing it softly. There were no windows inside this new room, therefore no light seeping through the drapes. Only the rope lights guided her now. It took time for her eyes to adjust, a few seconds, maybe more, then, too late to cover her scream, she clamped her hand over her mouth.

Before her, on a long table, stood an entire row of heads. Her heart jumped to her throat. She couldn't pull air into her lungs, and after a minute, her fingers begin to tingle. Dizzy, she fell to her knees.

Get up, Susan!

Using the sword as a fulcrum, she managed to pry herself off the floor. Suddenly, her common sense kicked into gear. She was in a wax museum. Those heads—they weren't real. Her chest loosened, and she resumed breathing. This had to be the art studio. Maybe there was another entrance. It made sense the artists would want to avoid walking through the public areas. Squinting against the darkness, she felt her way along the wall again until she was stopped by heat wafting toward her, warning her not to touch what was up ahead. In the dark, she saw shadows. No, not shadows. White vapor dissolving into black air like smoke into a night sky. That sweet scent she'd smelled earlier was so strong here—as if someone had set a thousand candles aflame. The vapors triggered a spasmodic, uncontrollable cough. When her fit finally subsided, her mouth opened in a gasp. Then, as if compelled by some unknown force, she reached out her hand, waving it over what she now could see to be a bubbling cauldron of molten wax.

Those footfalls again.

The door creaked open.

He was coming for her.

Chapter Four

Friday, October 4
11:00 A.M.
Hollywood, California

BACK AT THE Sky Walk Hotel, Spense stood at the window of his room, staring down onto Hollywood Boulevard below. At Caity's suggestion, they'd booked adjoining rooms on the same side of the building and same floor where Selena Turner had stayed. Caity had the idea that exposing themselves to an environment experienced by the killer might trigger some sort of insight into the crimes. Spense agreed it was a good idea, and he liked the idea of keeping Caity close.

The trip back from Boulder had been a quiet one. On the plane ride, Caity had kept her eyes closed, and though he knew she was exhausted, he doubted she'd been sleeping. More likely she was avoiding any conversation about what had transpired with her mother—and he didn't blame her for that.

Given Arlene Cassidy's cold demeanor toward her daughter, and Caity's equally chilly response, it'd taken all of his self-control not to intervene further. He'd wanted to take Arlene by the shoulders and shake her until she saw how badly her daughter needed her. He'd itched to pull Caity aside and reason with her, help her see that Arlene's professed lack of interest in Thomas Cassidy's case was merely a symptom of how deeply she'd been devastated. The woman couldn't seem to deal with her husband's execution in a rational manner. But out of respect for Caity's wishes, he hadn't interfered . . . much. Instead, he'd bitten his tongue . . . mostly, and folded his hands in his lap, leaving the two of them to work things out on their own until the Bible study group arrived. After the group left, Arlene had asked a few questions about the Falconer murder, then gone to bed, claiming a headache.

Her behavior reminded him of a person in shock. Though the news of her husband's exoneration should've been welcome, it had changed the landscape of her familiar, if painful, world. Spense knew it would take time for her to adjust. When you carry a burden that long, you're bound to remain a little bent, even after the weight is lifted.

The sound of Caity moving across the room broke his reverie. When she was close enough for him to smell her freshly shampooed hair, he turned, and the lost look on her face made him wonder if he should encourage her to talk about her mother. "You want to talk about Boulder?"

"No."

"Okay." Reaching out, he tweaked her nose, and the smile that came across her face changed everything. Curiosity replaced the hurt in her eyes.

"Checking out the lay of the land?" she asked, pushing her shoulders back and seeming to stand a bit taller in her bare feet.

His vibrant, ready-to-roll Caity had returned—and all it had taken was one touch from him. He was good for her, and that, he knew from the way his heart was expanding in his chest, was good for *him*.

Skirting him, she placed her hands on the windowsill and tugged upward. Nothing happened. "Spense, I need your guns."

She was playing it cool and light, and he was happy to go along. Grinning, he flexed his biceps and shook his head. "Not even these guns can open that window." Tapping one corner of the glass with his index finger he said, "See here, it's nailed shut."

She frowned, and even though they both knew the window was not going to budge, she tried again.

He gave her the *what's-up?* face.

"I just want to see how hard it would've been for Selena . . . or her killer . . . to pry the window open if it was sealed at the time of the attack. And look here . . ." Dropping her hands, she examined her palms, then held them out for Spense to inspect the redness and creases that proved her effort. "It would've been too difficult. No way the window in Selena's hotel room was nailed shut like this one."

According to SID, the scientific investigation division of the LAPD, Turner's window had been found open with no sign of damage, so . . . "No, it couldn't have been sealed, like it should've been. The SID report also says all the windows in the hotel were subsequently inspected, and at least a few others weren't up to code. The hotel isn't denying it failed to secure the windows in certain guest rooms, but they've all been taken care of now. The Sky Walk is ancient, so while Selena Turner's open window may reflect negligence, I wouldn't ascribe any nefarious motives to the management. I doubt the killer deliberately selected accommodations where he could shove her out the window."

That earned him another smile.

"Agreed. Premeditated murder by unsealing a window? Even for my wild imagination, that would be a stretch. Still, the window was most likely closed *and* locked when Selena rented the room for the day. She wouldn't have had time during the attack to both unlock and open it."

"Are we officially working the profile now? Or do you need . . ." When she shot him a warning look, Spense stopped midsentence. If she did need time to recoup from her visit home, she'd never admit it. And the clock was ticking, with Jeffers expecting some sort of preliminary profile by tomorrow.

Nodding, she said, "Not to draw premature conclusions, but it seems obvious to me that the Selena Turner and Adrianne Simpson murders are connected."

Apparently, Caity was not only a good shrink, she could read minds, too—at least she could read *his* mind. And it was that sixth sense that made her especially suited to profiling. Not that there were any *real* psychic forces involved in this type of work, but a good profiler needed highly developed empathic abilities. A good profiler needed an almost uncanny knack for seeing the world from another's point of view, and that included the killer's. More than once, Spense had been on the business end of a raised eyebrow or an elbow jab followed by: *Boy, you got the mind of a murderer down pat.* People look at you funny when you can divine exactly what happened at a crime scene even before the forensics come back. "The murders are connected, yes . . . but that doesn't necessarily mean there's a serial killer at work."

Her brow knit, but she didn't press him for an explanation. Caity was smart enough to know there was more than one set of causal hypotheses for any given configuration of facts. Locking onto a single interpretation without considering other alternatives was almost always a mistake. "Let's look at the murders individually first. We'll start with Selena Turner—the first victim."

"The best place to begin is at the beginning I suppose." Caitlin went to the desk and grabbed the accordion file that contained the crime-scene and environmental synopses, photographs and ME reports. She offered half the material to Spense, but he shook her off. "I had my fill of these on the plane while you were playing Sleeping Beauty."

"Sleeping Beauty?" Caitlin lifted a disapproving eyebrow, even as she chased away her own silly fantasy of Spense waking her with a kiss. *Get a grip.* "We've got serious matters to deal with here," she said—as much to remind herself as to scold him.

He lifted one shoulder. "Sorry."

"No worries." She looked around for a place to sit then, deciding rather quickly against the bed, crossed the room, and settled into a suede wingback chair that smelled of cleaning fluid.

Grasping the accordion file, her stomach balled up into an uncomfortable knot, and the muscles in her chest contracted. She knew from experience the file's contents would provoke a disturbing sense of intimacy with the UNSUB. Then she took a big breath, pulled out a sheaf of papers, and dove into reading. If the photographs and reports evoked powerful images, great. After all, that was why she'd come: to help the police get inside the mind of the killer. And she couldn't very well achieve that end if she wasn't willing to go into a dark place. The only way to understand what drove a person to kill, at least the only way she knew, was to put herself in his head, to empathize with him. Walk a mile in a murderer's shoes. Terrifying? Yes. Sickening? Positively.

For a moment, she saw her work through her mother's eyes, and the knot in her stomach tightened. She could understand how her mom might wonder if her daughter took some kind of voyeuristic pleasure in the *salacious* details of the murders. But pleasure was definitely not what her work brought her. Nightmares were more like it.

Screw Mom's damn, judgmental attitude.

Lives were at stake. If these two deaths really were the work of a serial, who knew how long it would be before he . . . or she . . . struck again? And so what if when Caitlin distanced herself from assigning any moral value to the experience and simply looked at the crimes as puzzles, like Spense had taught her to do, she actually enjoyed her job? Solving puzzles was challenging and fun. Again, her mother's voice piped up in her head: *Murder is fun?*

I love you, Mom. But I have work to do, and I need you to shut up now . . . please.

She let out a long breath and closed her eyes. When she opened them, Spense hovered over her, a menacing look on his face. He reached out and grabbed her by the shoulders, pulling her to a stand. Her heart began to race. She was deep in it so quickly. That odd sensation of looking around the room with someone else's eyes was already taking hold. She started to shake off the surreal feeling but stopped herself. That was why she was here.

"Up for a little role-play?" Spense asked.

That wicked expression on his face meant he was beginning

to put himself into the killer's mind-set. He obviously wanted to reenact the crime to see if they could fill in the missing details before starting on a formal profile. So far, all they really knew was that Selena Turner had been stabbed in the neck with a sharp, pointed object, then, somehow, wound up flying out a hotel room window onto the Walk of Fame below.

While a reenactment was a good idea, Caitlin didn't relish the idea of playing the victim. Taking her time, she carefully slid the papers and photos back into the accordion file. "Sure, only how about *you* play Selena."

Spense tilted his head, studying her. "It seems likely, assuming statistics hold, that the killer is male. Not to mention the fact that semen was found on her breasts. To get the best sense of what might have happened to Selena Turner, I think I should take the part of the aggressor, and you should take the victim's part." His gaze probed hers as he spoke, and when he leaned in close, her hand went to her throat before she could hide her discomfort.

Suddenly, Spense straightened, backing away from her. "Or we can do it your way. I don't want to hurt you, if you're worried about your side or anything. I really should've thought of that before."

He meant her left side, where she'd been shot and stitched up and torn open and stitched up again over the course of the last couple of months. But her wound was mostly healed now, just a little sore. "It's not that." She wasn't a control freak or anything, she simply knew from experience that ever since her father's arrest, being grabbed or having her movements restricted in any way made her sick to her stomach. Thoughts of her father living out his days, confined to a tiny jail cell, intruded on her at the oddest moments. There had even been nights she'd slept in a closet, forcing herself to experience his pain as a show of solidarity. But, of course, that never made anything better and only intensified her anxiety. She hadn't shut herself in a closet since her father's exoneration, and there was no point putting herself in an uncomfortable situation today. It really shouldn't matter which part she played in their reenactment. "But if you don't mind, I'll play the killer," she said. Without waiting for permission, she reached for Spense's shoulders.

He bent at the knees to accommodate her grasp, then with a quick, awkward twist, easily secured his release. "Sorry. Let's try again, and this time I'll put less muscle into it."

As they struggled, Spense seemed to be trying hard not to overpower her with his superior strength, but even with him being mindful to match his abilities to those of a small woman, his height made realism impossible. This simply wasn't going to work. Spense had been right, and she'd been foolish not to realize that from the beginning. If they were going to get any true sense of what had taken place between Selena and her attacker, Caitlin was going to have to suck it up. She pressed a hand over her nervous stomach. "Let's switch back."

"Are you sure?" His tone let her know if she showed him the least bit of vulnerability he'd call off the reenactment altogether.

"Positive." She infused her voice with confidence and rubbed her hands together as if eagerly anticipating her part. "Go!"

Spense resumed his original stance, towering over her, moving in too close, and before she could blink, he had her by the shoulders again. She wanted to scream. "You grab me. I scream," she said, forcing a measure of control into her already shaky voice.

"Don't make another sound!" He jerked her against him, locking his arms tightly around her back, giving her no wiggle room. No *breathing* room. "You fucking do that again, and I'll kill you."

Selena's body had been half-dressed, with her shoes still

strapped to her feet when she hit that sidewalk, which meant she'd been wearing stilettos during the attack. Caitlin slammed her bare heel down on Spense's instep.

"Bitch!" He growled as his body jerked, giving her just enough room to get one arm free.

She yanked the only thing she could get her hand on . . . his ear. Spense let out a yowl, and she broke free of him, but he was between her and the door, blocking her escape.

She bolted to the window, reached up to its lock, but Spense was on her again in an instant. No time to unlock the window, which seemed to confirm her earlier theory that it'd been opened before the attack, but *why*?

Spense caught her and whirled her around to face him. Gently twisting one arm behind her back, he faked a punch to her right cheek. Even though she could tell he was being careful of her left flank, and his grip on her wrist wasn't half what it ought to have been, her entire body trembled with fear . . . and rage. This might be role-play, but the adrenaline pumping through her veins was very real. She jabbed Spense in the gut with an elbow and managed to spin back around to face the street. She found herself staring at the crowds milling on the Walk of Fame below. It was far too easy to put herself in Selena's head. *If I scream, someone will hear me. If I scream, someone will help. If I scream . . . he's going to kill me.* "I stick my head out the open window."

Spense pressed his body into hers, his hands beneath her breasts, lifting her off the ground.

She'd be bent over, halfway out the window if it were open.

Nowhere to go. I'm trapped. Desperate, she fought with everything she had to break his hold on her. She kicked his shins wildly, clawed at his hands. He might be handling *her* with kid gloves, but she was giving it her all. She *was* Selena Turner. She was fighting for her life, and she had no choice. "I scream."

"I told you not to do that." Only it wasn't Spense's voice she heard. It was the cruel, calculated voice of a murderer. Her head was swimming. The muscles in her legs burned from kicking. Raising her head, she gulped in air, trying to keep her head above the turbulent black water of her own fear. Then something cold and sharp lightly touched the side of her neck as Spense simulated the stabbing.

Nowhere to go.

She felt the cold touch of the object on her neck again. Looking right, through blurry eyes, her gazed homed in on the awning beneath the room Selena had occupied. "I'm bleeding. Terrified. Disoriented. I see a fire escape, but it's too far away for me to jump onto it. I'll never make it."

"I *warned* you not to scream." The killer whispered the words in her ear, his breath hot on her cheek, and she knew—with absolute certainty—if she stayed in this room, she'd die. Her eyes fell on the awning again. It was her only chance.

"Spense!" Her voice came out gravelly and surprisingly weak.

He lowered her feet to the floor, releasing her so quickly she almost fell.

She'd spoken his name, and he'd seemed to understand right away that she was done with the reenactment. The unsteadiness in her legs, and the pounding of her pulse, were good indicators she'd called a halt to the drama none too soon. And besides, she'd just had a small epiphany.

"You okay?" Spense asked, his eyes taking careful stock of her, reaching one hand out as if preparing to steady her. "You look a little seasick there, sailor."

"Fine." She waved him off with her hand. "Spense . . . Selena wasn't pushed out the window. She *crawled* out. Or at least she tried to." Caitlin pointed to the awning. "She knew she was going to die if she didn't escape, and she thought the awning might break her fall. She had to go for it."

He nodded. "And then, understanding that Selena's climbing out the window would increase the risk of his getting caught, he tries to pull her back inside."

"But she's fighting for her life. They struggle. She doesn't give up. Not until she's free . . . and falling." Caitlin pressed her palms against the cool glass of the securely sealed window, her heart aching for Selena. She swallowed hard before turning back to Spense. His pupils were dark and dilated, and she could see he was feeling Selena's anguish, just like she did. She could barely stand but managed to make her way over to the lovely corner desk. With one finger, she traced the geometric designs that inlaid the exotic dark wood of the desktop, then folded herself slowly into a swivel chair. They'd have to talk through the rest of this sitting down. "What were you using to stab me?"

Spense seated himself beside her, then opened his palm, revealing the object he held.

Oh. "A corkscrew." The ME had suspected an ice pick had made the puncture wounds on the victim's neck, but who the hell had such a thing these days? Her guess would be serial killers with elaborate fantasy lives and lots of time and ice on their hands.

"I grabbed it off the nightstand on my way to the window." When Spense had ordered a bottle of wine earlier, she'd found it a bit odd, since he usually avoided alcohol. Now she realized he'd ordered it because a bottle of chardonnay had been found chilling at the crime scene.

"Of course. That would mean, though, that the killer didn't bring the murder weapon with him to the hotel. And that suggests he wasn't *planning* to kill Selena at all."

"Agreed. The first murder is too disorganized to have been premeditated. No one uses a corkscrew and leaves a window open when they're *plotting* to stab someone to death. And the bruises found on Selena's wrists and her dislocated elbow are consistent with the killer's attempting to pull her back inside the room."

Their gazes met and held. The attacker wasn't showing off. He hadn't wanted Selena's body to fall onto Hollywood Boulevard for all the world to see. And even though the murder weapon hadn't been found at the scene, the killer had left plenty of trace evidence. DNA from beneath Selena's nails, for example, was cooking— along with the seminal fluid found between her breasts. This first murder had been impulsive, irrational, and brutal. Like Spense had said, *disorganized*.

"So how does that fit with the second murder? Adrianne Simpson's body was deliberately posed on the SLY tour bus, like a big neon sign flashing: *Pay attention to me*."

"It *doesn't* fit. That crime scene was sanitized with great care. Not a single print was found on the bus, yet it carries scores of passengers every day. And those differences between the crimes put quite a damper on the serial-killer theory."

"Still . . . the victims are undeniably of a type—blond, mid to late twenties, college-educated."

"And don't forget they were both stabbed in the neck. I'm interested to see if the ME confirms the wounds on both women appear to be from the same object." He got up and paced the length of the room a time or two, then sat back down. "That window is really eating at me. *Why* was it open?"

"It was a beautiful day. The obvious answer would be *fresh air* . . ." She offered this up without conviction.

"Selena was with a man in a hotel room in the middle of the day without her top on. It's pretty clear their meeting was meant to be clandestine. Secret sex. And the UNSUB was worried enough about his privacy to have Selena sign them in, making sure no one saw him with her. Only a fool would open the window and drapes under those circumstances."

"It was a second-floor room. So the chances of being seen were low."

"Sure, but if someone in that office building across the way had an inclination and a pair of binoculars, he could've gotten an eyeful. Maybe it wasn't *likely* they'd be seen, but it was possible. So why risk it? I'm not saying there had to have been an earth-shattering reason to open that window, but *something* must've prompted them to do it."

"And you think that something is important."

"Maybe yes. Maybe no. I'm just trying to understand the *motives* of the people in that room."

He made a good point. Sometimes a seemingly inconsequential detail could break a case wide open.

Spense pulled stationery and a pen from the desk drawer and scooted his chair closer to hers. "There's a lot to suggest this *isn't* the work of a serial murderer, but then again, there's a lot to say it might be. I say we get started on that profile."

Chapter Five

Saturday, October 5
9:00 A.M.
Hollywood, California

TODAY PROMISED TO be one of those ubiquitous Southern California days. The kind where the sun shines down from a shimmering, baby blue sky just brightly enough to toast, but not burn, your skin, and a honeysuckle breeze catches beneath your hair at the exact moment a sheen of perspiration begins to tickle the back of your neck. In Phoenix, where Caitlin had grown up, such a perfect-climatic trifecta occurred about ten seconds out of every year. If you blinked, the warm day would have already been replaced by scorching desert heat, and the soft breeze would have changed to a gustnado—a pseudotornado of dust. Not that she minded the Arizona weather, it was only that she noticed the way flowers and the smiles on people's faces seemed to flourish in the temperate climes of Southern California. Caitlin loved flowers, and Los Angeles served up a feast of both the wild and cultivated variety. So when the time came for them to deliver their Fallen Angel Killer profile to Jeffers, she asked Spense to indulge her in the mile or so stroll from the Sky Walk Hotel to the Hollywood police station—or as Jeffers had called it—the cop shop.

Without hesitation, Spense agreed, and just minutes later they reached the turnoff from Hollywood Boulevard and headed south on Wilcox Avenue. Beside her, Spense took long strides, and she had to move quickly to keep up with his pace. His arms swung at his sides, making her fingers itch to take hold of his hand—but she didn't. The memory of his lips pressed to hers was seared into her brain, and whenever he touched her, even if it was only to put his hand on the small of her back to guide her through a doorway, she melted. Though it had only been a few days since they'd talked of going to Tahiti together, it seemed a lifetime ago. Since then, they'd been assigned a new case, and while her body might be eager to take the plunge with Spense, her brain was screaming *danger*. There were so many things to consider: their differing world views, his habit of riding in on his big white horse even though she didn't require a rescue . . . and then, of course, there was the case. What if giving in to their attraction compromised their ability to work together to catch a killer?

Spense pulled up short to pick a California poppy for her.

"Thanks," she said, tucking the flower behind her ear and feeling too warm and happy—and confused—to remind him the poppy would have brightened far more days if left undisturbed.

A wide grin, one that lifted his lips slightly higher on the right side than on the left, split his face. How could that slight imperfection make a smile so devastating? Neither Spense nor she had the time for haircuts these days, and his usually close-cropped dark hair had gotten wilder than she'd seen it before. With his long hair and rugged good looks, he could've been a movie star. And given the way her heart raced when he tipped his shades and gave her a playful wink, she was his biggest fan.

Danger.

A sudden gust of wind cooled her cheeks, and when she touched her hair, the flower was no longer there. As they crossed first Sunset Boulevard, then De Longpre Avenue in silence, she wondered if Spense's mind was on the case, or, if like her, he was thinking of something altogether different. With effort, she refocused her attention on the approaching meeting with Jeffers and his second in command, a lieutenant Enrique Martinez—just in time. She spied a black-and-white POLICE sign in front of an edifice up ahead. They'd reached their destination.

Hollywood station had about as much architectural panache as a loaf of bread, and its light brown bricks carried an orange tinge, making it appear as though the building had been the victim of a bad spray tan. With a quick whiff of disappointment, she noted there were no surrounding flowers and only a few small bushes. But water was precious here, and the xeriscaping had no doubt been installed to conserve that limited resource. Besides, the station wasn't entirely without charm. Tall, thick-trunked trees with full green canopies lined the sidewalk, and an unexpected, old-timey lamppost stood sentry out front. The station was, in fact, rather lively compared to the barren white apartments and dilapidated bail-bonds office across the street.

Leading up to the front entrance, she noted embedded sidewalk stars, similar to those on the Walk of Fame. Apparently nothing in Hollywood went untouched by the entertainment industry, not even its police force. Strange though, to find stars so far off Hollywood Boulevard. Wondering who had been unlucky enough to be relegated to this distant location, she stopped and crouched on one knee to get a better look.

Oh no.

Her hand went to her heart as understanding dawned. These sidewalk stars weren't for celebs. They were monuments, honoring Hollywood police officers killed in the line of duty. As she counted the stars, her breathing sped up. There were far too many.

"Guess there's more than one kind of fallen angel in LA," Spense said softly, then offered his hand, pulling her back to her feet.

Without warning, her vision darkened, and she stretched out her arm, waving her hand around, feeling for the reassurance of brick. When she found it, she took a step back and slumped against the wall. "Stood up too fast," she said, before Spense could swoop in with his questions.

He yanked off his sunglasses, and his eyes widened in apparent concern. But this was no big deal—just a slight drop in blood pressure from too much sun and too little fluid. She made a mental note to stop for Gatorade on the way back to the hotel.

"It's nothing. I just need to do a better job of staying hydrated, so I don't get dizzy." But . . . there was something else. "Spense . . ." she hesitated. "Something Jeffers said has been bothering me—he said I've been batting for the wrong team." Her gaze went to the sidewalk memorials for the officers killed in the line of duty. The stones reminded her of the time she'd spent at her father's grave, and she couldn't help thinking of the families of these brave men. She'd always followed her conscience in her work, but she could understand how some people, like Jeffers, might view her as the enemy.

Spense moved in closer, so close she could feel his body heat transferring to her, making her blood expand and pound in her veins. For a moment, he said nothing, and she wasn't sure he'd heard her. But, finally, he raised an eyebrow in seeming challenge. "Well, kid. I can't say you haven't driven me crazy at times. Always up in my face about protecting the rights of one motherfucker or another."

Her chin jerked up. She no longer needed the wall—her own spine was all the support she required. "And who's to decide who's worthy of having his rights protected? You? Your copper buddies? Last time I heard, in this country, *motherfuckers* have rights, too. If they didn't, we'd all be screwed."

"There's the Caity I know and love." The big grin spreading across his face told her he'd been baiting her.

Her face flushed hot. Because she'd not only bitten the minnow, she'd swallowed the hook whole. His point was made, however. Someone had to look out for the rights of the accused, and how could she ever doubt her past work when she'd played at least some small role in freeing more than one innocent man? But . . . at the same time, she couldn't deny that she was beginning to believe the best way to protect the innocent was to see to it that the guilty were correctly identified in the first place. If they'd caught Gail Falconer's real killer to begin with, her father would be alive today. Her head cleared, and her pulse beat fast and hard. She knew she was in the right place, doing the right work. "I guess it's like we said before."

"When before?"

"Back in Phoenix, when you convinced me we should work together."

"Remind me. How did I do that again? I mean apart from my pure animal magnetism?"

Now that she thought about it, she might've mostly convinced herself, but what did it matter who got the credit? "You asked me which side I was on, and I said, something like *if the truth is a side, then I'm on that one.*"

"Ironic, isn't it? To think we'd been on the same team—the truth team—the whole time we were butting heads, but we simply couldn't see it. Maybe one of these days, Jeffers will figure it out, too." His hands lifted toward her shoulders as if to help her.

She shook her head.

"You got your land legs back?" Spense asked.

By way of an answer, she pushed through the door to Hollywood station and held it open for Spense. "Let's roll."

Chapter Six

Saturday, October 5
9:15 A.M.
Hollywood, California

THE PRETTY GIRL kneels on the sidewalk in front of Hollywood station and reverently touches the stars, one by one. Then the man in the suit reaches out his hand to help her stand. She gazes up at him, her eyes shining with admiration. The adoring way he looks at her suggests love's first blush is waiting for them just around the corner.

How nauseating.

As I focus on the shadows that fill the gentle hollow of her throat, anticipation sparks within me. My fingers long to close around that delicate neck. In my head, I hear her strangled cry as she realizes, too late, that *I'm* her destiny. How much longer must

I wait before I can smell her fear? Touch my tongue to her cold, lifeless lips?

Who am I?

That's the very question I asked myself when all this began, and every day since. I had to dig deep within to find the answer, recall my most difficult moments, relive my worst days. And then I used that pain to find the strength to carry out the task at hand. You see, murder isn't for the faint of heart. Killing isn't a task for an ordinary person.

But I am extraordinary. I am filled with righteousness, and so I have every right to take what I desire.

Be very careful.

I am not who you think you see when you bump into me on the street or sit next to me in the coffee shop.

Closing my eyes, I remember last night. My pulse leaps beneath my skin when I recall the look on the angel's face while her life drained away. Then I open my eyes, and the thrill disappears, leaving behind it a gaping hole that demands to be filled.

I cannot stop.

I cannot rest.

Those two over there, striding with such purpose into the station, have come all this way to find me, and instead, I've found them. Like you, they don't see me at all and yet . . .

Here I am.

Chapter Seven

Saturday, October 5

9:15 A.M.

Hollywood, California

INSIDE HOLLYWOOD STATION, the lobby seemed as nondescript as the building's exterior. While Spense flashed his creds and spoke with the desk sergeant, Caitlin perused a handout purporting to answer frequently asked questions:

Do we treat celebrities differently? No. Stars are treated the same as everyone else.

The corners of her mouth twitched. According to what she'd read, Hollywood was one of a very few police stations in the country that didn't release mug shots to the press. But, of course, that wouldn't have anything to do with its celebrity-rich demography.

Spense put away his wallet, and the desk sergeant buzzed them into the captain's office, but not before delivering a frown and a highly territorial look that Spense later described as *the stink-eye.* Judging by the officer's expression, the Hollywood division had not yet been made aware the Los Angeles chief of police had called in the BAU. Thus the profilers' grand entrance at the station was the equivalent of a cat jumping out of a bag into a room of highly displeased canaries. Spense gave her one of his winks, and she blew out a breath. *Truth team,* he mouthed.

Dressed in full suit and tie, seated behind a mahogany pad-footed desk and flanked by certificates, photographs, and commendations, Captain Lionel Jeffers looked every bit the part of commanding officer—even with his wrinkled puppy brow and untamable gray eyebrows. He motioned Spense and Caitlin into his office, and when they entered, her attention was immediately diverted to a younger, magnetically handsome man, balanced on the edge of a Queen Anne wing chair that had been upholstered in expensive-looking red fabric. The man, also dressed in plain clothes, though his were not so fancy as Jeffers's, appeared to be attempting to make as little body contact with the chair as possible. He reminded Caitlin of a kid who'd been sent out to play in his Sunday best and warned not to get mud on his knickers. He lumbered to his feet, and side by side with Spense, their heights seemed almost equal. His coal black hair, however, was a good three shades darker, and his skin a buffed bronze. Like Spense, his profile was rugged, but his aquiline nose gave him a more aristocratic air than Spense's *man of the people.*

"I'm Rick," the man introduced himself in a rich, bass voice that sent unexpected shivers across Caitlin's skin. Or maybe it had more to do with the way his warmed cocoa gaze traveled from the tips of her toes up to her face, resting there a second longer than was polite.

"My right hand, Lieutenant Enrique Martinez." Jeffers came to a half stand and quickly reseated himself. "The lieutenant does a hell of a job managing my detectives for me. He'll be sitting in with us today, and later he'll be the one who conveys the Fallen Angel Killer profile to the rest of the task force."

Task force, Caitlin had learned, was the kind of term the public found reassuring. It might mean a team of ten men working a case, or it might mean one hundred. But clearly, Jeffers had relegated Spense and her to an advisory role. He was compartmentalizing them. And maybe for now, there was some justification for keeping the investigators and profilers separate. But sooner or later, they'd need to compare their profile of the unidentified subject—the UNSUB—against the leads that were coming in, so that they could revise it accordingly.

"It's a pleasure." Again, the lieutenant's deep voice had a physical impact on her.

Noting Rick Martinez's friendly smile and open stance, she decided she was glad he would be the one interpreting their profile to the Hollywood detectives. "Mine too. I'm Caitlin Cassidy," she replied, offering her firmest handshake.

"Spense," Spense said in a terse voice. Then came his clipped follow-up, "FBI."

The only other seating in the room was a couch, also a Queen Anne, done up in gold fabric that coordinated well with the red wing chair. It didn't take a profiler to figure out the captain's office had been decorated by a doting wife. The room, almost claustrophobic with commendations and plaques, made it clear Jeffers was both devoted to duty and far too busy to select his own furniture. The captain obviously was, as the cliché goes, the kind of cop who bled blue, and she suspected the lieutenant did as well. Selecting the end of the couch closest to Martinez, she seated herself and suppressed a smile as the big man returned to his awkward, end-of-chair perch.

Spense dropped onto the couch next to Caitlin, just far enough away to be appropriate, yet close enough to send the signal to anyone who cared to receive it—like Martinez—that they were more than colleagues. It was a small gesture. One that made her stomach flutter, but also set off warning bells in her head. It was hard for a woman to be taken seriously in a *cop shop*, and she preferred to keep things highly professional in such a setting.

Stretching his arm over the back of the couch and opening his knees until his leg touched hers, Caitlin saw Spense shoot Lieutenant Martinez a look. One that was every bit as possessive as the stink-eye they'd gotten from the desk sergeant earlier. If Spense was going to act like a jealous lover when they hadn't even . . .

"Great to meet you both." Though Martinez seemed to address Spense, he kept his gaze focused on Caitlin. "So you're the profiler who's got the captain's shorts in a knot. Not to worry. His bark is worse than his bite." Like a typical cop, the lieutenant seemed fond of sprinkling multiple metaphors into the conversation.

"I'm not worried," Spense ground out.

"And my shorts aren't in a knot." Jeffers narrowed his eyes at his lieutenant, but his voice held no rancor. The two clearly had a familiar and trusting relationship. Their mutual respect was apparent in their tone, if not their words. *Good.* Since Martinez seemed at least somewhat receptive to their input, maybe he could smooth the way for them with the captain. Now, if only Spense would take his alpha-dog attitude down a notch.

"Rick is full of shit—I got no stick up my shorts or anywhere else either. But I don't make any bones about the fact that no BAU bullshit is going to run this investigation."

A flicker of movement started up in Spense's jaw. "You mind if I ask how come this case didn't get kicked to RHD?" The Robbery Homicide Division of the LAPD worked high-profile murder cases across geographic boundaries, so it made sense they'd be involved here.

Spense had spoken slowly and carefully, and Caitlin surmised he was working hard to keep himself under control. She bit her lower lip, willing him not to antagonize the captain or Martinez.

Jeffers crossed his arms over his chest and leaned forward. "If you think RHD detectives got bigger dicks than my men, Agent Spenser, then you're an asshole."

"Their dicks may or may not be bigger, but RHD is certainly endowed with more of them. So I'll ask again—why not kick this to them?"

Hearing the challenge in both men's voices, she could easily imagine them jumping to their feet and circling each other with their fists up.

After a moment of glaring at Spense, the captain dropped his gaze. "Serials *are* their specialty."

"But?" Spense persisted.

"But," Jeffers shrugged and leaned back. "When I argued this was Hollywood's case, they backed off. Robbery Homicide wasn't all that eager to take credit for a potential public-relations nightmare."

"You fought for this." Spense's tone conveyed a grudging respect. His shoulders dropped, and the two men looked at each other, still seeming to size each other up, but with a hair less animosity. Smiling, she let out a soft breath.

Jeffers nodded. "Both murders happened on my turf. And I don't walk away from my duty that easy. Robbery Homicide is, however, making whatever resources we need available. So it's all hands on deck . . . but ultimately this is *our* show. I'm sorry if the BAU bullshit remark offended, but after making a stand that my detectives should lead the charge, I can't afford to screw this thing up."

Caitlin straightened her back, deciding there was no way to sugarcoat what she had to say. "Well, then, since you don't want the bullshit version, you won't mind me telling you that although we've brought you your profile . . . as the chief requested . . ." She put the barest emphasis on the last part to remind Jeffers that although this was still his case, his was not the *final* authority. "We also brought you problems."

"What kind of problems?"

"Like whether or not the same person is responsible for both homicides."

Jeffers scrubbed a hand over his face.

Spense jumped in. "That would be good news . . . if we could actually rule out a serial killer . . . but we can't. What we can say is that the second murder has all the markings of a serial. But the first murder is simply too impulsive—unplanned and disorganized—to fully connect the dots to the second murder. For example, we don't believe the UNSUB intended for Selena Turner's body to wind up on the Walk of Fame at all. Therefore, we can't say leaving the bodies in popular tourist spots constitutes a signature for some Fallen Angel Killer."

"But both bodies *did* wind up in popular tourist spots," the captain objected.

"Sir." Rick held up a hand. "I'd like to hear them out."

So Martinez really was interested in their profile. And he should be because the practical burden was on him and his detectives to catch this UNSUB. The captain might have the nominal responsibility, but the actual investigation was being conducted by the lieutenant's detectives. The real heat wasn't in the captain's kitchen, it was at the homicide table.

"I never said I wasn't going to hear them out." For the first time, Jeffers seemed to be growing impatient with Martinez's informality, his lack of deference to the captain's rank. Jeffers turned to Caitlin. "How did you arrive at your conclusion—that the body wasn't meant to wind up on the Walk of Fame?"

"We wanted to get a feel for what might have happened," she paused, giving Spense a chance to take the reins, but he motioned for her to continue. "So we conducted a reenactment of Selena Turner's murder in Spense's hotel room. Based on that reenactment, we determined Selena Turner likely climbed or fell out of that window in an attempt to escape her attacker."

"When you say you *determined* it, do you mean you have evidence to go along with that hypothesis, or is it just your hunch?"

"It's an educated hunch. When Spense and I analyze a scene, we're looking at behavioral clues, and that's based on years of training and experience. Call it a hunch if you will, but at least acknowledge we have a track record behind us." Well, at least Spense did. Hers was a bit shorter. But so far, she was one for one with her profiles.

Jeffers shook his head. "Maybe so, but the forensic evidence points to the fact that Selena's murder was planned . . . not impulsive like you said. The ME's initial assessment is that Selena Turner was stabbed in the neck with a sharp, slender object such as an ice pick. And yes, ice picks do occasionally come in bartending kits, but Martinez already checked with the Sky Walk management, and they do *not* provide ice picks to their guests. In fact, they don't use ice picks in the hotel at all. Which means the killer had to have brought the murder weapon with him and removed it when he left. It was premeditated murder."

"Except we think it was a corkscrew," Spense interrupted.

"Again you *think*. Based on what? Your educated hunch again? I like my conclusions to be supported by *facts*." When Jeffers frowned, his eyebrows nearly touched.

"We'll get the facts, sir." Martinez said. "Both women had shallow puncture wounds to the neck that were too small in diameter to have been made by a knife, thus the ice pick supposition. I'll check with the ME. Find out if Turner's wound could have come from a corkscrew. Given the arterial spray when Miss Turner hit the ground, she was definitely still alive when she went out the window. I'd have to say that goes *against* premeditation. Tossing a vic out a second-story window—a potentially survivable fall— while she's still breathing is a big risk for a killer to take."

Jeffers nodded. "A crazy-ass risk. But we got a crazy-ass killer on our hands, so who knows what was going on in his head?" His eyes darted from Spense to Caitlin as if it had suddenly occurred to him it might be of some use to have a shrink and a profiler on his team. He pointed at Martinez. "There was an open bottle of wine on scene. Check with room service. Maybe whoever brought the bottle up remembers if he opened the wine for the lady and took the corkscrew back with him, or if he left it so she could open the bottle later." His brows worked his forehead, and he fisted his hands on the desk in front of him. "We'll follow up on this crime-of-impulse theory for the Turner woman—but if you're asking me to believe, based on nothing but an unscientific reenactment and your so-called insight into the mind of a killer, that these murders aren't connected, I'm not buying what you're selling. If there's not a serial murderer out there, how do you explain the second blonde?"

"We can't." Caitlin met the captain's eyes. She intended to be straight with him.

"It can't be coincidence that another beautiful blond *actress*," his voice dripped with sarcasm on the word *actress*, "was stabbed in the neck and displayed bare-breasted in an SLY tour bus parked just off Hollywood Boulevard."

"Agreed," Spense said. "Which is why we went ahead and constructed a profile. We just need you to be aware . . ."

"It's full of holes?" Jeffers kicked back in his chair and snorted.

"That it might need revision," Caitlin said.

"So where is this genius report of yours, anyway? The lieutenant and me are all ears. Aren't we, Rick?"

"I am, sir. Last night I was reading about that mad bomber case that happened back in the day. They say the profile was accurate right down to the double-breasted suit the killer was wearing at the time of his arrest."

"That wasn't a Cassidy and Spenser profile, though, now was it, Rick?"

Had a shadow of mirth flashed in Jeffers's eyes? The tension in the room had started out thicker than bone, but now seemed more like just a bit of tough skin. She decided this might be the right moment to try to cut through it with a little humor. "Absolutely not. *Our* profiles are much more accurate." Then, figuring she could always claim dirt in her eye, she dared a wink at the captain. To her surprise, he threw back his head and laughed. "You do have spunk, young lady."

Ignoring the *young lady* part, Caitlin smiled her thanks, then passed around copies of their report. It looked neat and tidy in its laminated binder, but she knew the contents were anything but. There were just too many unanswered questions. "The primary support for a serial-killer theory is that both victims were of a specific type—same age, same hair color, same lifestyle—and the posing of the second body. The killer spent a great deal of time with Simpson, taking care to set a specific scene. That suggests her murder fulfilled a unique fantasy for the killer, one that he's played out in his imagination many times and is likely to act on again in the future."

"Our UNSUB will be male and old enough to have segued from an elaborate fantasy life into the real-life enactment of those fantasies through his crimes," Spense said. "On the other hand, given the youth of his victims, the killer is not likely to be middle-aged. He'd be closer to his victims' ages. So late twenties to early thirties at most."

"*Why* would he be close to his victims in age?"

"You said you wanted facts. The epidemiology of crime tells us killers are similar to their victims more often than not. In this case, the age of the UNSUB is a conclusion drawn from a statistical probability. If I speculated as to why, I'd be bullshitting you, and we've already established we're not here to do that," Spense replied.

Jeffers shuffled the papers in his hands, but his eyes were focused on Spense. He was listening—attentively.

Caitlin cleared her throat and picked up where Spense left off, "We have a killer around thirty years old, between five-foot-seven and five-foot-nine. From the defensive wounds on her body and her dislocated elbow, we know that Selena put up a hell of a fight. And she managed to get out the window despite the UNSUB'S attempts to yank her back in. So the killer couldn't have been that much stronger than she was. The angle of the wounds to the necks in *both* women tell us the killer was taller than his victims—but the shallowness of the wounds suggest he didn't have enough of a height and weight advantage to be able to drive the murder weapon deep. Of course, if the weapon does turn out to be a corkscrew, that's harder to embed than a knife."

"Or an ice pick." Jeffers reminded her. "Education level?"

She raised a pleased eyebrow at the captain.

"In for a penny," he said.

She was warming up to Jeffers, or maybe he was warming up to her. In any event, she had to give him his due. He obviously hadn't wanted their interference with his case, but he was evaluating everything put before him anyway. "Given the meticulous planning in the second murder, and the fact that the UNSUB managed to escape without being noticed in both cases, his IQ is above average. Some college is likely—he may even have some postgrad work under his belt."

"But he's not a genius." Jeffers's eyes shifted nervously around the room. Apparently he didn't relish the idea of having to outwit an evil genius. Nor did she. The case they'd just come off of in Phoenix had been all the more challenging because the UNSUB had been incredibly smart. Then her gaze fell on Spense, fiddling with his Rubik's cube.

She covered a smile. Despite having been labeled as intellectually handicapped for the first half of his childhood, Spense was a gifted profiler. He might not have as many letters after his name as she had after hers, but he could easily discern the truth from a pack of lies, and no one could solve a puzzle faster. In the unlikely event their UNSUB turned out to be brilliant? *Oh, well.* He'd be no match for the man sitting next to her.

"I doubt it. Selena's murder was simply too unsophisticated, and the methodology, the stabbing in the neck, is too crude. Geniuses go for a more complicated MO. Untraceable poisonings for example. Something that utilizes their skill set, challenges both them and the authorities. Besides that, these victims were medium risk. They weren't homeless, but neither young woman had close family or a regular job. That makes it less likely the killer would be known to her inner circle and easily identified, so again, not that much of a challenge for someone who's looking to prove how intelligent he is. This killer doesn't seem to be saying *I'm smarter than you*, so much as *I'm important. Please notice me.*"

"But he does have the social skills to lure the girls," Spense added. "The SID reports suggest he killed Adrianne Simpson on the bus itself. So he had to have had enough smarts to come up with a good reason to get her there and enough charm to keep her on board until he was done with her. Our guy's married, personable, and has an IQ between 115 and 130. Hell, let's call it. His IQ is 120."

"That's pretty specific." Martinez, who'd seemed supportive to this point, openly rolled his eyes at Spense.

"That's a rough estimate," Caitlin hurried to say. Just when they were making headway, earning some credibility with the locals, Spense had to start showing off. "He means he's above average, but below genius so that's . . ."

"One twenty." Spense said. "Wait and see." He stretched his legs and put his hands behind his head. Smiled.

"Employed?" Pointedly ignoring Spense, Jeffers directed the conversation back to Caitlin.

"Probably. But most likely underemployed, or at least he *be-*

lieves he's not being properly utilized in his chosen profession, and that's a source of resentment."

"Got it. Five-foot-seven to five-foot-nine married male, medium build, late twenties to early thirties, employed at a job he resents. IQ . . . 120. Elaborate sexual fantasies." Jeffers gritted his teeth. "I'd prefer to know exactly how you came to each data point. That way, I'll know which of them I care to put stock in."

"Of course. That's why we've included a point-by-point explanation for each profiled characteristic. You'll find a lot more detail in the formal report we've given you. We explain the source of each conclusion, whether it's based on epidemiology, forensics from the crime scene, psychological theory, or simply our own expert opinions. We're here to help, and we don't mind answering questions," Spense responded with diplomacy, though a vein had begun to bulge in his forehead.

"Then answer me this . . ." Jeffers made a big show of pulling a coin from his pocket. "Heads or tails? Do we or do we not have a serial murderer in town?" Rick Martinez's admonishing look didn't stop the captain from continuing. "'Cause if you can't answer that one simple question, you two are about as useful to me right now as a quarter, maybe a dime, if I'm being honest. I don't need the BAU to swoop down here, just to tell me to flip a damn coin."

Caitlin sprang to her feet. She was fine with being polite while others neglected to behave with courtesy. She was a professional, and that was part of the job. But there was no reason to sit around and be insulted indefinitely. They'd delivered their profile, and they'd told the truth. "We cannot answer that *simple* question at this time. We have several possible theories, which you'll find outlined in our report if you choose to read it. But the truth is we simply don't have enough data points to draw a definitive conclusion." She refrained from adding *despite the fact the press, the public, and the LAPD have prematurely made up their minds.*

A series of beeps sounded, and Jeffers and Martinez both began working their BlackBerries. They exchanged glances, and Jeffers said, "You said you needed another data point. Well, then you're in luck . . . We got ourselves another DB." He yanked his tie, then ran his index finger inside his collar before finally popping open the top button of his shirt. "And I don't just mean another dead body. I mean another dead blonde."

"She's at Waxed. Wanna come along?" Martinez aimed his words at Caitlin.

"Won't that contaminate your work product?" Jeffers seemed annoyed that Martinez had extended them an invitation to an active crime scene.

Spense rose and shoved his hands in his pocket. "The profile basics are already there. At this point, it's not only reasonable but necessary for us to be given more access to the investigation." He pulled out his key ring. "We'll meet you there."

"We walked from the hotel," Caitlin reminded Spense.

Rick opened the office door. "No worries. We can take my car. Cassidy, you ride shotgun. Spense, I'm afraid you're in back. I've only got room for one beautiful passenger up front."

Chapter Eight

Saturday, October 5
12:00 P.M.
Hollywood, California

NEVER A PATIENT man, Spense was nearing the end of his rope. What should've been a ten-minute trip from Hollywood station to Waxed wound up taking well over an hour for no good reason. Martinez had detoured for a briefing with the deputy chief, but just as they'd reached their destination, an adjuvant informed them their meeting had been canceled, and they had to make the reverse journey back to Hollywood in heavy traffic.

Spense repositioned his long legs, trying to work out the ache that had developed from being cramped up in the backseat. Backseats were for prisoners and short people—not six-foot-four special agents. He suspected from the dank smell that the last passenger had been a gym bag containing sweaty tennis shoes and a rotten banana. What's more, during the entire ride, Martinez had continued his open flirtation with Caity, and while Caity hadn't exactly flirted back, she hadn't shut the guy down either. Barely resisting the temptation to call Martinez out, Spense pressed his hands over his buzzing ears. From his delightful position in the vehicle, he caught bits and pieces of their animated conversation, but the crackle of the police radio, mixed with the sounds of the streets impeded his comprehension.

Martinez had his window down, and while Spense was grateful for the fresh air, his brain was overstimulated. Multiple threads of sound such as these always seemed to find a way to wind tightly around his neurons, choking off his ability to focus. As a result, he found himself wishing he could stick his fingers in his ears, like he'd done as a kid whenever he'd needed to concentrate. But he was all grown-up now, so instead, he shoved down his irritation with the chirping couple up front, imagined himself putting on a set of noise-canceling headphones, then sat back and worked his cube. By the time they got to Hollywood Boulevard, his thoughts were as sharp as if someone had opened up his cranial vault and blasted the dust off his circuitry with canned air.

After scouting the area, they found parking and approached Waxed on foot. By now, the place was crawling with uniforms, and yellow crime-scene tape had already gone up. It was impossible to keep the discovery of another dead blonde secret—but if the press got wind of FBI profilers on-site, it would only fuel the media flames that were already threatening to blaze out of control. So the trio used the private employee entrance in the alleyway.

As the door closed behind them, Spense spotted a cameraman accompanying someone he recognized—a popular SLY reporter. The man snapped their photograph, and *poof* went the slim chance of keeping the FBI's involvement out of the news. It wouldn't take much digging to identify Spense as a profiler, given his past court testimony in highly visible cases. Captain Jeffers wasn't going to be happy, but Spense knew something like this wouldn't have stayed quiet more than a day or two at the most anyway. Museum personnel, who'd made the horrific discovery this morning, were inside waiting to be interviewed, and they couldn't be compelled to keep silent.

As they ascended the steel stairs that led from the ground floor to the second level, Spense isolated the sound of Caity's heels tapping against metal. The sharp clicks triggered a question. Had the third victim worn heels? If so, she would've likely held on to the railing for security. He noticed Caity wobbling slightly, keeping her hands glued to her side, obviously not wanting to disturb the crime scene.

"You were on the horn with SID in the car. They lift any prints off this rail yet?" Spense asked Martinez.

"Didn't find any," the lieutenant called back over his shoulder. "We think the UNSUB and the vic must've come in through the gift shop that adjoins Perks—the all-night coffee shop. Plenty of prints there." His footing slipped, and he reached for the handrail. "In fact they found so many prints at the gift-shop entrance, it's going to be nearly impossible to get a clean set."

"The victim was brought in this way," Spense said. "Otherwise, they'd have found overlapping prints here, like they did at the other entry. The killer probably grabbed the rail like you just did, and then had to wipe it down. Tell SID to do an extra sweep of this stairwell for trace evidence."

Spense opened the door to the second level, holding it for Caity. She stepped into the A-list party room and did a double take. He didn't blame her. At first and even second glance, the statues appeared real. It was like walking in on an exclusive Hollywood soiree.

When Caity's hand went to her throat, he followed her gaze to the one figure that, ironically, seemed the least lifelike. The beautiful young blond woman had less color in her skin than the wax figures surrounding her. Nude from the waist up, she'd been posed on the lap of Waxed's replica of Tom La Grande, her short skirt hiked, her legs wound around his waist. Her arms had been wrapped around his neck, hands fur-cuffed together, helping to balance her in place. La Grande's trousers pooled around his ankles. The young woman's panties, if she'd been wearing any in the first place, were missing in action. Her blue eyes were fixed into a terrified, *help-me* stare.

Rage flashed through him, pulsing hard in his veins, and he welcomed it, revered it almost, because he knew he could use that anger as a whetstone to sharpen his focus. He filled his lungs with air, then let it out in a long, controlled breath.

"Do we have an ID on the angel?" Martinez asked the uniformed officer, who was busy dusting the chair and surrounding area for prints. Clearly, Martinez had connected his own dots, and at this point, Spense could not disagree with the assumption inherent in his use of the term *angel*. With the discovery of yet another dead body *posed* bare-breasted at a popular tourist attraction, Captain Jeffers's question had just been definitively answered: There was indeed a serial killer running around Hollywood. And given the UNSUB's preference for beautiful young blondes, the Fallen Angel Killer moniker seemed a good fit.

"Driver's license in the purse looks to match the vic. So, yeah, probably."

Spense snapped on the gloves offered him, then moved in for a better look at the body. Sure enough, there were several puncture wounds in the area of the carotid artery, but something important was missing. "No blood?"

"He cleaned up." A uniform flashed a megawatt flashlight around the room, and a million dirt particles, fibers, and more lit up, but nothing that appeared to be wiped-up blood.

"Nobody cleans up that good." Martinez shook his head.

Spense agreed. "Besides, there's no sign the place has been washed. Look at all the dust."

"If cause of death was a bleed-out from a carotid-artery stab wound," Caity said, "there would've been arterial spray. I don't see how the UNSUB could've removed *every trace* of that bloody mess without disturbing anything else." She arched a brow at Martinez. "So we all agree she wasn't killed here . . . at least not in this particular room."

Caity's words called to mind a significant problem. There were many rooms in Waxed. LA's newest addition to its collection of celebrity museums had opened to the public less than six months ago, and Spense figured its investors weren't going to be pleased with either the damage done to the establishment's reputation or with having to shut the place down for the time it would take to clear the scene. The museum, with three separate floors subdivided into numerous sections, wasn't going to be easy for the crime-scene technicians. Hundreds of tourists tracked through the premises on a daily basis, and the guests were even allowed to touch the statues, so fingerprints, fibers, and DNA would be abundant—and most of it would likely be useless. It was going to take days, maybe even a week or more to comb through the entire place for evidence. If this case had been a public-relations nightmare before, this new murder took things to a whole new level.

For now, the techs, along with more than a little help from the officers who'd arrived first on scene, seemed to be concentrating on gathering evidence from the area directly surrounding the body, and from the body itself. It made sense, but they'd have to cover the entire museum to get a clear picture of what had happened here.

"The UNSUB may not have killed her in the A-list room, but from a logistics standpoint, I'd say she had to have been killed *somewhere* on-site," Spense stated the obvious. "It would be virtually impossible to cart a dead body up Hollywood Boulevard without being noticed."

"A dead body sure, but the UNSUB could've done her elsewhere, then brought her into the museum in a trunk or even hidden inside a big instrument case, like the kind for a bass fiddle," Martinez offered doubtfully.

"That would be awfully risky hauling a dead body around in a bass case—not to mention heavy," Caity said. "No. I think our victim was lured to Waxed, then killed somewhere on the premises. Is there a storage room or a janitor's closet or . . . what about an art room?"

"I remember reading that Waxed planned to build an on-site studio. That way they could bring the sculptors here to craft the statues and maintain better quality control," Martinez said.

Spense watched as Caity, too, pulled on gloves and ran a finger over the blonde's swollen hands. When the skin indented, then failed to rebound, Caity jumped backwards. "Dear Lord. He dipped her hand in wax. I-I didn't see it at first." She inspected the left hand carefully. "Just the right one though."

The wax coating the woman's right hand was paper thin. Through its milky, semitransparent sheen, Spense noted the blue veins that had risen to the surface and been molded into tracks; the ruddy, bubbled texture of the skin, so unlike the creamy smoothness of the victim's other hand. He wasn't the squeamish type, but this last cruel act, added on top of the rest, turned his stomach.

"Why would he do that?" Martinez looked from Spense to Caity and back. His expression suggested he was every bit as repulsed as Spense. "I get that he's a sicko, but he didn't do anything special with the hands in the other murders."

"Could be any number of reasons, the most obvious being the availability of hot wax. On the flip side, a changing MO may represent a learning curve, or increased confidence on the killer's part. But I have another theory. Why don't we take a look at the room where the statues are made?" Spense addressed Martinez, who nodded to one of the uniformed men on scene.

"Follow me," the officer said, then escorted them to the third floor via an elevator. He pressed a button that opened the back doors instead of the front, and when they stepped directly into the museum's elaborate art studio, a chill crawled up Spense's back.

Life-size wire frames, waiting to support yet-to-be-sculpted bodies, were posed around the room in much the same way the finished statues lounged in the public areas. Adding one more layer of creepy to an already bizarre atmosphere, three heads, or rather plaster casts of heads, stared at him from a wooden tabletop. The surface was heaped with paints and sculpting tools of every sort. Moving forward, he accidentally kicked a large basket that had been divided into two sections: One part contained red threads and the other what looked to be human hair.

"Try to be more careful, if you don't mind," said a man in a white lab coat, his chagrined inflection rising with every word.

The fellow's pocket was monogrammed. *Gustav* didn't strike Spense as the SID type. He looked him over, and noticed paint splattered on the coat. Okay. Not LAPD. An artist.

The two officers flanking Gustav nodded at Martinez. "This guy makes the statues. We only found out about this room a few minutes ago. Apparently, he entered the studio by a separate entrance just minutes after the manager discovered the body. Claims he didn't know anything was up and hasn't left the studio all morning. His story checks out, so we were just about to kick him."

"It's not a story. These walls are soundproofed to keep the noise from the museum from disturbing me while I work." He raised an eyebrow. "How long did it take *you* to realize that I was here?" Gustav brought out a wounded inflection. "And as I was saying, please take care with my studio. The contents of that basket are more valuable than they seem. We creators pay careful attention to every detail in order to make the statues realistic. That's human hair, obtained ethically, of course, and each hair will be sewn individually onto the scalp."

Creators? Not artists? Perhaps Gustav had a Frankenstein complex. Spense made a mental note that the guy was also medium build, around five-foot-nine, and no older than thirty. Maybe he fancied himself a brilliant sculptor but hadn't had commercial success. Maybe he felt his talents were wasted replicating celebrity mugs at the wax museum.

"And as I was just explaining to these officers, the acrylic eyeballs"—Gustav swept his hand over yet another basket—"will be painted with the utmost precision in order to capture the exact color and pattern of the star's iris, and these . . ." He dipped his hand into the first basket and pulled out a fistful of red threads. "These will be fixed to the whites of the eyes to simulate their vasculature. You see it's my attention to this type of detail that makes the statues real."

"You mean makes them *seem* real, don't you?" Caity asked quietly.

"Well, yes. But to me, they are my masterpieces. Sometimes, I guess I get a little carried away and forget my darlings are not actually living."

"It must get lonely being locked away with only dolls to keep you company," Spense ventured.

"Not at all." Gustav's voice cracked defensively though Spense couldn't tell if he'd taken offense to the suggestion that he was a loner, or the term doll, or both.

Gustav smoothed his hands down his coat three times, then launched into a diatribe, as if someone had asked for a full rundown on the creation of wax statues even though no one had. Perhaps it was nerves that made him drone on and on. After all, there was a dead body out front, and the place was crawling with cops. In fairness, it would've been odd if Gustav hadn't been thrown a bit off-kilter. After a minute or so, Spense noticed he'd tuned out and forced himself to snap back to attention.

"And here"—the verbose Dr. Frankenstein gestured to several large cauldrons along the wall—"is where we heat our Japanese beeswax to 165 degrees Fahrenheit, the perfect temperature for casting the stars."

"Thanks, Gustav." Martinez, apparently fed up with the unsolicited art lesson, tilted his head toward the door. "You're free to go now."

"But I'm more than happy to stay and answer any questions that come up. No one else will be able to explain certain facets—"

"Go *now*," Martinez repeated. "Leave your information with the sergeant posted at the door, in case we need you later." He held up one finger. "You always come in on weekends?"

"Not always. Curtis . . . Mr. Pendleton, asked me to work on a special project."

"You give that information to these detectives already?"

"Yes, sir. But I don't mind repeating myself."

"I'm sure you don't, but it won't be necessary." Martinez jerked his chin toward the elevator, and Gustav reluctantly took the hint. Once the elevator doors closed, Martinez faced Spense and Caity. "You think this is where she was killed? I don't see any obvious blood spatter, but with all these paints and what not, who knows. We'll have to wait for the full report to be sure."

"It makes sense he'd do it here," Caity said. "These surfaces are designed for easy cleanup." She looked around at the yards of plastic, protective coverings, the industrial-strength cleaners, and an assortment of sharp tools. "You wouldn't need to bring a thing with you to do the deed here. This room is practically its own murder kit." She whistled.

Martinez pulled out his phone and took photos of the various tools on display.

Good idea, Spense thought, given that some of the finer chisels appeared as though they might make a similar hole to an ice pick . . . or a corkscrew.

No point speculating. The ME should eventually be able to tell what type of weapon had been used on the victim. Spense stared down into the fragrant cauldron of molten wax. "As for the hand dipped in beeswax, I don't believe it represents a change in MO." He was visualizing their earlier reenactment of the Turner homicide.

Caity's lips parted slightly. "It's like the window!"

"Exactly." Then Spense realized that while he and Caity might be able to read each other's minds, Martinez had no clue what they were talking about. "Initially, the assumption made by investigators was that the UNSUB had deliberately pushed Selena Turner out the window of her hotel room. But Caity and I believe her fall was the *unintended* result of a struggle."

"What does that have to do with the vic's hand being dipped in wax?" Martinez said.

"Like the tumble out the window, you're assuming the act was deliberate. But I don't think the UNSUB changed his MO at all. He didn't intentionally dip this woman's hand in wax as part of a bizarre ritual. That simply doesn't fit. Posing a sweet-faced blond beauty bare-breasted at a Hollywood tourist attraction . . . that fits. But not the waxy hand."

"So now you're extending an assumption from your totally unscientific reenactment of the Selena Turner murder to this one."

"Yeah. But we'll know soon enough from forensic findings if our theories are on the right track. We'll know if Turner's wound was more likely to have been made by an ice pick or by a corkscrew, and whether or not room service left behind a corkscrew that later went missing. So take our conclusions with a grain of salt if you want, but I believe that just like Selena went out the window during a struggle, this poor girl stuck her hand in a cauldron of molten wax by accident—when she was trying to fight off this conscienceless freak."

He noted the censure in Caity's eyes at his description of the UNSUB as a *freak*, but even if she found the term offensive, he found it apt and didn't regret it. No matter how disturbed the individual, Caity seemed to believe there was some shred of humanity remaining within. He didn't. And no matter how much he respected her, sometimes he wondered if she could ever accept him just as he was. Because he damn sure wasn't going to turn into some politically correct version of a special agent. Not even for Caity would he pretend to be someone he wasn't.

She heaved a rough sigh that didn't reassure him. As Spense considered the umpteen possible meanings of that sigh, Martinez pulled his detectives aside to dole out assignments. After a few minutes of hand waving and *yes, sirs*, they scattered in different directions. Then the lieutenant led Spense and Caity to an office on the second floor.

There, Curtis Pendleton, the manager of Waxed, was curled in a fetal position on a leather love seat, a sweater pulled over his head. As they entered his private sanctuary, he threw off the sweater and sat up with exaggerated effort. Good choice. A cardigan over the eyes isn't a reliable means of concealing the truth and tends to make you look like you're either guilty, an asshole, or both.

Spense noticed the man's Adam's apple bobbing up and down nervously. Pendleton's gaze fell on each of the intruders, then settled on Caity, probably because he found her to be the least threatening by virtue of her demeanor. She responded with a friendly yet professional smile. Martinez took the lead, making introductions. Then Spense and Caity relaxed against the wall, assuming an observational role, allowing the lieutenant to control the interview.

Martinez switched on a recorder, mumbled into it, then started with the most obvious question. "The statues in this museum are worth a fortune. So how the hell does Waxed not have a state-of-the-art security system? How could someone break in, commit murder, and nobody's the wiser until the place opens for business the next morning? It doesn't add up."

Pendleton whispered something into his cuff, looking as if he were about to cry. He didn't cry, but he did wipe his nose on his shirtsleeve. "Do I need a lawyer?"

His reaction took Spense by surprise, and from the look on Martinez's face, the lieutenant hadn't expected it either.

"Did you kill or conspire to kill that young woman out there? The one who's currently sitting pretty on Tom La Grande's lap?" Martinez asked.

Pendleton shook his head so hard and so long, Spense thought he might give himself a migraine.

"Then no, you don't need a lawyer. You're not under arrest. But if you want one . . ." Martinez shrugged his indifference.

"No. I really just . . . I really want to help." Pendleton's voice began to vibrate dangerously. His sleeve went to his nose again. "Because this is all my fault."

Spense tried to catch Caity's eye, but she was busy digging Kleenex from her purse. She approached Pendleton and offered him the travel pack.

"Thanks." He accepted the flowery tissues and blew his nose.

"That shirt looks expensive." Caity shot him a reassuring look before resuming her duties holding up the wall alongside Spense.

"Mr. Pendleton understands he's free to go at any time and is declining representation." Martinez spoke into the recorder. "Let's get down to business then. Let me put it another way. Does this place have a security system?"

"Of course. And it's state-of-the-art, just like it should be." The manager's hands shook as he crumpled multiple tissues in his fists, then set them gingerly on the coffee table in front of him.

Spense could think of two obvious reasons why the security system hadn't caught the break-in last night. Either it wasn't turned on, or the secret passcodes were exchanged freely among the staff.

"So then," Martinez coached, "it must've been pilot error. Which pilot?"

Pendleton's chest heaved, but no sound came out, and no tears fell from his eyes. "Me. I'm the screwup. Like I told those other detectives, I've already called the alarm company, and it appears the closing employee set the alarm as usual. Then, at midnight, it was turned off again."

"Who turned it off?"

"The security code entered to disarm the unit was . . . mine."

"But you weren't here. Did you give your code out to any of the employees? Maybe someone new who didn't have his own code set up yet? Is that what you mean when you say it was your screwup?"

"I'm going to get fired for this, aren't I?"

Nobody answered. Spense wasn't without empathy for Pendleton, but if he'd improperly managed the security codes, his *screwup* was in fact a firing offense.

"I didn't give out my information. But my code—oh I know what you're going to think—how stupid can a person be? It's just that I've got so many damn passwords and pin numbers, and I can't keep them all straight."

"So maybe you had to write it down. You left your alarm code lying around on your desk, maybe, or in a drawer," supplied Martinez.

"No." More violent head shaking from Pendleton. Spense could feel his own headache coming on. "But the code I use is . . ." Pendleton cringed, "the same one that opens the back door—the private employee entrance. But I swear, I never told anyone. No one *knew* I was using that as my security system code. In hindsight, I suppose I should've realized it would be easy to figure out."

"How many employees have the code to the back door?"

Pendleton gulped. "Only three people have an alarm code—the opener, the closer, and me—and they're all different sequences. But there's a single door code, and all of our employees have it. It hasn't been changed since we finished the building, so there are construction workers who may still be able to enter . . . I'll get you a list. We rely on our burglar alarm, not the door code, for security. I swear I never imagined anyone would try plugging the door code into the alarm system. We also have video cameras, but they'd been switched off, too."

Caity leaned over and whispered in Spense's ear, "He wouldn't admit to such a bonehead move, one that doesn't even exclude him as the doer, if it wasn't true. I believe him, but he's acting awfully hinky. I think he's holding something back."

Martinez saw her whispering and used a hand gesture to give them the go-ahead to jump in. Caity ambled over and pulled a chair up near the manager. "I'm terribly sorry for your troubles. I know how devastating it must've been to be the one to discover this poor young woman, and I can see how you'd feel responsible. But, Curtis . . . may I call you Curtis?"

He nodded.

"The fact of the matter is you are *not* responsible for this young woman's death. We've got a killer loose in this city. If he hadn't brought her here, he would've taken her somewhere else. *He's* the one responsible for that beautiful young woman's demise. Not you. But your input may very well help us catch him. We're going to need you to tell us *everything* you know. Think hard. Perhaps there's something you're leaving out. Something the stress of this terrible morning made you forget to mention."

A sob shook his body, and this time when his chest heaved, tears streamed down his cheeks. Caity reached out her hand and gently rested it on his shoulder. A minute or so passed before he collected himself enough to answer.

Then he tossed another wadded-up Kleenex on the table. He'd used up the entire travel pack by now, so Spense could only hope he'd man up. He wasn't looking forward to seeing a grown man with snot on his face. "This wasn't our first security breach. Someone disarmed the alarm around 10:00 P.M. Thursday night and broke into the museum. Whoever it was didn't steal anything, so I didn't get too worked up about it."

Martinez took back the reins. "You say you didn't report it because nothing was taken. If nothing went missing, how can you be sure someone broke in? Maybe your closer returned for something left behind, then simply forgot to set the alarm again."

Pendleton lifted one shoulder. "I wasn't one hundred percent certain of anything. That's another reason I didn't rush to action. And I guess I didn't want to get into trouble. I knew I'd have to come clean with the owners about my security code."

Martinez waited, allowing him to take his time. Clearly, he was having a rough go of it, and pressuring him would only make him cry again, thus drawing out the interview.

"When I came in yesterday morning—Friday—the alarm was off, but everything looked the same as always . . . at first. But then I noticed one of Richard Gere's fingers was missing. He had a bunch of dents in his head, and his clothes didn't look right, like they'd been messed up and someone had tried to put them back together."

"Could Gere's statue have been damaged during the daytime by a tourist? They're allowed to touch the figures, right?" Caity asked.

"Maybe, and yes, that's part of the draw. The tourists are encouraged to physically interact with the statues. But since nobody saw anything and the alarm was off when I came in, I figured it hadn't been any of the visitors. Our staff is mostly kids, and my thought was that someone had snuck his friends in after hours and accidentally knocked Richard over. I knew it was as much my fault as anyone's, so I put the damaged statue away and arranged for one of our artists, Gustav, to come in today and make the repairs. I'm paying him out of my own pocket. I thought that way no one would get canned. Not whichever dumb kid broke in for a lark, and not me either. Gustav would take home a little extra cash, and no one would ever be the wiser." He kept his gaze on his feet as he spoke. "I was planning to change my security code right away. I was going to do it last night before I left, but it was late, and I couldn't find the damn instruction booklet. It was my wife's birthday, so I . . ." Burying his face in his hands, he started up again. When he finally came up for air, he said, "Now a woman is dead because I couldn't remember where I put the instruction book. It's all my fault, and I-I don't even know her name. Do you have her name?"

In spite of Pendleton's theatrics, Spense felt for the guy. He was going to have to live with this stupid mistake the rest of his life.

"We can't release that information yet. Next of kin has to be notified. We need a positive ID from the family," Martinez answered. He dragged his hands through his hair. "I'm really sorry."

"Please, tell me her name. I don't want to have to think of her as *that woman*." Pendleton's voice was barely audible.

The atmosphere in the room was saturated with his shame.

Wincing, Martinez pulled a notebook from his pocket. Flipped it open. He waited a beat, then met Pendleton's gaze. "Her name is Brenda Reggero. She was twenty-three years old."

Nobody spoke for a moment, then, mercifully, a knock at the door broke the strained silence. A uniformed officer poked his head in and said, "We found something in the stairwell, sir . . . looks like a lucky charm."

Chapter Nine

Saturday, October 5
5:00 P.M.
Brentwood, California

THE CUP OF warmed milk Lucy had given her clattered in its saucer. Susan's hands were shaking badly by the time the woman on the television said, *We'll bring you more on this breaking story as details become available. I'm Kourtney Kennedy signing off for SLY Entertainment, your source for all the star news all the time.*

It had been *him*.

The man in the Charlie Chaplin mask was the Fallen Angel Killer.

She hadn't overreacted after all.

She'd smashed him over the head with the painted wooden sword and made a run for it. On her way out the museum's back door, she'd tripped over her lost purse. Her lucky charm had fallen

out, but her pepper spray was still there, and she'd been fully prepared to gas Mr. Chaplin, but . . . he hadn't even chased her down
the stairs. He'd just let her go, and so she'd thought she'd pushed
the panic button for no good reason. That the whole latex glove
thing had been an innocent part of Charlie's kink.

She'd been sure she'd made a big mistake, attacking one of
Lucy's VIP customers like that. It had taken her a while to work
up her nerve, but then she'd dropped by Lucy's place to apologize
for her rash behavior. She'd planned to beg Lucy's forgiveness,
explain that she was *uber* suspicious because of those two *fallen
angels*.

But now, here was Kourtney Kennedy, SLY news anchor, breaking the story of another dead girl. And this fallen angel had been
found at Waxed. No way that was a coincidence. The FBI, Kourtney reported, had even been called in to assist the LAPD.

The freaking FBI.

It was a miracle Susan was alive. "We've got to go to the police,"
she told Lucy. "I'm absolutely certain the man who met me at
Waxed is the Fallen Angel Killer." She sipped her milk, hoping
the tryptophan really would calm her down. She was getting so
paranoid, she was half-afraid to drink from the cup because she
hadn't poured it herself even though she was with *Lucy*. Man, she
was really starting to lose it.

"With all this terrible news, it's no wonder you're frightened,"
Lucy replied on a heavy sigh. She tossed her long, stylishly cut
blond hair and put her hand on Susan's wrist to help balance the
saucer. "Careful, Gina. You're spilling."

Lucy's place in Brentwood was the kind of house Susan dreamed
of owning someday. All tasteful modern décor, put together by a
designer who'd formerly worked for an associate of Nate Berkus,

interior decorator to the stars. Lucy had class, like Susan wished she had. The last thing she wanted to do was spill milk on Lucy's off-white divan. Carefully, she placed the cup and saucer on Lucy's acrylic coffee table, one that had been hand-painted by a local bum down in Venice. A sure sign you've made it is when you can be charitable to the less fortunate and get a banging coffee table at the same time. Susan's brain was going off on tangents now. The realization of what her fate might have been, had she not trusted her instincts, made her woozy and scattered her thoughts. Lucy's voice undulated weirdly in the air, and Susan had to work hard to comprehend her words. As she watched Lucy's cherry red lips moving in slow motion, the milk soured in her stomach.

"I'm so sorry for what you went through. But, Gina, honey, I don't think it could be the same man. And besides . . . we can't go to the police. What you did was illegal, remember? You were going to exchange sexual favors for money."

"But I didn't actually do anything. And he didn't pay me. So . . ."

"You broke into Waxed. That's far more serious than solicitation. If this really *is* the Fallen Angel Killer, and he finds out you went to the police, he'll surely come after you."

"But he doesn't know where to find me. He doesn't know my real name." Again, that niggling paranoia. Lucy knew her real name. Lucy knew how to find her. *Lucy* was the one who'd set her up with a serial killer.

"I bet it wouldn't be that hard to track you down." Lucy released Susan's wrist, and her charm bracelet jangled in the process.

Susan had always loved that Tiffany bracelet of Lucy's, but now, inexplicably, she found its rattling completely irritating. "I-I get your point, but I don't see how we have a choice." She lowered her voice, though there was no one else present to overhear. "You know who the killer is."

"Fuck you, Gina." Lucy jumped to her feet and planted her hands on her hips. "Do you honestly believe that if I knew who the killer was, I'd keep it a secret just to save myself from a pandering charge and jail time? Of course it would probably mean losing my entire business . . . everything I've worked to build." She wrapped her arms around her waist. "But . . . no. If I *did* know this man's identity—which I don't—if I did believe he was the Fallen Angel Killer—which I don't—I'd go straight to the cops." She fixed Susan with a hard gaze, one that said she wouldn't be swayed. "But since I have no idea whatsoever—no idea at all who he is—there isn't any point in going to the police. Your story is completely unsubstantiated. I doubt they'd believe a word either one of us said, and it could ruin us both. Not to mention, it would put us in terrible danger."

"How could you not know his name? You vetted him. You vet all the johns." An unbidden thought disconcerted her. Maybe she'd been naïve, counting so much on Lucy's integrity. "Don't you?"

"Always. Except in this case I didn't need to vet him because he called me on the phone. Nobody has my private number unless they have a legit referral. It's not like you can look me up in the book, baby." Lucy smiled, her whitened teeth glowing garishly against her red, artificially inflated lips. Some of Lucy's class seemed to be flaking off, allowing a cruder version to peek through the genteel veneer. "He said he was Ryan Winters. Am I supposed to *vet* Ryan Winters?"

"Oh my God. He claimed to be this year's *hottest man alive*, and you believed him?"

"I recognized the voice—at least I thought I did. So I . . . yes.

I believed him. After all, he's fresh out of rehab, and remember a few years back when he got caught with that hooker in West Hollywood? He's obviously the type of man who enjoys a lady's company on the side. Everyone knows his voice, and it sounded exactly like him, so I had no reason to doubt his identity."

"Everyone knows his voice yes—and half the town does Ryan Winters imitations. How could you send me out there like that? To meet someone you'd had no personal contact with. Especially at a time like this, knowing there's a serial killer on the hunt." Susan's world was tilting. She'd pinned her future on Lucy's promises. She cared for this woman like a sister, and she'd believed Lucy cared for her. She didn't remember getting to her feet or balling her hands into hard knots, but suddenly she was all but on top of Lucy, shaking her fists at her. She actually had her backed into a corner.

"I couldn't imagine a *safer* john than *Ryan Winters*. I'd have to have been crazy to turn down his business. A client like that could take my company to a whole new level." Lucy's eyes widened. "I told you I *believed* him." She cowered, like she was afraid of Susan.

Imagine that. Maybe Susan was more of a badass than she realized. After all, the freaking Fallen Angel Killer had let her go. Somehow, that thought straightened her spine and cleared her head a bit. Lucy was her friend, and she didn't want to frighten her. Dropping her fists, she stepped back.

Lucy let out a long, slow breath. "I didn't realize until you showed up here today and told me your story that it wasn't him. If I'd known that at the time, I wouldn't have sent you. The man you described is obviously too short and poorly built to be Ryan Winters."

"Of course it wasn't Ryan Winters!" Susan slapped her hand

over her mouth. She wasn't herself. She didn't want to scream at Lucy. Her heart was pounding out of her chest, and her blouse had gotten all sweaty. She needed to get control of herself. *Just breathe.* "I'm sorry. I shouldn't yell at you. I'm sure you had no idea I'd be putting myself in danger. This isn't your fault." But what she was also thinking was that now Lucy *did* know. That now they both had a chance to stop the Fallen Angel Killer before he struck again. No. Not a chance. A responsibility.

"I'm sorry, too." Lucy took Susan by the hand and led her back to the couch politely but firmly, like she was a concertgoer who'd strayed from her ticketed area and had to be put back in the cheap seats where she belonged. "And I suppose I should have been more careful. Gina, you have my word that I'd never have sent you if I'd thought for one minute there really was a serial killer out there. But at that point, I'd only lost two girls, so you see, I thought the whole thing was just an unfortunate coincidence."

Susan's knees gave out, and she dropped onto the couch. She had no anger left in her anymore. She was back to her initial state of shock and disbelief. "*You* lost two girls?"

Lucy's lashes fluttered, and Susan could see tears forming in her eyes. Lucy looked away. The color drained from her cheeks as she bent over and opened the coffee-table drawers, rummaging around until she found her e-cigarette. "Anyway, you got away, so whew! Good for you, you clever girl."

Fake smoke jetted from the end of Lucy's cigarette. Susan didn't smoke, but at the moment she found herself wishing for a drag off Lucy's nicotine stick. She still couldn't wrap her mind around what she'd just heard. "Are you saying Selena Turner and Adrianne Simpson both worked for you?"

"I'm not saying anything. You know I'm a vault." Lucy turned a pretend key near her lips. "I don't divulge my johns' identities, and I keep my girls' secrets, too. You wouldn't want the others to know you worked for me, now would you? That's the only way a business like mine, with such high-end clientele and high-end girls can work. One of my escorts is the daughter of an Oscar winner, you know."

Susan shook her head. She hadn't known that. Lucy was indeed good at keeping everything private. Then a question presented itself that made her fight to keep down her well and truly soured milk. "Did Ryan Winters call for dates with the others, too? Did you send me out to meet a man who'd already killed two of your escorts?"

"God no." Lucy's hand shook as she brought the cigarette to her lips. "I suppose since I've let it slip they were my girls already, and since they've passed on and no longer require my discretion, I might as well tell you the whole truth." Lucy's sympathetic gaze swept over her. "And after what you've been through, I think you deserve to know whatever details I can provide. It was one my regulars, not that phony Ryan Winters, who called for Selena. And I hadn't set Adrianne up with any of my clients in over a year. So she obviously made her own arrangements—I have no idea who she went with." She paced back and forth, puffing the e-cigarette. "Arranging your own dates is a practice I strictly forbid. How can I be expected to keep my business afloat if you girls give out your personal phone numbers to the johns?"

"You mean how will you get your 60 percent? But I thought you said that was a safety rule. For our own protection."

Throwing her hands up, Lucy looked at her, almost gratefully. As if she'd forgotten that her intentions had always been good, and Susan had just reminded her what a lovely madam she really was. "That rule certainly *is* for your own safety. Look at what happened to poor Adrianne and Selena . . . Brenda, too. If they'd only followed protocol and not tried to go rogue with their own arrangements, they'd be alive right now."

To clear the tangles from her brain, Susan shook her head. She was pretty sure what Lucy had just said made no sense at all—and Lucy had slipped in another bombshell revelation like it was nothing. "The woman at Waxed was yours, too?"

"Not exactly. Like Adrianne, Brenda had gone off on her own. She stopped returning my messages a few months back. And from what we just learned on the news, she obviously made herself a date with the wrong man. So you see, this is precisely why you girls need me. I'm your protector, and without me, you're exposing yourself to all kinds of lowlifes, *murderers* even."

Maybe Lucy was in denial. Or maybe she couldn't face what she'd done because apparently she'd been an unwitting accomplice to murder. No wonder she was afraid to go to the police. "But, Lucy, you're the one who set me up with a killer. And Selena, too."

"No. No. No. We don't know for sure your Charlie Chaplin is this Fallen Angel person."

So now it seemed Lucy had changed her position. First he wasn't the killer, but now she didn't know for certain that he was.

"And like I told you before, I didn't set Selena up with the same man as you. *Her* john was one of my regulars. I'm positive he didn't kill her."

"How do you know?"

"Because I just do, and because he just wouldn't. Besides, he cannot possibly be the same man who met you at Waxed."

She didn't see how Lucy could know that for sure. Maybe the

john did a killer Ryan Winters imitation. Who could say for certain? Unless . . . "Too tall. Like Winters?"

Lucy took a protracted drag on the e-cig. "Yes. Sure. He's too tall." She grabbed hold of Susan's shoulders and pulled her back to her feet. "Listen to me, Gina. I know you feel sorry for those girls. Believe me, I pity them, too. And if I had any information that could stop this devil"—she paused and made the sign of the cross, though Susan had never known her to be religious—"I wouldn't care what happened to me. But I do care what happens to *you*. I don't want to think about the consequences if he finds out who you are. I want you to get out of town. Lie low until this all blows over. So, here's what I'm going to do. I'm going to give you the full twenty-five hundred you would've earned had you fulfilled your end of the bargain and gotten the money from Ryan Winters."

"He wasn't Ryan Winters." Her arms were starting to go numb from the grip Lucy had on her shoulders.

"You know what I mean. Had you stayed long enough to collect from this . . . Charlie Chaplin character."

Character seemed a rather benign way to describe a serial killer and made her wonder if Lucy even believed her story. "If I'd stayed any longer, I'd be dead." She shoved Lucy's hands off her. She could barely think straight, but she was more rational than Lucy by a mile.

Breathe in; breathe out.

Lucy had plenty of reason to be frightened, too. After all, the killer had Lucy's private number. He probably knew exactly where she lived. With a shudder, Susan cast a wary glance over her shoulder. What if he was hiding in the other room or lying in wait in the garden or . . .

"Stay right where you are." Without giving Susan a chance to respond, Lucy went to the bedroom and returned with a purse and a fistful of cash. "You want the twenty-five hundred or not?"

The crisp scent of all that green started a war between Susan's conscience and her instinct for self-preservation. What began as a close battle, however, ended abruptly when she remembered that the reason she'd made it out of Waxed alive had nothing to do with her conscience. "Yes," she answered, feeling an immediate sense of relief. It was over. She didn't have to do anything more. She'd tried her best to be a good citizen, but it hadn't worked out. Hanging around Hollywood would be a dumb, futile move, and while she might be a natural blond, she'd never been stupid.

But her relief lasted less than a heartbeat before guilt sucker punched her in the gut, nearly doubling her over from its force. "I want the money, and I'll blow town as soon as I can, but I still think we have to tell the police what we know. All three fallen angels worked for you, Lucy. The man who tried to kill me called you on your private line, and you said yourself *no one* has your private line except your clients. Don't you see? The Fallen Angel Killer is most likely either one of your regulars, or close enough to someone you know to get your number."

Lucy folded her arms across her enhanced breasts. She'd once bragged to Susan she'd gotten her implants as a high-school-graduation present from her parents. Susan didn't know for what she envied Lucy more—parents who'd understood peer pressure and hadn't judged, or those nice moneymakers up top.

"No. I don't see that at all. There could be any number of explanations for this whole situation."

"Such as?"

"*I* don't know, but I'm sure there are several," Lucy said, and waved the bills under Susan's nose. "For your own safety, do not go to the police. I insist you take this money and get out of town *now*."

"I don't have anywhere to go." Susan was thinking aloud. She couldn't go back to her parents, not after the life she'd been living. And her only friends now were her personal trainer and Lucy herself. If Lucy kicked her to the curb, she'd be lost. Flat-out lost. It seemed she'd not only lost her four-leaf-clover charm last night, she'd lost her *luck*.

Lucy emptied the entire purse full of cash onto the couch, then went to the wall and removed a large, framed portrait of her pet poodle, revealing a built-in safe. She motioned for Susan to turn her back, so she did. She could hear the beeps as Lucy entered the combination.

"You can turn around now."

After rejoining her by the couch, Lucy removed a rubber band from a roll of money and began peeling off bills. "This is over $5,000, Gina. I want you to consider it your severance pay."

"You're firing me?" She could hardly believe what she'd just heard. She'd grown dependent on this life . . . and on Lucy. She didn't want to give either of them up. But Lucy wasn't leaving her any choice. She gritted her teeth. Didn't Lucy care about her or the rest of the escorts at all?

"Yes. I'm firing you—because it's the only way I know how to protect you. If you had the sense your maker gave you, you'd realize what you're suggesting, going to the police and all, is just plain crazy." Lucy hesitated, and Susan held her breath, hoping Lucy would change her mind and let her stay. "Besides, you can't turn tricks in Hollywood anymore. Think about it, my darling. From here on out, you'd surely be afraid any john I found you would turn out to be this murderer."

But Susan knew she'd have nothing to fear once the police caught the killer. She shivered as the full implication of Lucy's words slowly sank in. Was Lucy considering continuing with business as usual under these circumstances? That backbone Susan had discovered when she was up against Charlie Chaplin was still holding her upright. She knew she had to be willing to face the consequences of defying Lucy if she was going to hang on to her self-respect. "I won't let you keep sending out escorts."

Lucy pulled a slipcover off one of the decorative pillows on the sofa and filled it with cash. "Really, Gina, listen to what you're saying. And after all I've done for you." Then Lucy shoved the case at her.

She needed the money. She had no choice—at least that's what she told herself. She took the pillow case.

"That's what I thought." All business now, Lucy strode to the front door and held it open. "If it makes you feel any better, I promise I won't send out any more girls until this is all over. I've learned my lesson, and I'm sorry it had to be at your expense. Believe me, I can't afford to lose any more girls. And . . . I'm not heartless, you know."

Susan arched a brow at Lucy, disbelieving. She'd trusted her once, but she wouldn't make that mistake again.

"I swear on my momma's grave I won't send out any more girls until they catch this bastard. So you can take this money and get out of town with a clear conscience." With a knowing smile, Lucy pointed to the pillowcase stuffed with small bills. "You've got my word, Gina. Now then, do I have yours that you won't go to the police?"

Chapter Ten

Saturday, October 5
7:00 P.M.
Hollywood, California

IT HAD BEEN a long day, and Spense thought it showed in Caity's demeanor. Though her wide smile was bright enough to light the entire city, he'd caught her covering a yawn a time or two, and she'd shifted in her seat more than once. He highly doubted that the straight-backed chairs in the Sky Walk's main dining room, thinly padded and built more for show than comfort, could be blamed for all of that fidgeting. Her side must be bothering her, but for whatever reason, she seemed to feel the need to cover up her pain.

Every time he saw her, he was convinced she'd grown more beautiful in the interim—whether their time apart had been a day or merely an hour. Though, of course, that was impossible. *Wasn't it?* Tonight, her long hair had been brushed until it shone. It cascaded over her shoulders, drawing his gaze to the tempting cleft between her full breasts. For dinner, she'd changed into an Egyptian blue dress with a sweetheart neckline. The color, which was nearly identical to that of her eyes, brought out their sparkle and the richness in her dark hair.

She was stunning. Heart-stopping. Breathtaking.

Always the poet, he said, "Nice dress."

"Thank you." She looked up at him through thick black lashes, dialing up the voltage that was already crackling between them. Then she innocently shifted her attention to their server, as though she had no idea what she'd just done.

"Nice to see you again," Caity addressed Six-Pack, who had also gotten dolled up for dinner service. The server with 'tude had traded his skintight T-shirt for a skintight white button-down shirt—mostly *un*buttoned—and ironed black slacks. The high-heeled leather boots he'd worn with his more casual Herby's outfit had been exchanged for a different pair. Either that, or Spense had failed to notice those gigantic silver buckles at lunch the other day.

Whereas both Caity and Six-Pack had upgraded their attire for the evening, Spense had gone a different direction. Special agents were expected to suit up every day, rain or shine, to reflect well on the Bureau. During his limited downtime, Spense liked to relax. A different woman might've had something to say about his jeans and polyester knit shirt in the fancy dining hall, but in the elevator, Caity had simply smiled at him and remarked that his Old Spice smelled wonderful.

"It's a pleasure to see you, ma'am . . . and you as well, sir," Six-Pack intoned, eyeing Spense dubiously.

"Great to see you, too." Personally, Spense could've used a

change in scenery, both in restaurants and waiters, but for Caity, who seemed genuinely delighted to see the server's familiar, if disdainful, face, he managed to screw on a smile.

"You folks staying here awhile?" Six inquired. Spense decided right on the spot to shorten the kid's nickname. Weren't waiters supposed to wear name tags or introduce themselves at some point? If Six had ever told them his name, Spense couldn't remember.

"How long you in town?" Six rephrased, apparently determined to get an answer.

"Our business is somewhat open-ended at the moment, Horatio. I'm guessing we'll be seeing each other around for at least a little while longer," Caity replied.

No way Spense could have missed a name like Horatio. Except that he had. He ducked his chin. He'd been too focused on Caity to pay attention to anyone else in the restaurant. *Horatio?* What kind of a woman would saddle her son with a name that all but guaranteed he'd never eat lunch with the cool kids—ever—as in not even once? Then his ears warmed, and he suddenly felt a strange kinship with Horatio. Henceforth, he resolved, he'd try to be nicer to the guy.

"Oh good!" The server did a silent clap, dropping his superior attitude upon learning they'd be around long enough to leave him multiple tips. Or maybe Spense was being too hard on him, maybe Caity's natural friendliness was bringing out the best in Horatio. Like it did with most people.

Like it did with Spense.

Correcting his posture, he suddenly wished he'd put on a tie. Or polished his shoes. Caity deserved as much. And who knew, maybe this dinner could turn into something more. He could tell there was something as yet unspoken that had her keeping her guard up, but hey, if anyone could win a woman over, it was him.

As he listened to the server recite the dinner specials, Spense had to admit he did it with panache. Even the brussel sprouts sounded appealing when Horatio described their special sauces and kissed his fingertips. But Spense wasn't into fancy. "Garden burger. Gimme a salad instead of fries."

Both Horatio and Caity shot him a disappointed look.

He tugged a piece of lint off the sleeve of his casual shirt. It might be too late to undo his regrettable choice in clothing, but the night was young, and sometimes little things can make a big difference. He supposed it wouldn't kill him to order a nice meal. "Hang on . . . I'll have the grilled Ono . . . and . . . the brussel sprouts Francine."

"Excellent choice, Sir!"

Caity beamed at him, never taking her eyes from his face as she placed her order. He did his best to remain cool in front of Horatio, but the way she was looking at him had his heart thumping and made it nearly impossible not to beam right back at her.

Brussel sprouts.

It was ridiculously easy to please this woman.

He wondered if she'd be ridiculously easy to please in other ways.

Horatio disappeared, and Spense reached his hand across the table. Caity hesitated. He wiggled his fingers insistently, and, eventually, she extended her hand. He took it and slid his grasp lower. As he circled his thumb across the supple skin of the inside of her wrist, he *thought* he heard her make a soft noise in the back of her throat. A jolt of pure heat flashed through him. Easy or hard, it didn't really matter, because either way he wanted to get down to the business of pleasing her as soon as possible. Between her injuries, her family business, and, of course, their work, he hadn't yet had an opportunity to make his big move.

"Penny for your thoughts," she said.

"They may not be fit to print," he answered honestly.

A flush climbed from her neck to her cheeks.

Imagining himself dragging his chair next to hers and whispering in her ear just *exactly* what he wanted to do to her, he tugged on his jeans, crossed his legs, and dropped a napkin in his lap. At this rate, he'd be lucky to make it through dinner. "I . . ." What was he waiting for? Even if that dress she was wearing wasn't the signal he thought it was, those wide take-me-*now* eyes were for sure. "I've been mentally unzipping that pretty dress of yours since before we stepped into the elevator. I want to make love to you, Caity."

A SPLIT SECOND before Spense opened his mouth, Caitlin knew what he was going to say.

She pulled her hand from his but didn't drop her gaze. "I want you, too, Spense."

His answering look made her forget how to breathe. Placing her hand on her stomach, she concentrated on inhaling and exhaling until she got the hang of it again. She trusted Spense with her life—trusting him with her heart wasn't as easy. "But, if I'm being honest, I have reservations."

The flicker of disappointment in his eyes made her all the more aware of her own frustration. When she was away from Spense, even for a short time, she couldn't stop anticipating the moment he'd next come around the corner and flash her that cocky grin of his. And when she was with him, it took all her self-control not to stare into his golden brown eyes like a love-struck goose.

"If you're worried about the FBI, don't be. I'm not your superior, so the Bureau's sexual-harassment policy doesn't apply. There's nothing in the rules that prohibits us from *fraternizing.*" He emphasized the last word with an eyebrow waggle.

She knew the rules were no big deal to Spense, but he had no idea how hard it was for her to ignore even the *unwritten* ones. Her reputation was at stake, and her ability to command the respect she needed to do her job. But for him she'd be willing—make that eager—to set aside her professional boundaries *if* she felt certain it wouldn't compromise the case. She swallowed hard . . . there were other things, too. Up until recently, they'd been rivals, and she knew how much Spense loved a challenge. She imagined he'd feel darn good about adding her to his *win* column, and she couldn't entirely tune out that small voice whispering in her ear that she might be just another puzzle he was determined to solve. "It's not that, exactly. I mean that's part of it. You don't see a conflict of interest?"

He leaned back and placed his hands behind his head. "No. I don't."

She arched an eyebrow. "Okay. So let's take a scenario. I admit it's far-fetched, but what if the police needed to use me as bait to catch—"

Dropping his hands, he jerked forward as if a shot had been fired off in the restaurant. "*Nobody* is going to use you for killer bait."

His reaction was so swift, so unrelenting, she winced.

His gaze swept over her. "What's wrong? Are you in pain?"

Even if she was, that wasn't the problem. Maybe the hypothetical she'd proposed was extreme, but just today he'd overreacted to Martinez's flirtatious overtures. If she'd embarked on this conversation in the hope of resolving her concerns tonight, that hope had just vanished. Besides, her flank was indeed aching, and that suddenly presented her with an honest way out of making a decision—one way or the other—that she might later regret.

"I guess I am a little sore," she said, then searched the room for Horatio. Why did servers always appear at the most inopportune moments, but when you truly needed them, they were never around? Ah! Thank goodness. From the corner of her eye, she saw him approaching their table.

"I'm a complete ass. I noticed you fidgeting earlier, but I guess I got caught up in how sexy . . ." Spense's voice trailed off when he caught sight of their waiter.

"I brought Ono for the lady." Horatio sidled up to the table with a dinner plate on each arm.

"Oh, no. The Ono's for the gentleman. I had the filet," she teased, trying to snap her attention back to the business of dinner—but it was more like a slow rebound. Knowing the moment had passed, she sighed—both with relief and disappointment.

Horatio crossed his arms with the hot plates and slid the correct meal in front of Spense and her respectively. "Your candle's out." He addressed Spense and proffered an exaggerated wink. "We can't have that. I'll be back in a flash to rekindle the flame."

Her cheeks became a flambé. She held her water glass against her face in an attempt to cool down fast. Definitely time for a change of subject. And there was something that had been on her mind ever since Waxed. "I'm not sure I could really call this a connection, but what do you think—"

"About the Tom La Grande coincidence?" Spense finished.

"Yes." So Spense was ready to change the topic as well, and he'd also noticed that La Grande's name had come up in one of the witness field interviews that had been provided along with the crime-scene materials for their profile. "La Grande was supposed to have been at Robb's star ceremony but never showed. Does *not* being present at the scene of one crime, and having your wax replica present at the scene of another constitute a meaningful connection?"

"A lot of cops believe there's no such thing as a coincidence, but I'm not one of them. The truth is, sometimes random events just happen in a way that makes them seem . . . *non*random." He shifted in his seat, removed his napkin from his lap, and used it to dab at a bit of sauce that was dripping from the edge of his plate. Apparently talk of the homicide was cooling both their jets.

Good.

"On the other hand, the UNSUB chose to pose Brenda Reggero with Tom La Grande at the museum. Out of all the stars, why select him?" Spense asked, spearing three brussel sprouts onto one fork.

"He had to pick someone. Maybe it was easier to pose her because La Grande's statue was seated."

"Right. But serial killers *need* to communicate with the authorities and the public. And since he left no note or cryptic clue at either scene, at least not one that we've found so far, I have to wonder if the UNSUB'S choice of statue might have been his way of sending us a message."

"No question posing her in a highly sexual manner was designed to get our attention. Every choice he made was likely orchestrated for a specific purpose. I'm not sure what our UNSUB was trying to tell us, but I do think La Grande deserves a closer look," she said.

From out of nowhere, a hand reached over her shoulder, causing her to jump in her chair. Horatio flicked his lighter, then lit their table candle. As her heart rate returned to normal, she wondered how long the server had been lurking and whether or not he'd heard any of their discussion. They were seated in a secluded spot in the back of the room, and they'd barely spoken above a whisper, but if he'd made a deliberate effort to eavesdrop . . .

Horatio shifted from one foot to the other, then circled the table inspecting the cloth for debris. Using a wooden stick, he swept the crumbs onto a plate and deadpanned, "We'll save these for later, in case you decide to order the bread pudding."

Spense snorted. Caitlin was grateful she'd already swallowed the water she'd been sipping. Horatio waited for their appreciative guffaws to settle down, then looked around, perhaps keeping a lookout for his supervisor. "You two are the profilers on the Fallen Angel Killer case, right? I saw your pictures on TV. Did I hear someone mention Tom La Grande?"

Great. So he had been eavesdropping, and the news had already spread that the FBI had been called in

"We can't discuss the case," Spense said.

"Sure. I know that," Horatio said, pulling a chair up to the table. "But I'm not after any inside information here. Yes, I do hear a lot of gossip, and I could make some good bank selling my stories to the press—you'd be amazed at the things I've seen at this hotel—but I like my job, and I got my integrity."

It was hard to believe that in this town, anyone would refrain from leaking what he knew for cash. Everyone seemed to be doing it. Even family members sold their famous relatives out on a routine basis. But Horatio looked and sounded sincere.

"Still can't discuss the case," Spense repeated.

"But you can listen, can't you? I got some information I think might interest you. I thought about calling that cop I saw you with the other day, but frankly, I think the guy's a dick. I'd rather talk to the two of you."

Caitlin tried to picture the witness list in her mind's eye, but she didn't recall seeing a *Horatio* on it. "Were you working the day Selena Turner was murdered?"

"I was. And that's what I wanted to tell you. I was right here in this very dining room, looking out onto the street through that window when her body bombed onto the pavement. A couple of cops asked me had I seen Miss Turner or noticed who she was with earlier. I told them no, because I hadn't." Leaning forward, he dropped his chin close to the tablecloth. "But then, today, when I saw on the news that the last fallen angel was posed with Tom La Grande's statue, something clicked in my brain. I don't know if it's important, but I can't seem to stop thinking about it."

Kourtney Kennedy had been the first to include that detail in her newscast. Whether she'd pried it out of someone on the museum staff, or whether she had sources inside Hollywood station was hard to say—Caitlin hoped it wasn't the latter.

By now, Spense had pulled a notebook from his jeans pocket. He opened it, and said, "I'm going to take notes if that's okay."

"Sure," said Horatio. "But there's not much to take down. It's only that I saw Tom La Grande at the bar that morning. I watched him toss back a shot of whiskey and head upstairs. He took the elevator bank that goes to the block of rooms overlooking the Walk of Fame—where Selena Turner was staying." Horatio's mouth turned down at the corners, and he went a bit misty-eyed. His emotion appeared to be genuine.

"Did you know Miss Turner?" Caitlin asked.

On a long sigh, he said, "Not personally. We weren't friends or anything. But she hung out at Herby's a lot. I waited on her more than a few times. She was a sweet kid. Always said *thank you*. Always left me a nice tip."

"Did she stay at the hotel much?"

"I don't know. And I never saw her with La Grande, if that's what you're getting ready to ask."

It had been. Horatio was a bright guy. "Was it unusual for La Grande to be at the hotel or to order whiskey before noon?" Caitlin followed up.

"Not particularly. I've seen him here a time or two. He's usually half-baked and doesn't like to shoot the bull like some of the other celebs do. He just likes to be left alone and drink in peace." Horatio smiled at the origami bird he'd just fashioned from a napkin. "Anyhow I overheard you say that he no-showed his buddy's Walk of Fame ceremony that day. And that's when I realized I *had* to say something. It doesn't make sense, La Grande standing his pal up like that if he was already here at the hotel. If that's the reason he came down here in the first place, why didn't he stick around for the ceremony?"

Chapter Eleven

Sunday, October 6
6:30 P.M.
Los Angeles, California

SUSAN HAD NEVER been the heroic type, and right now her knees were knocking so hard that old woman eyeing her from the Skirball Cultural Center information desk probably thought there'd been one of those surprise Southern California tremors. With her blue hair and crinkled-paper face, the lady reminded Susan of her grandma—the one who used to say you never know what you're capable of until there's no one else around to do it for you. She must've been onto something, because as her mom was always quick to add, the good Lord only knew Susan was the most selfish girl on the planet.

Anyway, she missed her grandma, and she hoped the blue-haired lady was some sort of sign that she was doing what Granny would've expected her to do—the right thing. It was weird to think how much faith her grandmother had had in her, and that was probably the reason Susan couldn't let this thing go. Some asshole was out there killing whores like her, and now she finally and truly understood Granny's words.

No one else was going to do this for her.

So here she was, dressed in the frump-a-dump church dress she'd gotten for Christmas the year she left home, with a scarf wound around her head as a poor man's disguise, waiting to meet Kourtney Kennedy. Susan had left an anonymous message on the SLY tip line, and she wasn't even sure she'd dropped enough tidbits to entice Kennedy into meeting her today. She'd stayed in town on the mere chance the reporter would show—and to think she could've been lying on some beach in Florida, where the Fallen Angel Killer would never find her.

Lucy had made a number of valid points, especially about not going to the cops. They'd probably interview Susan and make her promise not to leave town, or worse, book her for solicitation, then put her right back out there with no protection at all. Then she'd have to contend with Charlie Chaplin all over again, and this time she might not get away. Since she was no hero, going to the cops wasn't really an option.

Kourtney Kennedy, on the other hand, seemed like the perfect solution to Susan's dilemma. They were around the same age, so Kourtney should be easy to talk to, and she seemed nice on TV despite obviously being a fame whore. Plus, reporters have to keep their sources confidential. Susan knew this was true because she'd just seen an episode of *The Newsroom*, where Jeff Daniels went to jail rather than reveal his source. SLY might be *entertainment* news, but the same principles surely applied.

She lowered herself onto a bench at the farthest end of a long corridor, twisted her hands, and stared at the bronze bust of Albert Einstein on a pedestal in front of her. She'd asked Kourtney to meet her at the Skirball Museum because she was afraid to go back to her house, and this was a good place to hang out. She wanted other people around, but not too many. There were a lot of cool art and educational exhibits here, and tonight they were showing old black-and-white movies for free. Besides, the Skirball was the opposite of Waxed. Instead of honoring actors who pretended to be interesting people in films, this museum honored individuals whose *real* lives were interesting. People who'd made a difference in this world. She took a long, slow breath and noticed that her hands had finally stopped shaking.

Glancing furtively about, she spied a striking blond woman, dressed in an expensive-looking emerald green suit and super-high heels stalking down the hall—headed right for her.

You're up, Susan. Make Granny proud.

She pulled her chin high, removed her sunglasses, and looked directly at the woman. Man, Kourtney must have some great makeup artist. Susan had never seen such a beautiful creature in person. Kourtney was making good time, heading down the hallway on her long, supermodel legs. Susan had read that SLY ordered their anchor a custom-made peekaboo desk, just so everyone could see her legs during the broadcasts. Susan would never have legs like that, and she'd never be on TV either. She swallowed hard at the realization she'd have to stay in hiding her whole life unless they caught this bastard . . . and that definitely limited her career opportunities. Then she smiled inside because she recognized this familiar, self-interested part of herself a lot more than that other Susan, who was about to risk her life to help catch a killer for no personal gain.

"I'm Kourtney." The reporter, a little out of breath from walking so fast, sat down next to Susan. She might've been beautiful, but different layers of smell—perfume, cigarettes, coffee—made Susan want to slide a few inches away from her.

"I'm Su—" Fuck. She'd almost told the reporter her real name. Holy shit. She better slow down so she didn't make any more mistakes. "I'm Gina," she said. After all, the dude already knew her as Gina Lola, so what was the harm?

"You have a last name, honey?" Kourtney's voice was like thick, sweet cream, and it confirmed Susan's theory that she was a really nice person. She could trust her.

"Lola. My full name is Gina Lola, and I'm a . . . prostitute." She never called herself that in her business dealings; however, whatever Kourtney reported wouldn't help the police if it wasn't true. "A high-priced one. My johns are all rich, and some of them are famous."

"Oh my." Kourtney jerked her head sideways toward the information desk, leaned in and whispered. "I don't think she can hear us, but maybe we should take this outside. Besides, I need a smoke if you don't mind."

Sure. The courtyard would be much more private, and the last thing Susan wanted was to be overheard or draw attention to herself. Her guess was the blue-haired lady hadn't heard a word but rather was checking Kourtney out. Everybody with a TV knew Kourtney Kennedy. A few minutes later, they emerged from the Skirball's interior into the Taper courtyard: a large, paved area, with a giant reflecting pool and a smashing view of the Santa

Monica Mountains. The sun was just beginning to set, turning the water lilies in the pool into a virtual kaleidoscope of color. Suddenly, emotion clogged Susan's throat. It wasn't that her life had been exactly ugly up until this point, but she couldn't remember seeing anything quite so beautiful as these water lilies in this magic light before today. Something about this place gave her the feeling she could do more than she had done, *be* more than she had been. If she hadn't been scared out of her mind right now, she might've considered this one of the best moments of her life.

Striding the length of the terrace and back, she checked for visitors, but there was not another soul in sight. Just her and her new friend, Kourtney Kennedy. Eventually, the pacing started her knees bumping again. She found a lawn chair, turned it to face the sunset, and sat down.

You can do this.

Kourtney sat down next to her and pulled a small, handheld camera from her purse. The camera made a whirring noise when she turned it on.

Surprised, Susan yanked her scarf across her face, hiding from the camera. "Put that away, please."

"Look, I need confirmation—"

"No. Way." Through the sheer fabric of her scarf, she could see Kourtney was still aiming the camera her way. "Turn it off, or there's no story. I told you already, I have to stay anonymous."

Heaving a big, irritated sigh, Kourtney shut off the camera and set it aside. "You've already blown your anonymity with me— when you told me your name, remember? But there's nothing to worry about. I promise to keep everything confidential. I just need something to show my boss. Otherwise, he might think I made the whole thing up."

"Why would he think that?" She wondered if Kourtney had made up stories in the past.

Kourtney's eyes darted away. "No reason. Let's just say it would be best if I had some sort of verification. You know the networks are always making out like *our* news team over at SLY isn't real. Like we don't have ethics or standards or source things like they do, but they're wrong. I'm going to have a heck of a time getting my boss to air a story where I can't get another source for confirmation. So what do you say I just get a quick five of you on tape to prove you're not some figment—it'll be for my boss's eyes only."

Susan thought about this a moment. She trusted Kourtney, but not that much. "Sorry. No tape. Not even audio. You got a notebook, don't you?"

Kourtney nodded.

"Then use it or lose the story. This is the only way I talk."

After a few seconds of thinking about it, Kourtney seemed to realize she couldn't convince Susan to go on camera. "Then promise me an exclusive. Tell me you won't go to any other reporters, and I'll do whatever it takes to convince the powers that be at SLY that this story is too important not to air. Tape or no tape, confirmation or no confirmation. You'll be my Deep Throat." Kourtney grimaced, but Susan hadn't taken offense. She had a college degree, and she knew all about Watergate.

"No pun intended, I'm sure," she said, and unwound her scarf from her face.

"Sorry."

"It's okay. And of course this is your exclusive. I don't want to have to go through this more than once, and you seem—"

"You don't find me intimidating? Like the *real* reporters?"

Kourtney sounded surprisingly insecure for such an accomplished woman. She shouldn't take things so personally, but Susan could see that Kourtney had a big chip on her shoulder. And in a way, she could see why. People must assume Kourtney had only gotten to be an anchor because of her looks. But maybe Kourtney should be more honest with herself, because her looks might not be the only reason she'd succeeded, but in this town, they had to have been a factor. In this town, looking good was a job requirement, and no one knew that better than Susan. Susan had almost died for a boob job.

"I was going to say I picked you because you seem nice. And because everyone watches SLY. Besides, you're the one who came up with the Fallen Angel Killer nickname. I think you're smart, and you deserve to be the one who gets the story."

"Well, thanks." Kourtney flashed her million-dollar smile, then pulled out her smokes and shook two out of the pack.

Susan hesitated before accepting the cigarette. She bent and let Kourtney light it for her. After a couple of deep drags, a coughing fit started up, and she ground out the cigarette beneath her heel.

Kourtney lifted an amused eyebrow. "A prostitute who doesn't smoke. I'll have to mark that off my list of hooker stereotypes."

"Better cross them all off, if you ask me. I don't come from a broken home. I've got an education, and I make my own decisions."

"So . . . you don't have a pimp."

This was going to be tricky. She didn't want to blow Lucy's cover, but she had to tell the truth. Lives were at stake.

"I've got a madam, but it's not like you think."

"Oh?" Kourtney puffed three perfect smoke rings into the air.

"Like I said before, it's all high-class. My madam doesn't set me up with losers or abusers."

Kourtney wrinkled her brow. "Except for this last time."

Kourtney had just given voice to Susan's own doubts, but somehow that made her want to defend her friend more than ever. "Right, well, Lucy didn't know he was a bad dude because he claimed to be Ryan Winters on the phone."

The reporter choked on her smoke. "Are you telling me Ryan Winters is a client of this Madam Lucy?"

She was getting tired of explaining this point to people—first to Lucy, and now to Kourtney. "The man who called for me *wasn't* Ryan Winters. Ryan Winters is *not* Lucy's client. But it's easy to understand why Lucy wouldn't question him too much. I mean, he certainly *could* have been Winters. The guy does have a rep."

"Okay. Let's forget about Madam Lucy and Ryan Winters for a minute. Why don't you start from the beginning and tell me everything that happened that night at Waxed." Kourtney's tone seemed disappointed. Having smoked her butt down to ashes, she let it fall from her mouth without stepping on it.

Susan threw her leg out and stomped on it. When the butts cooled she'd pick them up and put them in her pocket. She wasn't a litterbug, and she'd didn't particularly like the fact that Kourtney had been so careless. If she was careless with a smoke, she might be careless with the information Susan gave her. But there was no turning back now.

She gulped in a breath of courage. She started talking, and she didn't stop until she'd gotten the whole story of Charlie Chaplin out. During the course of her tale, Kourtney broke three different pencils from writing so hard and fast. When Susan finished, her chest felt both sore and light at the same time, as if someone had been sitting on it for days but then finally thought of something better to do and had gotten off.

Kourtney scrabbled around in her purse and found a tissue, which she used to dab perspiration from her forehead. Regarding Susan with something that seemed like worry in her eyes, she asked, "You gonna be all right? You got money, a place to stay?"

"Yeah." She'd found a nice little motel in Brentwood after leaving Lucy's place yesterday.

"How can I reach you?"

She didn't plan to stick around, so there was no point in giving Kourtney her number. "Oh, well, you can't. I'm outta here in the morning. I don't feel safe with *him* around."

Kourtney crossed her legs at the ankles and touched Susan's hand. In an earnest voice she said, "Of course you don't feel safe. You're very brave for coming forward . . . but I'm thinking that if we're really going to catch this bastard, I might need to talk to you again. You said I could share this information with the public and the police."

"That's the reason I called your tip line. I hope the cops catch him before he hurts any more escorts."

"Exactly. And the police will surely have questions. I can be the go-between and leave your identity out of it, but in order to do that, I have to know how to reach you. Also, I don't think you should leave town. Not yet, anyway. I won't tell anyone where you are."

That feeling of someone sitting on her chest returned. "You think I'll be safe at a motel? You don't think he'll come looking for me after the story breaks?"

"No one will know you're still in town except me." Kourtney put money in Susan's hand and curled her palm around it. "I'm sure it's safe to stick around. You used a fake name, didn't you?"

Susan nodded. She wasn't foolish enough to register under either Gina Lola *or* Susan Smith.

"Then just be careful. Stick to the phony name. Don't use your credit cards or write any checks, and I'm sure he won't be able to find you."

Chapter Twelve

Monday, October 7
4:00 P.M.
Malibu, California

IT'D BEEN SURPRISINGLY easy, Caitlin thought, to persuade Lieutenant Martinez to set up an interview with Tom La Grande. She'd expected that with so little to go on—La Grande having been spotted at the hotel bar around the time the first victim tumbled from the window and the use of the star's wax statue as a prop in the third murder—Martinez wouldn't have jumped at the idea of casting suspicion on such an important celebrity. But the moment they'd suggested it, the lieutenant had begun making arrangements to question Tom La Grande. Now here they were, less than forty-eight hours since Horatio had given them the lowdown, sitting around a kitchen table at the Malibu home of Jamie Robb—that adorable kid actor who was now all grown-up and remarkably sane for his ilk. Present for the interview were herself, Martinez, Spense, La Grande, and Robb.

Jamie Robb and Tom La Grande, it seemed, had remained fast friends ever since they'd played brothers on the hit sit-com, *Family Rules*, more than twenty years ago. And like their TV counterparts, Robb had assumed the role of the good, dependable brother, while Tom had taken on the bad-boy mantle. La Grande, who'd been forthright about his gambling and drug addictions, had been in and out of rehab numerous times, and at thirty-one, was already on his fourth marriage. But despite his bad habits, a boyish charm still twinkled in his blue eyes, and his complexion remained clear. The highlights in his sandy hair were either natural or very expensive, and though he wasn't a tall man, he clearly worked out. And when he smiled, there was no doubt Tom La Grande had that *je ne sais quoi* that made a man a star, and that, coupled with some genuine acting talent, had carried him far in the business.

After refusing to come down to the station without a formal charge, La Grande had agreed to talk with them without an attorney present, so long as Lieutenant Martinez complied with two conditions. First, to keep his wife from getting wind of it, La Grande wanted the meet set somewhere other than his home, and second, he wanted his friend, Jamie Robb, present during the interview. Robb had never practiced law, but he'd graduated from law school and even passed the bar exam a few years back. La Grande asserted that although there might be certain things he'd prefer his wife not learn about, he hadn't done anything *unusually wrong for him*, and Robb's informal counsel would do for now.

Jamie Robb, an average-looking man, with a receding hairline and the beginnings of a middle-age paunch, bore little resemblance to that charismatic child star who'd delighted audiences for years, but he still had a wide smile and an easy way about him. After sending his wife and son out on a mission to find special ingredients for a gourmet dinner, their host was the last to join them at the table.

"Don't worry," Robb told them, easing his chair next to La Grande. "I sent them on a wild-goose chase. They'll have a heck of a time finding chocolate coriander, don't you think?"

"How come?" Martinez bit the bait.

"Because there's no such thing. But this way, they'll have the fun of a treasure hunt, and we'll have plenty of privacy. I'll make it up to them with one of my special dinners, though," he added, looking a little sheepish about having tricked his wife and son.

While Martinez set up his recorder, spoke to La Grande about the manner in which the interview would proceed, and asked for questions or objections from Robb—the attorney stand-in— Caitlin used the time to take in her surroundings. Despite the serious nature of the business at hand, she had to admit she was rather enjoying the circumstances in which she presently found herself. Robb's well-equipped galley was as elegant as any she'd seen in magazines. Outside the kitchen's opened glass doors, the Malibu surf pounded out the sound track to the lives of the rich and famous . . . And the view at the table was even more enticing than the beach.

Spense caught her staring and let his gaze linger on hers, caus- ing the sound of her pulse to amplify in her ears. The look he sent her made the moment feel as intimate as if they were dancing cheek to cheek. Breaking eye contact, she cast a glance around the table once more and couldn't help noticing that among all these powerful, seductive men, it was Spense who truly stood out. You might say he *out-fined* them all. Feeling a flush rise to her cheeks, she ducked her chin and forced her thoughts back to the case.

Focus.

She was here for the fallen angels, not the floor show. In his role as supervising detective, she expected Rick Martinez would take the lead and set an easy, nonthreatening tone—which would allow for either her or Spense to step into a *bad cop* role later on should La Grande prove uncooperative. In the meantime, keeping things light would throw the suspect off guard. As hard as it was to imagine him as a serial killer, La Grande was their prime suspect until they could cross him off their list. Although *prime* and *list* might not be the correct terms since La Grande was the only person on their radar. Perhaps that was the reason Martinez had been so anxious to interview the man. At the moment, there were no other leads, at least not any the captain had shared with his profiling team. Glad the lieutenant had been grateful enough for the tip she and Spense had provided to include them today, she pulled out a notepad and pen—not to take down the spoken content of the interview but rather to make note of any subtext she could pick up from the suspect's intonations or body language.

"I appreciate your sitting down with us, Mr. La Grande, and you, too, Mr. Robb. Please state your full names for the record," Martinez said.

"Our real names or our stage names?" La Grande asked.

"Both."

"I'm Thomas George Everett, my stage name is Tom La Grande."

"I'm James Robert Linnaeus, acting as Jamie Robb."

"Great. We'll try to make this quick and be out of your hair before your family gets home. Don't want to interfere with your dinner." Just as she'd expected, Martinez had started off on his best behavior.

"No problem," Robb replied. "Let's just get this done. Tom wants to clear up any misconceptions the police might have about his being somehow involved in this terrible mess."

"We want to clear things up, too." The detective directed his attention to La Grande. "Let's start by making sure I understand why we're doing this here. I get why you wouldn't want to come down to the station. But surely you don't expect to keep your wife in the dark forever?" Martinez probably wanted to distract La Grande with minor issues before getting to the good stuff.

"May I speak frankly, Detective?" For now, La Grande's posture remained open, cooperative. Caitlin made a note of it.

"I sure wish you would," Martinez said.

"I love Anita very much. She's my fourth wife," he addressed Caitlin as if she were the only person in the room in need of clarification on the matter, then turned back to Martinez. "Anyway, Anita's not like my first three wives. She's not in show business. She's a smart, good girl. A physical therapist. I met her after I busted my knee doing a stupid stunt in *Jammed Up*—back then it was all the rage to do your own stunts, but thank God that trend's fading. Anyway, as you may have heard, I've had my share of troubles. Most of them my own doing. Anita's been a saint to put up with me, and I promised her no more drinking. I swore I was on the straight and narrow. After the last time . . ." He hesitated.

He didn't need to finish his thought. Everyone here knew he was referring to the time he holed up in a Las Vegas hotel room with a porn star for three days and had to be air-evaced to the hospital with alcohol poisoning.

"Anita says this is my last chance. So I'm sure you can understand why I don't want her to know I had a drink at the Sky Walk Hotel before Jamie's star ceremony."

So far, Caitlin hadn't seen any tells to suggest he was out-and-out lying, but his rate of speech had slowed. He was picking and choosing his words, as if he were concealing something.

Lying by omission.

He still maintained that his only reason for being at the Sky Walk that day was for a ceremony that had never taken place.

"You don't want the little woman to know you fell off the wagon. Understandable. And believe me, nobody down at the station wants to make more trouble for you. You're one of our most popular citizens." A pained look came over Martinez's face. "In Hollywood division, our mission is to build a safe neighborhood for everyone and to maintain good relations with our community leaders."

Caitlin struggled to keep from smiling. He was quoting from the brochure she'd found down at the station. The one that said celebrities get the same treatment as everyone else. From the way his mouth was twisting, she suspected *community policing* was not the lieutenant's favorite activity.

"So if you could just tell me, in your own words, Mr. La Grande, how you came to be involved with these young women, we'll be on our way."

La Grande shook his head, a little of his composure seeming to crumble away with each jerk of his chin. "There must be some kind of mistake. I don't know why you think I have any information about these women because I don't."

Ah. Now, the tell came out to play. La Grande had touched two fingers to his lips before speaking. He was lying. She was almost certain of it, but she wanted to wait and see if he did it again in response to this same line of questioning.

"What was your relationship with Selena Turner?"

Two fingers to the lips, eyes jerking right. La Grande was definitely lying. Spense rose slightly on his haunches. He'd seen it, too.

"What? I had no relationship with that woman. And I'm sickened by what happened to that poor girl, Brenda? Was that her name? I'm deeply disturbed the killer chose to use my statue to demean her in that awful way. But surely you realize he could have picked any figure in the museum. This is just an unfortunate coincidence."

"What's a coincidence?" Rick tapped the heel of his palm on his forehead as if trying to catch the drift. "Oh!" He paused dramatically. "You must mean it's a coincidence that Brenda Reggero, the third murdered woman, was posed with *your* statue and that you had a close relationship with Adrianne Simpson, the second murdered woman."

Despite the lieutenant's nonchalant tone, his words sent a silent shock wave rippling through the air. It was clear from the way Robb's mouth dropped open that he hadn't expected this declaration any more than had Caitlin or Spense.

It didn't take Caitlin long to connect the dots, however. In their initial meeting with Jeffers, he'd mentioned that Adrianne Simpson's landlord was a public figure. They'd speculated that figure might have been acting as her benefactor—a sugar daddy in common parlance. Caitlin would bet an Arnold Palmer they were about to learn that the landlord in question was Tom La Grande. And *that* was the reason when she and Spense found a witness who placed La Grande at the Sky Walk on the day of Selena Turner's murder, Martinez had started humming like a honeybee in a candy store.

"I-I. You didn't mention that on the phone, but yes, I knew the Simpson woman. We had business dealings only. She was my tenant. You see, one of my many investments is a property in Laurel Canyon. Addie is an excellent renter. I mean, she *was* an excellent renter. I can see how you'd get confused about this. But I'm telling you, I had nothing to do with any murders."

"Where were you Friday night, then, say from midnight to six? You must remember what you did over the weekend."

"I can vouch for Tom's whereabouts on Friday," Jamie Robb quickly jumped to defend his buddy. Maybe a little too quickly. These men were like brothers, and Caitlin had to wonder how far Robb would go to protect him. If he really believed La Grande to be innocent, he just might be willing to give a false alibi.

"Tom called me Friday night from a bungalow at the Beverly Hilton. He'd been fighting with Anita, and he needed a shoulder. He's been working his program hard, and since he was tempted to drink, he wanted me to come over for moral support to help him stay sober." Robb must've seen the doubt in Caitlin's eyes, adding, "You can check with my wife when she gets home. She was here when Tom called. Anyway, I went right over. I stayed up with him most of the night. He finally fell asleep around sunrise, then I headed home because my wife had an early doctor's appointment, and I didn't want our son to go without breakfast. I asked the hotel manager to send someone to wake Tom at seven."

"You say your wife can verify all this?" Martinez looked as skeptical as Caitlin felt.

"Yes, and the manager at the Beverly Hilton, too."

"Okay," Martinez said. "Let's set Friday night aside for the moment. Where were you on the night of September 27?"

La Grande's fist came down on the table. "Christ, I don't know. Is that the night Addie died? I'll have my assistant look into it. I'm certain I can provide an alibi."

No fingers to the lips. Caitlin made a note. *Subject appears truthful in this regard.*

"Well, that's great. Be sure to have him call this man . . ." Martinez passed a card to La Grande . . . "Sergeant Rimes, he's sort of like *my* assistant. He'll take down the information and get right on confirming your alibi." Martinez's brow drew down. "Now my only problem is you can't alibi out for the morning Selena Turner was killed. Because we *know* you were at the hotel. A server recognized you, and you paid for that drink you don't want your wife to know about with a credit card. Since you never showed up for your friend's ceremony, I need to know exactly what you were doing at the Sky Walk that day . . . if you weren't stabbing Selena Turner and shoving her out a window, I mean."

La Grande covered his entire face with his hands, making it hard for Caitlin to read him. "I did not know Miss Turner. I did not push her out a window. I went to the hotel that morning because my dear friend, this gentleman at my side, who has stood by me through all my troubles, Mr. Jamie Robb, was supposed to be honored. I arrived early because it was quite important to me to be on time for Jamie's big day, and you never know about traffic in LA. Since I'd missed breakfast, I thought I'd just have a cup of tea and some snacks while I waited for the ceremony to begin. But let's face it. I should've stayed out of the bar. In no time, I weakened and ordered a drink. A whiskey. I only had the one. You can check my tab if you don't believe me. But you see I really am trying to be the man my wife needs me to be, so I've started taking a medication. I forget the name." He pulled a bottle of tablets out of his pocket. Spense leaned in and took a good look before La Grande handed it over to the lieutenant.

Martinez turned the pill bottle in his hand. "Disulfiram. Never heard of it."

"It's a medication prescribed to prevent alcohol abuse," Caitlin provided.

"Right." La Grande nodded emphatically. "And so you see, that's what happened."

La Grande seemed relieved, as if he himself had only just stumbled upon this version of the truth and found it to his liking. Caitlin dutifully wrote down her observation.

"No. I'm afraid I'm too thick to see." Martinez crossed his arms over his chest. "Explain it to me if you don't mind."

"This medicine. It makes you sick as hell when you drink, so you don't . . . drink. Only, I did. I know it was stupid, but I'm an alcoholic, and I didn't have my best judgment at the ready. I told myself one shot of whiskey wouldn't make me sick. I hadn't even taken my pill yet that morning, so I thought I could get by with it. Boy was I wrong. You see, the medication builds up in your system, and you can't drink for days, sometimes weeks after your last dose. Live and learn. Anyway, I got the shakes and the shits, and I knew I was going to hurl not once but many, many times. I couldn't go to Jamie's ceremony in that condition. I just couldn't. So I called my driver, and he picked me up and took me back home. And that's why I was at the hotel that morning but never showed up for the ceremony."

Spense scraped his chair back from the table and turned it to face La Grande, then gave him a slow clap. Caitlin didn't know what Spense had figured out just by looking at the bottle of pills, but clearly he thought he'd found a puzzle piece. And from the look on his face, she knew the *bad cop* had just entered the building.

La Grande held his breath so long, the skin around his mouth took on a bluish hue. Spense said nothing, just waited as if he had all day for La Grande to gather the courage to meet his gaze.

Finally, La Grande wheezed out his breath, and asked, "You don't believe me?"

Spense leaned in. "Not at all. I think you're full of shit. Great performance though."

Placing his hand on his friend's shoulder, Robb said, "You gave them what they asked for, Tom, an honest interview." He narrowed his eyes at Spense. "I think you should show Mr. La Grande some courtesy; otherwise, we're done here."

"I show courtesy when it's called for. Like for example if you invite me over for one of your family dinners, I'll bring my company manners. But this isn't a dinner party. This is a murder investigation, Mr. Robb, and company manners don't catch killers."

"I'm not a killer," La Grande protested in alarm. "Do I need a real lawyer?"

Robb's cheeks went apple red. "I think you might. I'll call Teddy Haynes right now if you want."

"No. Not the Torpedo. I'm trying to keep this quiet. I don't need him riding into town and stirring up a media frenzy."

"I don't see how you can avoid one. And if you think you may have some . . . liability . . ."

Interesting, that La Grande was averse to calling Haynes, who was reputedly one of the best criminal lawyers in the country. Caitlin would've expected a guilty man to be clamoring for the best defense money could buy. Noting the earnestness in La Grande's tone, she scribbled a notation in her book.

"I'll say again," La Grande's voice broke. "I'm not a killer."

"But you *are* a liar." Spense dragged his chair closer to La

Grande's until their knees touched and their eyes locked. "That's a pretty little story you just told us. But it's full of half-truths and outright fabrications. Suppose I tell you what I think really happened the day Selena Turner was killed, and you stop me if I get anything wrong."

"What is this, some kind of profiler grandstanding? I suppose you're going to hold up a card to your forehead and play Kreskin now." Robb's tone was irate.

"Who's Kreskin?" Martinez elbowed Caitlin and whispered his question in her ear.

"A famous mentalist," she whispered back.

Robb turned to La Grande. "Don't say another word until we get Torpedo on the horn."

"You don't have to say anything. Just listen." Spense spoke directly to La Grande, bypassing Robb altogether. "But if I get something wrong, stop me."

Smart, Caitlin thought. That way, La Grande didn't have to admit anything. He could always claim later he only kept quiet because he didn't want to talk without a criminal attorney present. And Spense was well within the law to press him since he not only was not in their custody, he'd officially turned down Robb's offer to contact a *real* lawyer. She had her pen poised and ready. She'd be watching La Grande's body language in order to gauge his reaction to Spense's statements.

"Here's what I think really happened. You arrived at the hotel with the plan to attend the ceremony for your friend's, Jamie Robb's, refurbished star. Just like you said." Spense seemed to be easing into the confrontation by starting with facts La Grande had already conceded. "And just like you said, you had a drink at the bar."

La Grande nodded. "That's right. Just like I already told you. I wasn't lying."

"Not about that. But you haven't been taking your medication. Not since a few days after coming home from the hospital, have you?" Spense reached for the pill bottle on the kitchen table. "This bottle is almost full, and the date on the prescription is six months old. The server who spotted you at the Sky Walk says you were your usual self that morning, not shaking or red faced or god-awful sick like a man on disulfiram would get within minutes of ingesting alcohol. You had no fear of downing a shot of whiskey because you weren't taking the meds. And a drink wasn't all you had that day. You'd scored something else earlier. I'm guessing H. And since you're the type who likes company when he parties, you arranged to meet a hooker, Selena Turner. You weren't just paying her for sex. She was to be both a play pal and a babysitter. You needed someone to make sure you didn't do too much damage, like last time in Vegas."

La Grande's lips began to twitch. Spense was on the money. Caitlin noted it.

"After tossing back a whiskey in the hotel bar, you headed up to the room Selena had rented for the two of you. And because you really did plan to attend Mr. Robb's ceremony, that part of what you said is true, you opened the hotel-room window."

"Christ. How did you know that?" It seemed La Grande couldn't help himself. Caitlin relaxed. If Spense got the suspect to admit everything, they might not need her notes at all.

"Shut up, Tom," Robb ordered, an undertone of anger in his voice.

"These ceremonies never start on time, and you didn't want to miss it altogether, but you also didn't want to curtail your fun any sooner than you absolutely had to. With the window open, you'd be able to hear when the master of ceremonies began the program. Then you could hustle downstairs in time to fulfill your promise without having to hang around and waste any more time than necessary with Jamie and his kid."

A flush slowly crawled up Robb's face. It had to be humiliating to learn that his so-called best friend had taken so little interest in the star ceremony—an event that probably meant the world to Robb.

La Grande's body trembled from head to toe, but he kept silent. Caitlin read that as meaning Spense had it right. If not, La Grande would've told him where he could stick his theory.

"We're going to need a DNA swab from you. When you give us one—and you will do so, either now, or later when we have a warrant—this is what we're going to find: The traces of semen on Selena Turner's chest are a match for you and only you. Because you're exactly the kind of asshole who thinks that as long as he doesn't stick it in, he's not cheating on his long-suffering wife."

A tear made its way slowly down La Grande's cheek. "I'm an asshole. It's true. But I didn't have sex . . . I just . . . I did come on her . . . but we never had intercourse. And I swear to you, I didn't kill her. Just like I said before, I planned to go to Jamie's ceremony. I *wanted* to be there for him like he's always been there for me, but I was too fucked up—you're right about the H. I couldn't let the press catch me in that condition. I should have realized that before, but like I said, I'm a fucking addict. I called my driver to come pick me up, and I snuck out the back way. But Selena was alive when I left the hotel room."

"What time was that?" Martinez interjected.

La Grande shook his head. "I really don't know. Like I said, I was too messed up. But my driver will know." He cast a sideways glance at Robb. "I'm so sorry, buddy. I'm a piss-poor excuse for a husband, and I'm a piss-poor excuse for a friend."

Caitlin noted Robb's throat working in a hard swallow. But whatever his reaction to La Grande's words, he seemed determined to hold his tongue.

La Grande's gaze traveled from Spense to Caitlin to Martinez. "I swear on my mother's grave, I am *not* a murderer."

No fingers to his lips. Genuine pain in his voice. She scribbled it all down, but she really didn't know if he was finally telling the truth or just a really great actor.

Martinez rose, moving slowly and deliberately, like he was trying not to spook a wild animal he'd ensnared. He walked around the table and stopped next to La Grande. "On your feet, please."

La Grande clutched Jamie Robb's sleeve. "I didn't kill anyone. I *liked* those girls. I never would've hurt any one of them. Please, you've got to believe me."

Robb's gaze froze on the pounding surf. "Of course I believe you. Let me call Torpedo. You deserve the best man to defend you, and I'm afraid that's not me."

"On your feet," Martinez repeated, leaving no wiggle room in his tone.

"Okay, okay, call someone, but not *that guy*. I don't want a media circus, Jamie. I can't put Anita through something like that." As he kicked his chair back and followed the lieutenant's instructions, everything about La Grande, his tone, his posture, his tears, spoke of a broken, guilt-ridden man.

She gripped·her pencil hard and scribbled into her notebook: *He's not the one.*

"Hands behind your back." Martinez reached beneath his coat and produced a pair of handcuffs. "Tom La Grande, I'm placing you under arrest on suspicion of murder. You have the right to remain silent . . ."

Chapter Thirteen

Tuesday, October 8
8:00 P.M.
Los Angeles, California

"YOU DON'T THINK he did it," Caity said, looking undeniably sexy with the moonlight shining on her toned legs as she brushed crumbs from her shorts and climbed to her feet.

With Tom La Grande, the prime suspect in the case, safely locked away in the Hollywood jail, Spense had taken advantage of the downtime to plan a special evening for Caity: a moonlit picnic in Griffith Park, to be followed by stargazing at the observatory—and a surprise. It wasn't the kind of romancing he was accustomed to, or even the kind he thought Caity expected . . . but it was the kind she deserved. And so here they were, kicked back on a checkered blanket on the grounds of Griffith Park with bellies full of apples and brie.

Still, though he definitely had more than work on his agenda tonight, the case was never far from his thoughts, because Caity was right—he didn't believe Tom La Grande murdered Selena Turner, or anyone else for that matter.

And if he was correct, that meant the killer was still out there.

"I don't," he said, then stood and folded the blanket, packed up their trash, and headed for the nearest waste barrel. The moon shone brightly enough that he hardly needed the flashlight, but he switched it on anyway, to be certain Caity wouldn't stumble.

"Me either. Everything I know about human behavior tells me Tom La Grande is not a serial killer. And when he insisted Selena Turner was alive when he left the hotel that morning, his body language indicated he was telling the truth."

After dumping the trash, they turned in the direction of the car. The Prius Spense had rented for the evening was parked at the trailhead.

Because Spense liked to view a case from multiple viewpoints, he decided to play devil's advocate for a minute. "It's pretty damning he was with Turner just minutes before she went out that window. And since he was high, he wouldn't really need much motive. I can see how things could've gotten out of hand—they might've argued, and then the drugs took over, and he reached for the corkscrew. The crime scene was certainly disorganized enough to fit that scenario."

She shrugged one shoulder. "I still don't buy it."

Neither did Spense. "The guy's a dick, but he lacks the initiative needed to kill. He's too busy getting stoned . . . but he is the right height, weight, and age for our profile."

"Other than demographics, he's no match at all. La Grande is at the pinnacle of his career. His personal life may be a mess, but he's up for another Academy Award."

They'd reached the Prius, and Spense unlocked it with the remote.

Caity lobbed the blanket into the trunk. "If anything, La Grande is *over*appreciated—he's certainly not underemployed. And he doesn't fit the most important part of the profile."

In unison, they said, "He's not an attention seeker."

Which was strange for an actor. Over the past twenty-four hours, Spense had uncovered a number of interesting facts about La Grande. For example, he'd never wanted to be a star. He hadn't chosen his own career path. Rather, it had been his alcoholic mother who pushed him into the limelight. She'd been a stage mom of the worst sort, and he'd reportedly tried, and failed, to get out of show business more than once. But he was simply too successful to quit. With all that money coming in, his inner circle wouldn't tolerate a career change. The guy had an entourage to support, and he couldn't walk away if his life depended on it. Which it probably did, given his appetite for drugs and his knack for getting himself into dangerous situations.

Caity leaned against the trunk and crossed her feet at the ankles, as though she was getting set for a long discussion. "He refused to hire Teddy Haynes as his defense attorney simply because Torpedo is a media hound who loves to try his cases in the press. It's almost as if La Grande values his privacy more than his life. He loathes media attention, whereas our UNSUB is willing to kill for it."

As fascinating as this discussion was, the big telescope at the observatory closed around ten, and if they didn't head up now, there'd be no surprise. It was time to refocus the agenda. "Hon."

She looked around as if she wasn't sure whom he meant, then pointed to her chest. "Me?"

"Yeah, you. This is supposed to be our time off. You wanna talk shop all night or catch the stars?"

"Definitely the stars."

"We can drive up to the observatory or—"

"I prefer to hike, it's such a beautiful night, and I'm not the least bit tired."

He was glad Caity had suggested they walk. It would give him a chance to test a claim she'd made earlier—that she was feeling good as new. Besides, in his line of work, it was hard to find a quiet moment, and even harder to find someone to share it with. Someone who really understood that he absolutely needed this time, this chance to experience an ordinary night, untainted by evil. He grabbed her hand and sucked in a long, cool breath of happiness.

THEY'D WALKED WELL over a mile, and Caitlin had hardly gotten winded at all—except for the time she'd stared too long at Spense, which apparently was like looking directly into an eclipse. Something about the curve of his mouth, the strong line of his jaw, the whole *Spenseness* of his profile, seemed to blind her to any and all obstacles in their path—at least for tonight. All he had to do was grin at her, and her heart lifted. What could it hurt to put her worries away for just one evening?

Then a set of stairs, wrapping up and around the observatory, suddenly appeared in front of her. While she'd been thinking of Spense, she hadn't noticed they'd reached their destination. The winding cement steps led to the roof and the Zeiss telescope. On the hike up, Spense had explained that Griffith J. Griffith, the park's founder, had been a fan of looking at the world with both the soul and the eyes. He was famously quoted as saying: *If all mankind could look through that telescope, it would change the world.*

With all her heart, she wished that to be true. And she certainly believed in never refusing to see what was in front of her. Yes, she might be spared the awareness of evil . . . for a while at least . . . but the cost of missing out on the good stuff was simply too great.

Keep your eyes open, so you don't miss a thing.

That was how she aspired to go through life.

As she began the ascent of what she was now thinking of as the "Stairway to Heaven", she began humming the old Led Zeppelin tune. Seeming pleased, Spense hummed along with her. She was having a lovely time when a heavyset man jostled her from behind. Perhaps he didn't find her humming charming. Looking over her shoulder, she realized the real issue was the throng of tourists unloading from a bus. Though visitors could take their time at the telescope once admitted, nine forty-five was the deadline to line up, and guests were vying to make it onto the stairs before the park officials roped them off for the night.

"Sorry," the man said.

"No problem." She smiled back at him, happy the bulk of the crowd was behind her. It was too easy for her to get claustrophobic in situations like these. But once they rounded the curve of the building, and she saw the crowd snaking up the stairs in front of them, her relief came to an abrupt end. A few feet later, the line was at a standstill, as people took their time looking through the telescope. Behind her, the heavyset man pressed close enough that she could hear his labored breathing.

She put her hand on her stomach. She was beginning to get that panicky feeling in her belly. A beat later, she became acutely aware of the dampness on the back of her neck and a tickle of perspiration between her breasts.

"You look a little done-in, Caity. You should've told me you were getting tired." It didn't take much to turn Spense into Mr. Mom. For a special agent, he could get fussy.

She shook her head. "That's *not* it. I promise you, I'm not the least bit fatigued. If anything, I've got too much nervous energy. It's just that I absolutely hate enclosed spaces. I can't stand being confined."

He arched one eyebrow in challenge. "Baby, we're outside."

"I know, but with all these people breathing down my neck, I feel trapped."

And that was no delusion. She was backed against the side of the building, and the only way off these stairs at the moment would be to dive over the edge. Which seemed a better option than possibly being trampled to death, now that she thought about it.

"Do you want to turn around?"

Elbowing her way through the crowd to get down didn't exactly appeal, but the idea of being trapped here indefinitely seemed worse. Much worse. Her knees had gone watery, and it was hard to get a deep breath. But if she turned around now, she'd miss her chance at the stars.

Spense grabbed her hand. "There's nothing to be afraid of, Caity. I'm right here."

"I know I'm behaving like a child, but I don't feel right."

"Your palm is clammy." He rested his ear against her chest. "And your heart's racing."

"I feel like I'm going to die. Right here, and right now."

"But you're *not* going to die. At least not here with me tonight." He brought her hand to his lips, and the oddest thing happened— that sick feeling in her gut vanished. The crowd seemed to melt away, like in one of those old movies, where the camera zooms in, and the rest of the room fades, until only the couple on the dance floor remains.

"Do you want to see the stars?" His voice was low and gravelly, making her breath catch in her throat.

She nodded.

"Then be brave. If I thought for one moment any harm would come to you, I'd flash my creds and part this crowd for you. But, I've seen you face down *real* danger, and I know how much courage you have. This isn't the time to doubt yourself. We'll do whatever you want, but just so you know, I really want to share this with you."

She took a deep breath. "I want to share this experience with you, too."

So they waited. And with each passing moment, her anticipation grew greater. With each step forward, she grew more determined to see, with her own eyes, the sights Griffith J. Griffith had talked about—the beauty that could change the world.

When she finally got her turn at the big telescope, she had to laugh at herself. "You were right. I'm still alive."

"I told you so," Spense said, lifting his hand and waving an attendant over.

She pressed her eye to the scope, and after a minute of adjustment, she could see the wide night sky. It was a breathtaking sight indeed. "I can manage. Thanks so much," she said, not wanting to take the attendant's time.

But Spense came up close behind her. "I've got a surprise for you," he whispered.

With her heart fluttering in her chest, she stepped back and watched Spense and the attendant work to aim the scope at a particular spot in the heavens. Then Spense gave the man a tip and motioned her over again.

She bent and pressed her eye to the scope, waiting a beat for her vision to adjust. And then all at once she saw it, a single brilliant orb surrounded by a halo of more distant stars. Spense laid his hand on her shoulder, and a shiver ran through her. "W-what am I looking at?"

"Your father's star."

Her knees threatened to buckle, but Spense locked his arms around her waist, supporting her. "I adopted that star for your father—for *you*. I've got a certificate with his name and coordinates and everything. So whenever you need to, you can look up and find him."

She tried to speak, but her throat had gone dry. She couldn't take her eyes off that bright light, couldn't think to ask what it meant to adopt a star. All she knew was that as she watched its energy pulsing before her, she felt her father's presence, and somehow, somewhere out there, in all that infinite space, she knew he'd found his freedom.

Chapter Fourteen

Tuesday, October 8
10:30 P.M.
Los Angeles, California

DESPITE THE CLEAR night sky above, humidity soaks the air. Filling my lungs, I savor the smell of damp leaves and rich earth. I can taste the promise of rain on my tongue. A storm is coming, which is a bit of much needed luck for me.

Weary of standing, I am now sitting cross-legged on the rocky ground, well hidden by a combination of darkness and overgrown brush. I don't need my mask yet, but I have it in my truck for later. The F-450 I rented—no one's ever seen me drive a big truck—is parked at a scenic pullout just a few hundred yards from here. Sighing, I raise my tactical night-vision goggles. I've no fear the lovers in the backseat of the Honda Element will hear me. They'll never discern my impatient breaths over their moans and urgent grunting.

My goggles are military grade, and I can see, quite clearly, the contorted expression on the young woman's face as she grinds her hips. Her tits bounce in and out of focus, and I can sometimes make out the bumpy texture of her areolas. While I am pleased with the performance of my binoculars, I take little pleasure in the show.

This is not the couple that interests me.

I lower my goggles and check my watch. It's after ten, and the big telescope has closed for the evening. That means my targets will soon return to the trailhead. Even if the Honda leaves now, I've missed my chance to cut the brakes on the Prius. I'm not mechanical to begin with, and though I've reviewed the procedure numerous times, I need to take my time to get it right. I have to be precise. Drill just enough, so that when the brake is pressed with sudden force, and not before, the line gives way. If I go too far, the driver will be tipped off. And this particular driver would spot the problem in a heartbeat. Then all my planning would be for nothing.

I smile, deciding it was lucky after all that the young couple thwarted me. Their presence at the trailhead saved me a fuck-up. Cutting the brakes was never the main plan anyway. It was just to give me an edge. Well, now I don't have that advantage, but I still have the element of surprise on my hands . . . and the good fortune of an approaching storm.

Chapter Fifteen

Tuesday, October 8
10:30 P.M.
Los Angeles, California

THEY'D WALKED WORDLESSLY all the way from the observatory to the trailhead parking lot, with Spense in deep concentration, as though the task of swinging the flashlight across the path to light their way took all his mental energy. Or maybe, like Caitlin, he'd turned his focus inward. Something had changed within her, and she was quietly fascinated by the difference. She didn't feel like the same woman who'd headed up the path only a couple of hours ago.

Strange.

But even the air smelled different. It was heavy with humidity, though, so that might account for its new sweetness.

"Looks like rain soon," Spense finally broke the silence. He searched the parking lot with his flashlight in much the same way she imagined he'd clear a building before entering on a warrant. The other cars were all gone, now. Only their rented Prius remained.

"You cold?" He reached out to open her door for her, and her heart suddenly swelled, at the sound of his voice, at the way he was always thinking of her and her comfort, her happiness.

"Not at all." Reaching out, she placed her hand atop his, before he could open the door. He turned his hand over and took her by the wrist, pulled her against him.

"Caity," he whispered against her cheek. His breath sent shivers over her skin, and the rasp in his voice made an ache start up low in her belly. She pressed against him, and he growled, gently curving a strong hand under her bottom, drawing her closer until she could feel him hardening against her.

She heard the flashlight clatter to the ground. In the moonlight, his eyes had a wild, demanding look that made arousal flare deep inside her. Turning her face up, she searched for his lips and found what she wanted. His kiss was urgent as his fingers probed, then found the top buttons of her blouse. He took his time, slowly undoing them one by one. Giving her plenty of notice, plenty of time to prepare herself for what was to come, but even so, she cried out from the thrill of his palm against her bare breast. Breaking their kiss, he pressed his lips against the hollow of her throat, the warm wetness setting every nerve in her body on fire.

As his fingers teased her nipple, her breath came in hard pants. Letting the pleasure unspool within her, she closed her eyes and arched against him. She was lost, falling deeper and deeper into a sensual abyss, when suddenly Spense jerked his hand away, and his body went rigid.

She opened her eyes, slowly coming out from under the spell of a kiss that had ended much too soon. Confused, she tugged her blouse to cover herself and looked up at him, searching his face for an answer. She wanted more . . . much more, but his eyes, so dark and hazy with need only a moment ago had turned clear and sharp. His gaze darted to all sides, letting her know his mood had changed. A wave of alarm washed over her, quelling her desire. He'd seen something . . . or someone. Without explanation, Spense grabbed the flashlight off the ground, then opened the door behind her and nudged her into the car.

"Is SOMETHING WRONG?" Caity asked, snapping her seat belt in place.

Spense's hands tightened around the steering wheel. It was probably nothing. The woods were full of small animals, and the wind had kicked up, likely rustling the leaves, but he could've sworn he heard a soft laugh coming from the bushes while they kissed. "I don't think so. But better safe than sorry. I thought someone might be out there—in the bushes."

"Oh." Her voice caught, and he almost regretted saying anything as he backed out of the lot and started down the park loop. "I didn't hear anything."

"Probably just kids, or my imagination. I'm sorry I startled you." He cleared his throat. "And even more sorry we had to . . . cut things short." He looked in the rearview mirror. The road was clear, deserted.

A light drizzle started up, and Spense searched around for the windshield wipers, accidentally hitting the power mirror button in the process. He'd never driven a Prius before, but he'd rented the midsize hybrid to prove to Caity he was environmentally conscious, like her—it was a small attempt at convincing her their value systems were compatible.

Safety first. He turned his focus to the road. Headlights flashed in the rearview mirror, and he drew in a breath. Where had that truck come from? It dropped back, and his shoulders relaxed as he remembered they'd just passed a scenic overlook. Probably teenagers.

The bank of clouds that had drifted in just minutes before now covered the moon. Then, as they hit a stretch of narrow curves, the rain began coming down in earnest. He switched on his brights. By day, this drive had its scenic moments, but by night in a rainstorm, the loop had little to recommend it.

Spense thought he heard the squeal of tires and cracked his window in order to hear better. The purr of an engine told him there was definitely another car approaching, then the headlights flashed in the rearview again. "There was a truck behind us a minute ago."

Caity turned around in her seat. "Looks like it's still there."

There was only one road out of the park from here, so there was nothing unusual about that, but call it gut instinct, or just experience, something had his radar up.

The truck flipped on its brights, all but blinding him.

Spense tapped his horn and flashed his lights, but the guy didn't get the message. "Moron." The truck sped up, closing in on them. "I'll pull over first chance I get."

The loop was paved and wide enough to accommodate daytime traffic, but on Caity's side it hugged a precipice for miles. At the moment, there was nowhere safe to pull off, and the driving rain cut his already poor visibility in half. His jaw clamped in anger. The asshole in the truck was putting them all in danger. As a warning, Spense tapped his brakes.

He heard the loud rev of an engine as the truck accelerated.

"Spense?" He could hear concern creeping into Caity's voice.

"Don't worry. There's got to be a safe pullout soon." He didn't want to frighten her any more than necessary. But . . . this guy was either impaired, or stupid—or he knew exactly what he was doing, in which case they were in real trouble.

Looking through his side mirrors instead of his blinding rearview, he could see the vehicle more clearly—a big truck, probably one of the Ford Super Duty models. *Great.* And Spense had picked a Prius to impress his girl. Chances were, however, that the driver meant them no harm—just wanted to go like hell on a wet, winding road, and was impatient with Spense's safe speed. "If you can reach the flashlight without unbuckling, signal him to pass us," he told Caity.

As she shined the beam out the window in a swinging motion, Spense slowed, hoping the truck would pass.

The truck moved left. They were on a straight, flat part of the road, giving him a good opportunity to make his move. Spense eased off the accelerator some more, noting the speedometer dropping to twenty miles an hour.

The truck came around the Prius, as if to pass.

"Well, there you go, buddy. Have a safe trip," Spense muttered under his breath. They were approaching a long section of curves. If this guy was going to go, he'd better hurry. As it pulled beside them, the truck slowed, too. "Caity take down the plates when he—"

Fuck.

Spense had just gotten his first good look at the driver. He was wearing a mask—it looked like some silent film star, but at the moment Spense was too busy to come up with his name.

"Charlie Chaplin?" Caity let out a surprised gasp.

The truck veered toward them, trying to force them off the road. Spense mashed the pedal to the floorboard, pulling ahead again. The truck dropped back, but Spense knew he was out-horsepowered. The man was taunting them, playing some kind of deadly game. He could overtake them anytime he wanted.

From his peripheral vision, he saw Caity scrambling in her purse. She pulled out her Ruger. The Ford's headlights were back in his rearview, but who knew how long it would be before the truck pulled beside them again.

"What are you planning to do with that?" Spense asked, forced to ease off on the accelerator further by an approaching curve.

"Shoot his tires out."

"You think you can hit his tires?" He didn't think it was doable, but that was Caity for you. She might panic in line for a telescope, but she was cool as Tom Cruise in a pair of Ray-Bans when it really counted.

She rolled her window down, and the rain whooshed in, stinging his skin like a thousand tiny needles. "It's worth a try," she shouted over the roar of the road and the wind. She unsnapped her seat belt and leaned as far out the window as she could, pointing the gun at the truck closing in behind them.

But there was no time to test her marksmanship. The truck was coming around the driver's side again. Spense had his foot on the gas. He was flying as fast as was safe on the slick, winding roads—faster. "Back inside!" he yelled, just as the truck bashed the side of the car. The Prius veered to the right, coming dangerously close to the edge of the precipice.

Spense's pulse went into overdrive, but he didn't panic. He'd *trained* for this, and he knew how to harness his adrenaline to his advantage. Judging by the way this motherfucker in the mask was driving, he'd gotten his car-chase lessons from the movies. If the truck hung back just a little and aimed its nose at their tail, it would cause them to do a 180 and lose control. But instead, this clown kept his nose too far forward as he tried to force them off the cliff.

In situations like this, he knew the simplest plan was probably the best—especially since he didn't have a complicated one. If Spense sped up, the asshole wouldn't need to force them off the road, they'd likely hydroplane and go flying off on their own. So Spense did the only reasonable thing he could. Instead of trying to outrun the truck, he eased off the gas, dropping behind. Now the hunter had become the prey.

Though Spense couldn't overtake him, he knew he'd confused the driver. The truck slowed, and Spense accelerated. Soon it was the Super Duty hugging the edge of the cliff. Spense clamped his jaw—he was about to give this motherfucker a driving lesson with a simple PIT maneuver. "Brace yourself!"

He slammed the nose of the Prius into the truck, right in the sweet spot.

Tires squealed and teeth rattled. But the maneuver worked.

The truck spun 180 degrees and stalled. Spense steered around him and accelerated, racing past the Super Duty. But his victory was all too brief.

The Ford roared back to life, then turned and bombed down the road after them.

Caity leaned far out the window again, this time firing off three earsplitting blasts. Spense was grateful for the rush of wind and rain, because its noise partially buffered the boom of her pistol, acting as a natural silencer.

In his rearview, Spense saw the truck swerve first to the right, then left. Gradually, the headlights grew smaller, then disappeared altogether. Caity might not have hit her mark, but she'd taken care of business just the same. She'd scared the shit out of the masked man, and the coward had done what cowards do—turned tail and run.

Above the ringing in his ears, he heard Caity whooping and hollering. She snapped her seat belt back in place. On his own—and in a more powerful car—Spense would've turned and given chase, but with Caity in the car, his priority was to get her home safely.

"Way to go, hon," he said, as a pair of antlers darted across the road.

The car jolted, its wheels slipping and hydroplaning on the wet pavement.

He heard Caity scream—just before a tree slammed into the windshield.

Chapter Sixteen

Wednesday, October 9
8:00 A.M.
Hollywood, California

WHILE SPENSE FILLED Martinez in on last night's car chase outside Griffith Park, the lieutenant paced the length of the detective's squad room at Hollywood station. He finally came to a stop too close to Spense, his black wingtip Oxfords all but touching the toes of Spense's brown Bruno Magli loafers. "Where's your partner again?"

Fighting the urge to step back, which was what this showboating detective expected, Spense canted forward until he could smell the burned coffee on the lieutenant's breath. "Cedars-Sinai."

"I know that. I mean what room. I wanna check in on her. Bring her some flowers maybe." His mouth tilted into a smile. "I bet you know what kind she likes."

He did. Any type of flower would please her, but she especially loved the pastels—pinks, purples, blues—regardless of the variety. "No need. They just wanted to observe her overnight for a mild concussion. She's probably being released late this afternoon." He stuck his hands in his pockets to keep from shoving Martinez out of his personal space—and out of his life while he was at it.

"So she's okay." Martinez sounded relieved.

The hairs on the back of Spense's neck bristled. It wasn't Martinez's job to worry about Caity. It was his.

Caity was his.

"No, she's not okay. She has a concussion." He pulled his hands from his pocket and cracked his knuckles in frustration. "Dammit." He was sick of visiting Caity in hospitals. He was the FBI agent. She was the consulting psychiatrist. If anyone was going to get hurt, from here on out, it was going to be him.

"I'd like to make sure Caity's taken care of. Maybe I'll just stop by before they release her anyway. What kind of flower did you say she liked?"

Spense's face flushed hot with anger.

"You don't like me calling her Caity?" Martinez's body tilted forward.

They were close enough to kiss, but kissing this jerk wasn't what Spense had in mind. One hand balled into a fist.

"You're not the only one who can call her that, you know."

But he *was* the only one who called her Caity, and he liked it that way. He counted to ten, but it didn't help. Without deciding to do so, he reached up and gave Martinez's shoulder a shove.

Martinez didn't even flinch.

"*I'll* make sure Caity has everything she needs." He took a deep breath, fighting back the desire to knock Martinez on his ass. "Got it?"

The lieutenant lifted his hands in surrender. "Chill out, buddy. I'm just trying to be nice here, but if you don't want me to bring her flowers, I won't."

Suddenly feeling a little ashamed that he'd cost Caity a bouquet of her beloved flowers, he relaxed his fists. He tugged at his collar. If she could see him now, ready to punch out the lead detective on their case for inquiring after her well-being, she'd be mad as hell. Martinez was right about one thing. It was time to chill out. They should get down to business. "I need to talk to La Grande."

Whether or not the actor turned out to be innocent, he had too many connections to the victims to ignore. He might know something that could help break this case wide open—even if he didn't know he knew. And now, while they had him in custody, they had leverage to get him to talk.

"He's lawyered up, I'm afraid. This time with a real criminal-defense attorney."

"Then get the new lawyer on the horn because I want to question La Grande, now."

"I'm in the room though." Martinez finally stepped back, giving Spense some breathing space and helping him remember they were on the same side.

"Understood."

One hour later, Martinez and Spense entered the interview room together and dragged chairs to flank Tom La Grande and his new attorney, Sutton Benoit. According to Martinez, Benoit was pricey enough, but his record wasn't all that great. Introductions were made, ground rules set, then Spense took over. He wasn't deferring to Martinez on this one. Spense suspected they had the wrong guy in custody. La Grande craved privacy whereas the killer craved notoriety. And both he and Caity had been convinced the man had been truthful when he asserted that Selena Turner was still alive when he left her hotel room. Not to mention that someone had tried to run Spense and Caity off the road last night, and he was having a hard time chalking that up to coincidence.

"I don't believe you killed anyone, Tom." Spense didn't bury the lead. "Let's get that out in the open, right now. But my friend, Detective Martinez, is going to need some convincing. So, you see, I'm on your side, just as long as you're straight with me. Any BS, any half-truths, though, and I'll be whistling Dixie while they cart you off to San Quentin."

"What is this? Good cop, bad cop?" Benoit asked.

"No it's smart cop"— Spense pointed his index finger to his chest— "stupid cop." He turned his pointer on Martinez, and the lieutenant's eyes flared. Spense had prepped him on his tactics, but he knew his tone had a sincere ring to it. "I'm afraid the detective is a slow learner. So we're going to have to spell things out for him. But as of right now, I don't know the alphabet, which is where you come in, Tom."

"What do you want me to say? I did *not* kill Selena Turner. I met up with her at the Sky Walk. I did some H while she watched. Then we fooled around, and I came on her tits so I wouldn't take any diseases home to Anita. Anita doesn't deserve to get herpes."

La Grande, on the other hand, was as deserving of catching a sexually transmitted disease as anyone Spense had ever met.

"You're missing my point. You've told us all that before. I need to know different things, so I can get Lieutenant Hardass over there to let you go. That means you've got to give me *new* pieces of the puzzle. Even if you think they might make you look bad."

"Like what?"

"Like, other than being dead, what do the victims have in common? You knew two of these women. So what can you tell me about them?"

"Not much."

"You just focused on their pussies?" Martinez spit into a hankie.

La Grande tugged at his hair and looked to his attorney. The attorney just stared at Martinez's soiled hankie.

"I'll say it again, I *liked* the girls. I found them through an escort service owned by Madam Lucille. Everyone calls her Lucy, though."

Martinez slapped his hand on the table. "Why the fuck didn't you say that before?"

"You didn't ask me. Is that important?" La Grande seemed genuinely confused. Apparently he had no idea that anyone connected to the girls would be a person of interest, potential witness, and possible suspect. If he'd known he could cast suspicion elsewhere, no doubt he would've told them about Madam Lucille from the get-go.

"Fuck yeah. It's important."

Spense kicked Martinez's ankle. He didn't want him taking over. "Tell us about Adrianne Simpson."

La Grande pressed the heel of his palms against his eyes. "Can I get a smoke or something?"

Martinez signaled to the camera. "Coming right up."

La Grande fidgeted, cleared his throat. "When?"

"It's coming," Spense said. "You rented out your place in Laurel Canyon to Adrianne Simpson. What was your relationship to her at the time of her death?"

Whispering to his client, the attorney nodded. It seemed he'd finally decided to do something to earn his keep. "Am I to understand that you're considering dropping all charges if my client cooperates?"

"No." Martinez folded his arms across his chest.

"Yes." Spense glared at Martinez—for show. They'd worked out ahead of time that they'd feign a rivalry . . . It wasn't that difficult to do. "You've got the wrong guy."

Benoit smoothed the sides of his oily hair. "I at least need a guarantee my client won't be charged with solicitation of a prostitute."

"I think we can manage that one," Martinez grumbled.

Benoit signaled his client to go ahead.

La Grande tapped the side of his hand on the table as if it held a pack of smokes. The guy had *addicted to everything* written all over his face. "All right then. I met Adrianne through Madam Lucy. Addie is . . . she *was* . . . a smart kid. I was half in love with her, I suppose."

Spense moved his hand over his mouth to cover a scowl. What happened to La Grande's loving his wife? "You must be devastated. I'm sorry for your loss."

"Thanks." He wiped the back of his hand over his eyes, sniffing.

"Please, take all the time you need. But . . . the sooner we get to the bottom of things, the sooner I can get my buddy to let you out of here."

"You know, I'm not accustomed to sharing my women. The way it usually works is that *they* share *me*. So I didn't dig it that much when Addie talked about Lucy hiring her out to other johns."

"And you didn't want the risk of disease, either, for Anita's sake." Spense sent him an understanding look.

"Exactly right. More than once I'd hear about Addie's pussy on break at the set—Lucy had a lot of character actors and stunt men for clients. It burned my ass that these jack holes thought Addie actually liked fucking them." He put one hand on his heart. "She was crazy about me; that's a given. So it was easy to convince her to quit Lucy for me. I set Addie up in a real nice place. I paid her tuition so she could go back to school. I gave her cash. She paid me rent by check. That way it was all on the up and up."

Spense felt a smirk coming on and stifled it. Apparently, La Grande considered himself a benefactor, when the truth was he was just another john. He might not believe he had to pay for Addie's company, but that's exactly what he'd been doing.

"So, pardon me, Mr. La Grande, but do you and Mrs. La Grande maintain marital relations?" Spense asked.

"Of course. I love Anita."

"So you were having active sexual relations with both your wife and your mistress, Addie. What were you doing with Selena Turner, then?" Martinez interrupted.

"Selena was more of a babysitter. I probably wouldn't have touched her if I hadn't been high. I don't like to cheat on Anita and Addie. But they both thought I was clean. After that fiasco in Vegas last year, I make it a point to have someone looking out for me whenever I indulge."

"And Brenda, she was one of Lucy's escorts, too?" Spense kept eye contact with La Grande, so he wouldn't look to his attorney. The actor hadn't yet admitted to knowing the third woman, but it made sense the pattern would hold.

After a tense pause, La Grande nodded. "Yes. I usually called Brenda when I wanted to get high, but she was sick the day of Jamie's star ceremony." He sniffed again, as if suddenly realizing he ought to act grief-stricken over her, too.

"Got it." Spense could hardly look at this man without his

stomach turning, but he made his tone sympathetic. "So you'd scored some H, and you arranged for Selena to meet you at the Sky Walk. The plan was to have some fun, then put in an appearance at Jaime Robb's star ceremony. Did you notice anything unusual about Miss Turner's demeanor? Did she seem worried about anything or frightened of anyone? Did she mention any recent arguments, maybe with another john?"

Maybe one of those stunt men. Last night, Spense had laughed to himself at the thought their pursuer must've learned to drive from big-screen car chases, but maybe he really *had* gotten his skills on a movie set.

"No. She was her usual sweet self. That's what you have to understand about Lucy's escorts. They're not really prostitutes. They're just regular girls like the kind who grew up next door to you. Only they get paid for sex. Lucy only takes quality johns. I can't think of anyone who would want to hurt Selena."

"So she wasn't worried. She hadn't argued with anyone."

"Now that I think about it, she did seem a little anxious about telling Lucy she was quitting. I offered to set her up, like I did with Addie. That way, Selena would be available on a moment's notice. But Selena was scared Lucy would get mad. Lucy was supposed to come by the hotel, and Selena wanted *me* to tell her she was leaving her, if you can imagine that."

"Lucy was coming by the hotel?" Spense asked. Suddenly, the lack of premeditation in the first murder made sense.

A uniformed officer entered the room with a pack of smokes, and Martinez gave the go-ahead to uncuff La Grande. Then the officer passed a note to Martinez, who looked at it and grinned. Benoit kept checking his watch, probably thinking about all the money he was making just sitting there with his mouth shut and

not doing anybody any good at all. Once La Grande had his cigarette going, they resumed the interview.

Spense had clicked on a new motive as soon as La Grande told
them Addie quit Lucy for him. Then, when he learned Lucy had
planned to meet Selena at the hotel, the puzzle pieces snapped into
place. "I suppose you had private arrangements with Brenda, too?"

La Grande nodded.

"So Lucy had a reason to be angry with all three women. They'd
betrayed her—for you." *Scumbag.* "She must've already been furi-
ous over losing Brenda and Addie. You think she might've snapped
when Selena told her she was quitting?"

La Grande's eyes widened. "Sure. Of course! Lucy was coming
by the hotel to meet Selena for brunch and collect her fee. She
must've come up to the room right after I left. Selena probably told
her she was finished, and Lucy lost it!"

Spense and Martinez exchanged a glance. It fit. The first
murder was impulsive, disorganized. Heat of the moment. *Satisfying.* After, Lucy could've carefully planned her revenge on the
other two girls, posing the bodies to make it look like the work
of a serial killer to lead investigators in the wrong direction. Was
Madam Lucy that smart? *Maybe.* After all, she'd been successfully
running an illegal operation for years, and the authorities didn't
have so much as a clue that she was in business.

"What's Lucy's last name?" Martinez was urgently taking his
own notes even though the interview was being video recorded.

Benoit put his hand up in warning, but La Grande wisely ignored him. "Hell if I know. But I have her number in my contacts.
Get them my cell, Benoit."

"You don't have to hand it over. They need a warrant to search
your phone," the attorney countered.

"I'm giving consent for the search. I want them to find that bitch."

Benoit nodded. "I'll see they get it."

"Good choice." Martinez got up and strolled to the window, lifted the bottom of the blinds, and peeked out. "Quite a crowd out there, Mr. La Grande. Looks like word somehow leaked out that you were about to be released."

"R-released? Already?" He fell back in his chair.

"You've got an alibi for the night Brenda Reggero was killed, and we've got hotel-security tape showing your driver leading you out the back way a good ten minutes before Selena Turner fell to her death."

"So you were going to let me go this whole time? And you tricked me into talking about my use of drugs and prostitutes."

"Not exactly. We were waiting on confirmation that you were out of town the night Miss Simpson was murdered—and we just got it from your assistant. Anyway, doesn't it take a load off your chest, knowing you came clean with the police? I'm sure your wife will understand completely—if you explain it to her like you did to us. If I were you, I wouldn't worry about a damn thing."

A uniformed officer, whom Spense recognized as Jeffers's adjuvant, poked his head in the room. "Captain needs you in his office."

Martinez nodded. "We'll be right there. Can you wrap up the details and get Mr. La Grande out of here? He's quite anxious to get home to his loving wife."

Shaking his finger at Lieutenant Martinez, Benoit rose. "You deliberately leaked my client's situation to the media, even after realizing he was innocent. I'm going to bring this up with my contact in the mayor's office. In my opinion, this calls for disciplinary action."

"You do that." Martinez walked over, his Oxfords toe to toe with Benoit. "But your boy just admitted he uses both women and heroin on a regular basis. If I were you, I'd get my client out of here before we decide to charge him with being an asshole."

Benoit's face reddened, but then he turned his back to Martinez and sat down with his client.

Spense and Martinez hurried to the captain's office, where they found him perched on the end of his desk, the remote to his flatscreen television in hand, the picture paused on a Viagra commercial. The door closed behind them, and Jeffers hit the PLAY button without preparing them for what they were about to see. Then Kourtney Kennedy, SLY news reporter, appeared on the screen.

Chapter Seventeen

Wednesday, October 9
10:00 A.M.
Los Angeles, California

CAITLIN SWUNG HER legs around the side of her hospital bed at Cedars Sinai and leaned forward, listening to the breaking news report. Her mild embarrassment at having to receive the NCAVC liaison, Jake Felton and the special agent accompanying him, one Dutch Langhorne, in a hospital gown was instantly forgotten as Kourtney Kennedy relayed her story.

According to the broadcast, a young woman, calling herself Gina Lola, had narrowly escaped an attack at Waxed. And this just one day prior to Brenda Reggero's murder. Though Kennedy was careful to note the story could not be confirmed by outside sources, Caitlin instantly realized it must be true.

Then the news switched to a minor celebrity encounter at a

local restaurant. Caitlin hit the mute button and turned to Felton. Acting as go-between for local law enforcement and the BAU profilers, Felton had provided introductions for them to Captain Jeffers. But neither she nor Spense had had reason to talk with him since, until today.

After retrieving Dutch Langhorne from LAX, Felton had stopped in to check on her condition, as well as get a report on the incident at Griffith Park. The BAU was keeping close tabs on her, as a consultant, and the SAC had asked Felton for a full accounting of her injuries. Langhorne, she'd learned, had flown in from Dallas to lead a seminar on hostage negotiation. Everything about both men screamed FBI—their tall, muscular builds, close-cropped hair, and especially their habit of scanning a room when they entered, as if looking for an imminent threat.

Now Langhorne turned probing blue eyes on her, making her aware she'd been slumping. It was hard to maintain good posture while sitting on a bed, but she did her best to straighten up. Something about the way Dutch Langhorne looked at her made her self-conscious. He seemed to be sizing her up with interest, though she couldn't imagine why. After all, he was merely tagging along with Felton and had no real business with her. Perhaps the Fallen Angel case had caught his attention in the media, and that accounted for his intensity. Or maybe he was just like that naturally.

"That's quite a wrinkle . . . if it's true," Felton said, referring to Kennedy's report.

"Oh, it's true all right," she responded without hesitation.

"What makes you say that?" Dutch arched a curious eyebrow.

Again, she didn't know what his interest in the case was. But he was FBI, so there was no reason not to speak freely in front of him. "Three things Kennedy mentioned haven't been made public, so the only way she could've known about them would be if her near victim is telling the truth."

"And those three things would be?" Felton asked.

"First, she mentioned she knocked over a statue while trying to escape her attacker. We know from the manager at Waxed that someone broke in the night *before* Reggero was killed and that a statue of Richard Gere was damaged. Second, this Gina claims she lost a lucky charm. After Spense suggested a second sweep of a back stairwell, a brass four-leaf clover turned up." She paused.

Dutch was eyeing her too closely again. There was something strangely familiar about him, but she was certain they'd never met. She'd remember a man like him. So handsome, with his piercing blue eyes, and that shock of red hair—he was anything but forgettable.

"And third?" Dutch leaned in, pinning her with his stare.

"Third—Gina said her attacker was wearing a Charlie Chaplin mask." Her heart started to trip in her chest. "The man who tried to run us off a cliff last night was wearing one, too."

"Are you certain?"

"Ninety percent. It was dark, but I thought it was Charlie Chaplin at the time. I said so to Spense."

Her phone rang, and she about jumped out of her skin.

"Sorry." She shrugged to her company, then looked at her caller ID. "I better take this one," she added on a sigh, as the men rose to their feet. "It's my mother."

Chapter Eighteen

Wednesday, October 9

11:00 A.M.

Hollywood, California

SLY HEADQUARTERS LOOKED exactly as it appeared on the air. Giant flat-screen televisions lined virtually every wall, metal trash cans sitting on the concrete floor overflowed with paper and candy wrappers, and in every red-and-black cubicle, reporters dressed in jeans, T- shirts, and backward baseball caps could be seen high-fiving each other and laughing. Spense's stomach growled. He hadn't had yet eaten, and the room smelled like cinnamon donuts and coffee.

With the exception of Kourtney Kennedy, SLY's showcase anchor, the reporters were college-age kids chosen for their youth appeal and charisma rather than their journalistic skills. Roland Pritchard, the genius behind this campy blend of gossip rag, tour company, and television show greeted Spense and Martinez, each in turn, with a firm handshake. Pritchard, a slight man of around five-foot-three, looked to be about forty years old. But Spense deduced he was much older since his perm and tie-dye T-shirt had gone out of style in the seventies.

"You must be the fuzz," Pritchard announced in a loud voice, confirming Spense's assumption. The man was around sixty. Throwing his arm out in an expansive gesture, he added, "Welcome to my humble pad. I've been expecting you." Then he whirled around. "But . . . where's that lovely headshrinker? I've been hoping to meet both Spenser and Cassidy ever since Kourtney first reported they were on the case."

"Dr. Cassidy couldn't make it. Where's Kennedy?" Martinez was in no mood, apparently, and, frankly, neither was Spense.

He believed in freedom of the press as much as anybody. In fact, it was his sworn duty to uphold the laws, including the First Amendment. But what Kennedy had done, meeting with a witness in a major crime investigation, all alone, and without informing the police, was both reckless and unethical. And if it turned out she'd withheld physical evidence in a criminal case, it was also illegal.

Pritchard beamed like a proud papa at the mention of her name. "Kourtney's in my office. If you'll follow me." He led them on a circuitous path through the cubicles. "I assure you, we want to cooperate fully with your investigation."

"Then perhaps you should've given us a heads-up prior to your broadcast," Martinez ground out.

"I called your commander, Captain Jeffers, prior to the show."

"Five minutes prior to airtime doesn't really constitute a heads-up. I shouldn't have to remind you this is an open murder investigation, and any information reported to the public may impact our ability to capture and prosecute the perpetrator. Not to mention, your broadcast might impact the killer's behavior in ways you're not qualified to predict. If there's another victim, you can consider the blood to be at least splattered on your hands."

"Oh, please. Get off your high horse, Lieutenant. We're within our First Amendment rights, and you know it." He hesitated, then pulled up short. "Naturally, we don't want to interfere with your ability to catch a serial killer. But I thought Tom La Grande, your prime suspect, was in custody. I spent two days consulting with my attorneys and investors before making the decision to allow Kourtney to run with this, and the pending charges against La Grande were a major factor in our decision to green-light the project." He arched an eyebrow. "La Grande's no longer in custody?"

"All charges against Mr. La Grande have been dropped." Martinez shrugged. "You can read about it in the *Times*. I believe I saw some of their reporters, and a few fellows from the *Herald* as I was leaving the station." He clapped Spense on the back. "Isn't that right, Agent Spenser?"

"Yep."

Pritchard's gloating expression evaporated once he realized SLY had just been scooped. Through a glass window, Spense spied Kourtney Kennedy's long legs as she crossed and uncrossed them, kicking a red stiletto on and off her heel while she waited. *This must be the place.* Pritchard held the door while they filed into his office. Then he hit a button, causing a privacy screen to scroll across the window.

"Please, don't get up." Martinez put out his hand to Kourtney, but didn't soften his demeanor. From her spot on the couch, she shook the lieutenant's hand.

Spense nodded a greeting, keeping his hands in his pockets. No matter how pretty the lady, he didn't cotton to her interference with the investigation. Pritchard relaxed against the wall, and Spense and Martinez pulled up chairs facing the reporter. With her looks, she could've been in pictures, as the saying went. Spense had to admit he'd watched her show more than once. Her reporting on the Fallen Angel case had been surprisingly on point and intelligent, though of course she'd milked the story for every sensational detail.

"Lieutenant Martinez, Agent Spenser; I'm honored to meet you." Kourtney spoke in a professional voice—one that provided a stark contrast to her miniskirt, red stilettos, and dramatized cleavage. "I want you to know I'll cooperate in every way I can. Something like this doesn't fall in the lap of a girl like me every day. You may think I'm all fluff and lipstick, but I promise you, I'm doing my best to treat this story with the seriousness it deserves."

Spense leaned forward, compelling her to meet his eyes. He couldn't say when or where he'd learned this trick, or even the mechanics of the move, but it never failed to force his target to look up at him. "This isn't a *story*, Ms. Kennedy. This is a murder investigation."

A quick breath whooshed out of her, and she blinked rapidly, as if wanting to drop her gaze.

"Don't look away, Kourtney."

"I-I'm not."

"Someone is out there, taking the lives of beautiful young women—like yourself. What that means is *you* don't get to decide what is or is not important. You don't get to decide what you will or won't reveal to the authorities."

"Or to the public," Martinez threw in, though Spense knew that was a bluff. "Who's your confidential informant?"

"I guess you never heard of the First Amendment, Lieutenant. The public has a right to know, and I have a right to report. The police don't get to censor the press. Not in the good ole US of A." Kourtney's gaze swept scornfully over Martinez. "And my *source* isn't an informant—she's a witness. A *victim*."

The lady had a pair. Spense gave her props for that, but he forced a disapproving scowl anyway. "Ms. Kennedy, I thought you said you were going to cooperate."

She threw up her hands. "Cooperate, yes. Kiss the LAPD's ass—no fucking way."

Spense choked back a laugh. *Good for her.* Spense wasn't kissing any LAPD ass either.

"Then we're all on the same page. Now then, we're going to need a full account of everything you know about this witness: her appearance, the name she gave you, how she contacted you, etc."

From beneath her pert bottom, Kourtney whisked out a set of bound papers. "I'm way ahead of you, Agent Spenser." She handed him the bundle, which still carried the heat of her seat. "The witness's name, or so she claims, is Gina Lola, and she works for one Madam Lucille, though she was very tight-lipped about the madam. Gina contacted me through our tip line. Everything I thought was important, you've already seen and heard in my broadcast. Everything else is here, in the report I made just for you. I knew you'd come knocking." Her gaze ping-ponged between him and Martinez. "Apparently, you gentlemen have me mixed up with some bonehead reporter you've seen in the movies. You know, the kind who goes to jail rather than reveal her source."

She kicked her shoe on and off one heel. "Well, I'm not that kind of reporter. I'm the kind who gets her story."

Spense believed the last part. Kourtney Kennedy was just exactly the kind of reporter who got her story—at any cost. But at the moment, he had no choice except to take her word that she'd disclosed everything. "Do you have another meeting set up with Gina?"

"No. I begged her to give me a contact number, but she refused." Kourtney batted her eyelashes. "However, if she reaches out to me again, you'll be the first to know."

Martinez squeezed one eye shut and looked at her dubiously with the other. "Aren't you going to demand we offer you some kind of exclusive access in exchange for your cooperation?"

"Not at all, Lieutenant," she purred. "You see, I already have exclusive access to the only living witness. That's why you're coming to me."

Chapter Nineteen

Wednesday, October 9
1:00 P.M.
Brentwood, California

SOGNI D'ORO, THE name of Susan's motel, meant *sweet dreams* in Italian. She'd hoped the name would portend a good night's sleep, but unfortunately she'd hardly gotten more than a couple of hours' shut-eye in one stretch since she'd arrived on Saturday. Pressing her nose against the door to her room, she peered out into the hallway through the peephole. After confirming that the woman knocking on the door claiming to be Kourtney Kennedy was one and the same, she undid the bolt, ushered the reporter inside, and slammed the door shut again, bolting it once more for good measure—even though it was two o'clock in the afternoon.

"You look like shit, sweetie," Kourtney said.

"Can't sleep." Susan threw her arms around her new friend,

hugging her longer than was socially acceptable. She hadn't seen a living soul in days.

"I've got some Valium in my purse. I should've left you some on Sunday." Kourtney filled a water glass and handed her the pill. "Go ahead. It's not like you've got someplace to be, and you look like you could really use a nap."

Susan swallowed the pill, grateful for even the hope of a peaceful sleep. She didn't feel safe at all. She'd read that the police had Tom La Grande in custody, but somehow, she couldn't believe they'd caught the right man. Yes, he was the same height, more or less, as the man in the Charlie Chaplin mask, but her gut told her it wasn't him. At least in the movies, La Grande had an exaggerated confidence in the way he carried himself, a certain swagger that she hadn't noted in her john.

"I brought you some things." Kourtney grinned, slipping a canvas bag from her shoulder. Then she kicked off her shoes and bounced onto one of the double beds. "This place is a wreck."

Susan frowned. She'd resolved not to set foot out the door of her hotel room until she knew she'd be safe. Thus far, she'd kept to her resolution, declining maid service and insisting room service leave her tray outside the door. She hadn't made her bed, but otherwise she'd picked up, and it was hard making due with the same towels and linens for days. She didn't want to waste a clean washrag just to dust. "Sorry."

"Don't worry. I get it. I shouldn't have even mentioned it, but hey look what I've got." She removed several packages of coffee, a large bottle of shampoo, and a tube of toothpaste from her bag. The shampoo was even the kind combined with a conditioner in the same bottle. Kourtney was the best friend a girl could ask for.

"Wow, I totally needed this."

"I figured you'd be shy about maid service. So just in case, I brought you the essentials. And I've got one more thing—" She pulled out a bottle of vodka. "I could use a drink. Let's toast to your celebrity."

"Go ahead. I don't feel like it." She wanted to keep her wits about her. She already regretted taking the Valium—it was a violation of one of her cardinal rules. But Kourtney hadn't given her much time to reflect on the matter.

"Don't mind if I do." Kourtney slugged back a shot, then poured herself another. "What a day I've had. I had a visit from the cops this morning. Seems they let La Grande go."

She paused, as if waiting for Susan's reaction.

Susan couldn't work up the energy to feign surprise. "I knew it wasn't him. Did the police have questions for me?" After all, that's why she was hanging around the Sogni D'Oro Motel in Brentwood. She wanted to get the hell out of town, but she needed to be available for the police. Thank goodness she had Kourtney as a go-between. She didn't trust the cops one bit.

"For one thing, they wanted me to tell them where you were. But don't worry. I told them I didn't know how to reach you. I promised to let them know as soon as you got in touch again."

Susan let out a relieved breath. "Thank you. I knew I could count on you."

"Of course you can. Reporter's code of honor and all." Kourtney tipped the bottle, then seemed to think better of it. "I'll leave the rest for you. Anyway, as I was saying, the coppers seemed particularly interested in Madam Lucy. Did you know those other escorts personally?"

Trust or no trust, she was glad she hadn't given Kourtney Lucy's last name or her address. "I didn't know the others. Lucy is such a stickler for protecting everyone's privacy. That's why she's able to get such high-class johns."

"Sounds like you think a lot of Lucy."

"She's my friend—at least she used to be."

"Even though she set you up with a killer? Your loyalty is admirable, but I think it's time you realize she wasn't looking out for you at all. On the other hand, I am. Just tell me her name, sweetie . . . It's for the police."

She shook her head.

"They just want to talk to Lucy about her clientele. One of her johns is probably the killer, so they're going to need to find her."

"I've given them a lot to go on already. They're detectives. Some of them are FBI. They should be able to track her down on their own."

"Okay. I won't press, but let me ask you this. If the person you met at Waxed was wearing a wig and a mask, how can you be sure of the gender? Could Charlie Chaplin have been a woman? I mean look at me, I'm five-foot-nine and a half. Could the man in the mask have been me?"

"I-I . . ." Her throat went dry, and she was having a hard time speaking, or not speaking so much as formulating an answer, because the truth of the matter was she really didn't know.

Could it have been a woman?

Could it have been *Kourtney*?

Her head pounded, and she became hyperaware of her surroundings. The realization hit her hard that if Kourtney Kennedy wanted her dead, all she would need to do was poison her . . . She noticed her throat burning. Was she imagining the bitter taste on her tongue?

All Kourtney would have to do was poison her . . . and then

stuff her in a suitcase and cart her directly out her sliding-glass doors into the parking lot. Susan went to the window, pulling back a corner of the curtains with trembling hands. Sure enough there was a red Beemer parked right in front of her room. Probably Kourtney's, just waiting for the reporter to make her getaway.

Take it easy. That Beemer's barely big enough for a suitcase.

Slowly, she turned. *Please, please don't let it be Kourtney. Not the only friend I have left in the world.* She forced herself to speak in a calm, steady voice. "I didn't think so at the time, but now that you mention it, Charlie Chaplin *might* have been a woman. No words were ever spoken between us. So you see, I really can't be certain one way or the other. Please tell that to the police for me. I think it might be important."

"That's why I'm here. As their emissary."

Kourtney bent down and slipped her shoes back on. Would she plan to commit a murder in stilettos and a designer suit? Susan looked at the bags of coffee, the shampoo, the toothpaste. If Kourtney were planning to kill her, she wouldn't have gone to the bother of bringing toiletries. A wave of relief swept over her, but it was immediately followed by a fresh wave of doubt. She simply couldn't trust her instincts anymore. She'd been certain her would-be assailant had been a man, but now, she realized anything was possible. Charlie Chaplin could've been *anyone*. Even Lucy!

She walked Kourtney to the door, then reached out, clutching her hand. "Lucy's last name is Lancaster, but that may not be her real name." She closed her eyes, unable to believe she was betraying her friend. "She lives on Silver Hollow Road in Brentwood, not far from here. I forget the address, but it's at the end of a cul-de-sac. A white, Spanish-style with a red clay roof. She usually parks her black Land Rover in the driveway. That ought to be enough for the police to find her."

"Thanks, hon. You're doing the right thing. Meanwhile, hang tight, and do *not* open this door for anyone."

As soon as Kourtney left, Susan slumped against the door, then felt it thumping against her back. She opened it, and Kourtney shook her finger at her. "I *told* you not to open this door."

Then they laughed. "Okay, okay, I promise."

As she closed the door yet again, her heartbeat slowed, and her muscles relaxed. Maybe it was the Valium kicking in, but she felt in her bones that everything was going to turn out just as it should. Then came that thumping again. She knew Kourtney was testing her, but she swung the door open anyway, just to tell her to chill. It was all going to be all right.

No one was there. She edged out the door, only a step or two, just enough, to see the elevator doors closing. But when she turned to go back inside, the hairs on the back of her neck raised a warning. Someone was behind her. Before she could scream, a hand clapped a rag over her mouth. Her nostrils stung as she gagged on a sickly-sweet smell. She tried to yell, but it was no use. Her lips refused to move. First her world went first fuzzy, then altogether black.

Help me.

Chapter Twenty.

Wednesday, October 9
4:00 P.M.
Brentwood, California

A COUPLE OF hours after Spense and Martinez had wrapped things up at SLY, the Hollywood division detectives located the *Madam to the Stars* via the cell-phone number La Grande had provided. Lucille Lancaster resided on Silver Hollow Road in Brentwood, and Spense, along with his new sidekick Martinez, headed out with a warrant to search the premises tucked into the lieutenant's breast pocket. Although Spense was hoping Lucy would cooperate, and things would go down easy, he expected, and had come prepared for, the worst. If she provided any resistance, they intended to haul her ass down to the station on a pandering charge—they had enough for that from La Grande's statements alone.

Martinez's city car crawled up the tight Brentwood streets,

which resembled back alleys more than roads. In this exclusive Southern California suburb, the lots came at a premium, and the multimillion-dollar homes were jammed together like cousins at a Thanksgiving table. Areca palms, bougainvillea, and a variety of deciduous greenery covered high privacy walls, obscuring all views of the homes from the roadway. They arrived at the gated entrance to Ms. Lucy Lancaster's place, and Martinez steered his car to one side of the street, then killed the engine.

Shaking his head, Spense stepped carefully out of the car. "Hell of a parking job," he said. Martinez had angled the vehicle halfway onto the sidewalk in order to leave room for other cars to pass on the narrow street.

Once they opened the gate, the madam's home came into full view.

A red clay-tile roof, casement windows, and period wood door lent an old-world charm to her elegantly simple hacienda-style home. The terra-cotta brick pathway winding through prolific gardens made Spense wish Caity were here. She would've loved the bright blooms of purples, reds, and blues, swaying in the yard. Spense knew some of the flowers by name since Caity had a habit of shouting them out excitedly whenever they passed a particularly fine display of California poppies, lupine, and his favorite of all: blue dicks. Lucy's house had less square footage than his mother's modest home in Phoenix, but Spense knew this little hacienda had not come cheap. Business must be booming for the madam.

After a quick hike up the path, they climbed the porch steps, then Martinez used the clapper to knock. With no answer after a full minute, he mashed the doorbell until it chimed. A few beats later, Spense heard footsteps passing near the door, inside the house, and a bright blue eye appeared in the peeper.

"Who is it?" a feminine voice inquired.

"I'm Lieutenant Martinez, LAPD, and I've got Agent Spenser, FBI with me. We'd like to ask you a few questions if you don't mind."

"Sorry, but I don't have time today. Come back tomorrow, please."

"We need to speak with you, Ms. Lancaster. Open the door." Martinez gave Spense a look that communicated *we're in for it with this one.*

"I'm not dressed."

Yep. This was not going to go down easy.

Martinez pulled an envelope from his breast pocket and waved it in front of the peeper. "We have a warrant to search the premises. Open the door, ma'am. That's an order, not a request."

"A warrant? Well, you should've just said so in the first place. Hang on. I'm not decent. I need to throw on some clothes."

It was four o'clock in the afternoon. She wasn't dressed? Since she was a madam, maybe that was plausible, though.

Footsteps scampered away, and he and Martinez exchanged a glance. Spense checked his watch, and let the minute hand run three cycles before asking, "You think she'd be stupid enough to try to make a run for it?"

"She'd be crazy to try it."

A black Land Rover was parked in the drive, so if she was going to flee, it would more than likely have to be on foot. No way could she outrun them, Spense thought, unless she were an Olympic-caliber athlete. But as unreasonable as it seemed for her to run, the back of his neck had begun to itch. Madam Lucy was a person of interest in a string of murders. Her *House and Garden* spread, and her cloying voice aside, she was potentially capable of mayhem.

Slipping his Glock from his holster, he nodded toward the side of the house. "I'm going to check around back."

Martinez smirked. "If we do have a rabbit, she won't get far."

Ten paces later, Spense rounded the corner of the house, just in time to see a leggy blond woman chesting an overnight bag, slip out the patio door. Unbelievable. She was making a run for it with *luggage*. He stepped away from the brick wall he'd been hugging and out into the open. "Hold it right there, ma'am."

She shot a look over her shoulder, dropped the suitcase, and blasted up the lawn.

In heels.

Spense loped after her, anticipating the path she'd take and hurdling a small hedge. His eyes searched her body, looking for a weapon, and sure enough, in her right hand, she gripped what looked to be a gun.

Not going down easy.

"Stop! Police!" he shouted a clear warning.

Lucy widened the gap between them. She reached her back gate and barreled through it a few yards ahead of him. Now he was chasing her down the alley between homes. With the crowded conditions, the last thing he wanted was to have to discharge his weapon. You never knew when a neighbor kid might dart out from a yard ,, or a pet. He didn't want to chance firing a warning shot in the air, since it could land in someone's yard, and he sure as shit didn't want to take aim at a woman on foot whose only certain crime was pandering.

To his right, he heard a barking dog. Knowing the dog might well be as dangerous as his fugitive, he took his eyes off the path to check over his shoulder. But no dog gave chase. The barking must've come from behind a fence. He looked ahead, and suddenly, the buttressed root of a fat tree appeared in front of him. His toe caught on the root, dumping him facedown in the dirt. He bolted to his feet, then rounded a curve in the road full tilt as Madam Lucy ducked behind a group of large shrubs.

"I can see you, Lucy. Drop your gun. Come out with your hands up," Spense panted, halting, and wondering if Martinez was still out front holding his dick, or if he'd be backing him up anytime this century.

"*You* drop it," she panted back.

For fuck's sake. "You do not want to do this, Lucy. I'm a federal agent. There is no way you can win a gun battle with me. Drop your weapon and come out with your hands in the air."

"Oh, I'm not planning to outshoot you. But I'm not dropping my gun. I've got more than one kind of weapon on me."

"D-don't shoot. P-please, just do what she says." Another saccharine feminine voice, this one all too familiar, floated out from the bushes.

Dammit to hell. "Kourtney, is that you?"

"Yes, Agent Spenser. It's me, and this maniac has a gun to my head."

"Okay, Kourtney, you're going to be fine. Just don't do anything stupid. I got this, okay?"

He heard whimpering. A *lot* of whimpering.

"Listen up, Lucy," he said in a grave tone, "I don't know what you have in mind, but I'm not going to drop my pistol. If I do, I got no leverage. You, on the other hand have got all the leverage you need. Like you just pointed out, you've got *two* weapons. Advantage—you." He waited for someone to object from behind the shrubs, but no one did. "Here's the plan. Either give me your gun or give me your hostage. You choose which one to keep."

More whimpering.

"Or, you could save us time and give up both of them right now. While you're considering your options, please bear in mind that as long as you hold a gun, I'm fully justified in the use of lethal force. You know what the word *lethal* means? It means I can shoot you dead and get a commendation for it. "

"You won't shoot a woman." Lucy's voice trembled just enough for him to know he had her.

"Not an unarmed one. Drop your weapon and kick it toward me. Then step out with your hands up. Send Kourtney out first if you want, but that's up to you. She's got no business lurking in the bushes to begin with."

"Why should I surrender when I've got a hostage?"

"Like I said, Kourtney got her own self into this mess, so if something happens, it's on her. Now, I can't be sure, but that looked a lot like a compact revolver I saw in your hand. Let me see if I can explain it better this time, Lucy. I'm a federal agent. A crack shot. I've got sixteen bullets in my *semiautomatic pistol*, and as long as you're armed, I'm authorized to use *deadly* force."

The gun thudded to the ground, then came spinning out from beneath the bush. Next, he heard a screech and a scream, then a loud crunch that sounded like a fist making contact with bone. A pretty blond charged out of the bushes, blood dripping from her nose.

Madam Lucy, he presumed.

Followed by Kourtney Kennedy. Kourtney shoved Lucy to the ground, jumped on top of her, and began pummeling her with her fists. Lucy kicked her feet and yanked Kourtney's long blond hair. Kourtney was definitely winning. Spense waited for Kourtney to get in a few good blows, then dragged her off the terrified madam.

Martinez ambled around the corner, a pair of cuffs dangling from his hand. He jerked Lucy to her feet, then turned to Spense. "Aw hell. Looks like I missed the fun."

Wednesday, October 9
6:00 P.M.
Los Angeles, California

CAITLIN HAD BEEN waiting all day for her doctor to give the final okay for to her to leave the hospital, and she didn't want to get caught in her gown by any more unexpected visitors. So when Spense entered her hospital room, she sprang out from under the covers fully dressed. He picked up the blanket she'd kicked off in the process and headed toward her with one of his usual bossy looks on his face. She sent him her most reassuring smile. Despite the goose egg on her forehead and the tiny row of stitches over her right eyebrow, she felt perfectly fine. She wasn't nauseous. She didn't have a headache, and she wasn't disoriented.

The doctor's concussion diagnosis had been an overly cautious *soft call.* "I'm not getting back in that bed, so you can just throw that blanket around your own shoulders." She pointed to the red goo on her tray table. "And you can eat this stupid cherry crap yourself while you're at it."

"If you insist." Spense swiped the cup off the table then, spooned the disgusting goo into his mouth, making appreciative noises all the while. He finished scarfing the snack, and said, "I'm not here to tuck you in anyway. I'm your ride."

Awesome. She was finally being released. She'd grown so impatient earlier that she'd been on the verge of signing herself out against medical advice. But after her meeting with Felton, she'd been more conscious than ever of how that might come across to the Bureau, and she didn't want them to think she wasn't exercising good judgment where her health . . . or anything else . . . was concerned. As it turned out, she loved profiling almost as much as she loved being teamed with Spense. So she'd kept herself in check, waiting patiently for Dr. Nguyen to declare that he'd cleared her CT scan, and her bump on the head didn't warrant keeping her another night, just like he'd promised to do hours ago.

"You bring the Prius?"

Spense gave her his worried look.

Ah. He must think her mind was mush. The rental had to be in the shop, and she should've realized that. The memory of last night, it seemed, had thrown her more off-balance than her supposed concussion. When she thought about that molten kiss they'd shared, she couldn't help but get light-headed.

"The Prius is out of commission. I rented a Hummer."

Her adoration of all things Spense took a temporary nosedive. "Why would you rent a monster like that when you could have your choice of vehicles?"

"You try PITing an F-450 with a Prius, then you can complain to me. If we'd been in a Hummer last night, we'd have had the upper hand. If we'd been in a Hummer, you might not have spent the day eating tapioca."

"It was Jell-O. You're the one who ate it, and if everyone would just drive a hybrid instead of a gas guzzler, our children might still have a planet when they grow up."

Our children? Maybe she really did have a concussion.

"I'm telling you, it's necessary."

She shook her head and noticed the tiniest twinge of an ache.

They did not need to drive around in a tank, even if a heftier vehicle might be in order while they were on a case. Last night, he'd had a different attitude. Had he only been pretending for her benefit?

He picked up her hand and brought it to his lips.

Her entire being softened in response. She didn't want to argue with Spense. Not today. She stepped closer and laid her head on his chest. "How was your day?"

He kissed the top of her hair, then proceeded to tell her one hell of a story about his trip to Brentwood and his encounter with a Madam Lucille. Caitlin found the part about Kourtney Kennedy particularly interesting. "So what explanation did the reporter give, after telling you earlier that she didn't know anything about how to reach Lucy?"

"She still claims that's the case. According to Kourtney, she was staking Martinez and me out, for the sake of the story. Supposedly, she followed us up to Lucy's place in Brentwood and hid in the bushes in the alley, waiting for a chance to sneak up to the house."

The story wasn't impossible. But . . . "I have a hard time believing that reporter has the surveillance skills necessary to follow two experienced law-enforcement officers without being spotted."

He nodded his agreement. "I suspect she knew how to find Lucy all along. I think she went up there on her own, chasing the story. Then, when she saw Martinez and me pull up, she hid in the bushes." He turned his palms up. "But I can't prove that. And at this point, I don't really care about Kourtney Kennedy. What I do care about is getting you out of this joint."

She was already at the door when his cell buzzed.

He raised one finger in the air. "I'm with Caity, and you're on speaker, Martinez."

"Did she get my roses?"

Spense grimaced.

"I did." Caity leaned toward the phone, but Spense took a step back, and she wasn't sure Martinez had heard even heard her thank-you.

"What do you need?" Spense asked tersely.

"We got DNA and more forensics back. Turns out the skin under Selena Turner's fingernails came from a *woman*. Captain wants all hands on deck at the station in the morning—0800 sharp."

"We'll be there." Spense hung up without a formal good-bye, and Caitlin got the uncomfortable feeling he was more than a little annoyed with Martinez. The two men had just been out in the field together, and they needed to have each other's backs. Their lives might depend on it.

"That seemed a little rude," she said, honestly.

"I told him not to send flowers."

She stepped away from Spense, more confused than angry. She didn't have to ask why he'd done such a thing. It was obvious he was jealous. Then another thought occurred to her, and she stuck her chin up. "My mother called a while ago. By any chance was it you who told her I was in the hospital?"

Chapter Twenty-One

A RAY OF sunlight warmed the backs of Susan's eyelids and seeped under her lashes. She tried to open her eyes, but her lids felt heavy, and she was too weak to make it happen. And too groggy to remember why her shoulder throbbed, or why her back ached. Curling into a tighter ball, she shivered against the hard, cold floor beneath her. Eyes still closed, she rubbed her hands over her arms and chest, only to encounter her naked breasts. The shock was enough to make her jolt into a sitting position. Her eyes flew open, and she squinted against the reed of sunlight straining through the bars of a steel cage.

Oh God.

This was not good. Not good at all. She'd forced her eyes open. Why couldn't she force her memory to return?

What the fuck happened to her?

She touched the top of her head and winced. A burning sensation covered her scalp like an electric shower cap. Her stomach hadn't been this sour since she'd drunk half a bottle of tequila and swallowed the worm her freshman year in college.

Once her eyes stopped stinging, she screwed up the courage

to let her gaze travel down her body. Her shorts were still on, but someone had stripped off the tank top and bra she'd been wearing earlier this morning. Or was that a different morning?

Think, Susan.

A long red scratch traveled down her right arm, and her side showed the faint beginnings of a fist-sized bruise.

Who did this to her?

She couldn't remember fast enough to quell the panic that was rising in her throat.

"Help me," she screamed, but her voice came out scratchy and soft. No one would hear a pitiful cry like that.

"Help me!" Better, but still not loud enough. She'd rest her voice a few minutes, then try again.

Meanwhile, keep thinking.

Her head was throbbing, but at last, she remembered something—the Sogni D'Oro Motel . . . and vodka. Kourtney had brought her vodka.

Kourtney Kennedy.

Then . . . In the hallway, someone grabbed her and covered her mouth with a bitter-smelling rag. She gazed furtively around and folded her arms to cover her breasts. That was all she could remember before waking up half-naked, locked in this cage.

Surely Kourtney hadn't done this.

The Fallen Angel Killer.

Of course, that had to be who'd grabbed her. All the victims had been found naked from the waist up. She crouched on her hands and knees and crawled to the door of the cage, her skin tender from the cold floor scraping against her knees. She grabbed the bars of the cage. Tried to shake them, but they didn't budge. Not even a rattle.

What had Kourtney asked her?

Could it have been a woman? Could it have been me?

A wave of sheer terror made her gut contract, and she hurled yellow bile onto the cage floor. Recoiling from her own vomit, she clambered to her feet, or tried to. Her head banged against the top of her cage. The roof wasn't high enough to allow her to stand erect.

The steel chute, which was longer than it was wide, seemed only about four feet tall. She stretched out her arms. The cage was wider than her arm span. Suddenly, she became obsessed with the dimensions of her new home. If she couldn't remember how she'd gotten here, at least she could walk the floor and count her steps. That was something, anyway. It gave her a sense of control.

One. Two. Three. Four.

Her cage was four feet wide. She did her hunched over walk lengthwise.

Six feet long.

What was four feet high and wide by six feet deep?

She had a feeling she'd seen something like this before. Yes . . . in Las Vegas . . . at a Siegfried and Roy show.

Dropping to the floor, she buried her face in her hands.

This was the type of cage used to hold exotic animals. She was in a freaking lion's cage. The sides appeared to be made of solid steel, and only the front was barred. She couldn't see around or behind her at all, only directly in front of her. She flopped onto her belly. Her cage was shiny and clean—at least it had been before she threw up.

A brand-new cage.

Didn't serial killers keep their prey in dirty cells in dungeons or warehouses? Weren't there always other cells, also filled with desperate hostages? That's how the movies portrayed these sickos. Maybe there was another cage in the room.

"Hello?" Her voice came out in a hoarse croak. "Is anybody there?"

Silence.

It was eerily quiet. Not only did she not hear other hostages, she didn't hear outside sounds like wind or traffic. She might be in a dungeon after all, or . . . a basement. She must be underground.

Resting her chin on her hand, she tried to come up with some sort of plan. She should be scared witless. She was a killer's captive now. That much was clear. Her hands did shake, and her heart did pound, but a little voice inside her head kept whispering:

Don't give up.

Somewhere deep, deep down inside, she believed that she could survive. And if she survived, then she could get away. Maybe not right this minute, maybe not even this week, but *someday*. After all, her captor, whoever he or she was, would have to come back eventually to check on his prisoner. Otherwise, why bother holding her at all? If he hadn't killed her yet, he was planning to return. And when he did, she'd watch him, study him, until finally she'd figure out her plan. It would come to her. It *had* to. But right now, every muscle in her body cried out for rest. Thinking and crawling around in the cage had used up all her energy.

She'd just decided to lie down for a nap when something in the darkest corner of the cage caught her eye. Blankets! Heaped in a pile. How had she missed that before? She crawled over and grabbed one of the thick wool blankets. Then she sucked in her breath. Beneath the blankets was an animal water feeder—the kind that allows you to leave your pet for days on end.

Days on end.

Chapter Twenty-Two

Thursday, October 10
8:00 A.M.
Hollywood, California

SPENSE HAD GRUMBLED during the short ride from the Sky Walk Hotel to Hollywood station about her needing to take it easy, but Caitlin was thrilled to be out of that damn hospital. And however confused she might be about her feelings for Spense, she simply couldn't think about such things right now. She was delighted that Martinez and the captain had specified they wanted her input, and it was imperative to keep her focus on the case. This was her job, and she wasn't phoning in sick over a soft-call concussion. Her brain worked perfectly well, and the last place she wanted to be was stuck in a hotel room, "resting," while this case broke wide open.

When they swung open the door to the station, she immediately detected a certain energy that had been absent before.

The place buzzed with the excitement of real police work being done. Solving a major crime wasn't an everyday event. She knew the duties of the officers more commonly involved meeting with community leaders and mediating neighbor disputes, or handling petty offenses. Even the homicide cases often involved a known perpetrator. Like medicine, police work seemed to be mostly by the numbers . . . until it wasn't. Days of pure boredom would suddenly be punctuated by a life-and-death dilemma, and it was those high-drama moments that provided the adrenaline junkies in both professions with a much-needed fix. Now, officers walked with renewed purpose in their steps, and even the stink-eye desk sergeant acted pleased to see Spense and her, buzzing them straight in to Jeffers's office.

Martinez jumped to his feet as they entered and, offering her a wide smile, reached out his hand. "You fit for duty, Cassidy?" When she shook it, he held on a moment longer than she'd expected. She registered his concern, and while she found it endearing, she didn't need yet another overprotective cop on her case—even if this one did look like Enrique Iglesias and had excellent taste in florists.

"Thanks for the roses, and thanks for asking." She looked from Martinez to Jeffers. "Let's get this out of the way. I'm okay, so we don't need to dwell on the car crash except, of course, as it relates to the investigation. I hear we have DNA."

Martinez looked as though he was about to protest, but then the captain shot him a look. He nodded. "We got DNA and more. But we can start with that. It seems the skin under Miss Turner's fingernails came from a woman. But we ran it through CODIS, and it's not a match for anyone in the convicted offender and arrestee databases," Martinez said.

"But the sample hasn't been checked against Lucy Lancaster?" Caitlin asked.

"Not yet. We've obtained a warrant for her DNA, though, and we're hoping for expedited results within the week. In the meantime, some of us like her as the Fallen Angel Killer."

Caitlin's head was spinning, but not from her supposed concussion. This represented not only a huge break in the case but a dramatic shift in direction. Forensics trumped profiles, but if Lucy Lancaster really was the Fallen Angel Killer, then Caitlin and Spense had been far off the mark. So far off, it was a wonder Jeffers wanted any more input from them.

Catching Spense's gaze, she shrugged.

Martinez continued. "All three victims worked for Lucy Lancaster. She's five-foot-eight, and thanks to her workouts, she has just enough upper body strength to have carried out the murders. We have a witness, Gina Lola, who could potentially identify our killer, but we haven't yet been able to locate her. Also, as of now, we're assuming our UNSUB is the same individual who tried to run you off the road."

"Because of the Charlie Chaplin mask." The driver had worn what looked to be a Charlie Chaplin mask, like the one Gina Lola claimed her john wore, but neither she nor Spense could be absolutely certain. It had been so dark. "And you think the Fallen Angel Killer is . . . Lucy Lancaster?"

"*Maybe* Lancaster. She doesn't own a Ford Super Duty, but she could've borrowed or rented one. Hell, she could've even stolen the truck. According to the SLY broadcast, Gina Lola claims to have been lured to Waxed by someone wearing a Charlie Chaplin mask and a wig. But Gina knew Lancaster well, and she never indicated to Kennedy that she thought her madam might also have been her would-be attacker."

"Hard to recognize someone in disguise." The police couldn't definitively finger Lucy as the doer—her DNA wasn't back yet. Unnerved by the idea a young woman was out there on her own, unprotected, and obviously afraid to contact the police, probably because she was an "escort," Caitlin said, "That broadcast put a big fat target on Gina Lola's back. We need to find her ASAP—not just for her testimony but for her safety."

Martinez stretched out his long legs. "Kourtney Kennedy still maintains she doesn't know how to contact Gina Lola. But after finding Kennedy in the bushes outside Lancaster's place, I can't say that I believe her. We could put her under oath and depose her, but if she's been lying to us, she'll probably refuse to testify. No matter what she said the other day, I bet she'd love the attention she'd get from going to jail as a martyr for freedom of the press."

"Given the fact that Spense saved Kennedy's hide yesterday, maybe *he* can convince her to give us what we need to locate the witness. And if not, you could always put a tail on Kennedy," Caitlin said.

"But back to Lucy Lancaster." Martinez brought the conversation back on point. "She has motive, means, and opportunity for all three murders, and no alibi for any of them."

"Her *motive* being that all three women had betrayed her, or were about to do so, by cutting her out of her share of the money and going off with La Grande on their own," Spense supplied. "She had access to all the women, so motive and opportunity, yes, I do see that. But . . ."

He paused, and Caitlin picked up his train of thought. "Why

would she go after Gina? As far as we know, she wasn't planning on quitting. And other than her height and IQ, Lucy doesn't fit our profile. The Fallen Angel Killer poses the bodies in ways that prove he . . . or she . . . craves attention. Lucy, on the other hand, doesn't appear to seek out the limelight. She normally operates behind the scenes, running a big business with absolutely no hope of recognition." Past madams to the stars had tooted their own horns, and that's what had led to their eventual downfall, but Lucy had been successfully flying beneath the radar. "In a town where fame is the drug of choice, Lucy Lancaster doesn't seem to be hooked."

Spense pulled his cube out, unscrambled it, and stuck it back in his pocket. "Not only that, the motive we're assigning her is *personal gain*. If Lucy did kill these women, it wasn't in the service of some highly developed fantasy. It was because these women put her business model at risk—at least that's what we're speculating."

The room suddenly went quiet as the volley of theories ran out. Then, after a few beats, Martinez cleared his throat, "There is one other issue to consider. Remember, I said we had more than DNA back."

"We have a minor forensic inconsistency among the murders," Jeffers lifted a letter opener off his desktop, turned it in his hand, and pointed it at his lieutenant. "But I don't think the ME's findings make Lancaster a less viable suspect in any way."

"Minor inconsistency?" Caitlin had a feeling they were about to find out whether the murder weapon had been a corkscrew or an ice pick.

"As you suggested earlier, turns out Selena Turner was stabbed with a corkscrew. On closer examination, the ME found impression marks on her skin consistent with the spirals on a corkscrew.

And her room-service attendant has now confirmed that he delivered an unopened wine bottle to Turner and left a corkscrew for her later use," the captain said.

So that fit with their original theory. Selena's murder had been *unplanned*. In a fit of rage, her assailant had grabbed the only weapon that happened to be at hand . . . a corkscrew. "Okay, Selena's murder was impulsive, the other two were obviously planned out. Any other inconsistencies?" Caitlin wouldn't exactly call the lack of premeditation a *minor* issue. It seemed Jeffers was reluctant to admit its importance. But it was human nature to resist admitting a mistake. Nobody likes to acknowledge when they've been wrong, but since new evidence had come to light, it was critical to have an open mind.

"The ME determined that a *different* murder weapon, most likely an ice pick was used on Simpson and Reggero." Martinez arched an eyebrow.

Jeffers shrugged. "MOs change as killers evolve in their skills. So Lancaster used a corkscrew on Turner, and it proved hard to handle, very inconvenient for stabbing. After the satisfaction of getting her revenge on Turner, her inner beast was unleashed, and she decided to go after the other two women who'd betrayed her before they could contaminate the waters and influence any more of her escorts to leave. When planning her revenge on Simpson and Reggero, she chose to use a similar, yet more efficient, weapon. She took an ice pick with her because it would be easier to stab someone to death with it."

With the DNA under Selena's nails pointing to a woman, Lucy did indeed seem the most likely suspect but . . . "It just doesn't add up." Caitlin sighed.

Martinez had been scribbling notes. He stopped and stuck his pencil behind his ear. "I like Lucy for the Fallen Angel Killer, but I have to admit we still have a couple of unanswered questions."

"Just a couple?" Spense laughed. "I'd say we've got a bona fide mystery on our hands. Did the search of Lancaster's home turn up anything?"

Caitlin sank lower into the couch cushions. Spense had had to leave Lancaster's place early in order to pick her up at the hospital.

"Not at all. We were hoping to find an ice pick or a corkscrew or bloody clothing, but we got zip. If Lucy was ever in possession of the murder weapon, she must've dumped it somewhere along the line."

"What about her black book?" Caitlin asked.

"If you mean a ledger with the names of her johns, the answer is no, we didn't find one. Either she doesn't keep records, which she insists is the case, or she's stored the book somewhere else for safekeeping. We've been leaning on her hard to get a list of her johns, but so far she's not cooperating, which is foolish on her part, given the fact that the men in her book would be possible suspects, and that could take some of the focus off of her. And guess who sent his lawyer over to help Lucy out in her time of need."

"La Grande sent Sutton Benoit?" Spense guessed. "La Grande must want to make sure she keeps her mouth shut about his dealings with her."

"Bingo. And so far, his plan is working."

The intercom buzzed, and the adjuvant's voice came over the speaker, "Captain, are you expecting Kourtney Kennedy and Roland Pritchard?"

Obviously not, given the way the captain's eyebrows shot up almost to his hairline.

"No. But, send them right in. I want to talk to that woman myself."

Before anyone had time to speculate on the reason for this visit, the door swung open, and Kourtney Kennedy swept into the room, followed by her boss, Roland Pritchard. Caitlin drew in a quick breath. Kennedy was beautiful, even more so in person than on television, but Caitlin hadn't expected to see scratches on the anchor's cheek or a burgeoning black eye. In an automatic gesture, Caitlin touched the stitches above her own eyebrow.

After brief introductions, the captain's adjuvant brought in more chairs, then excused himself. The room itself seemed to be holding its breath, waiting for the shoe to drop, or in Kourtney's case, the stiletto.

In her hand, Kourtney held a large manila envelope. She passed it to Jeffers. "I think this ought to prove my intention to cooperate with the police. The truth is, a story like this one could buy me a Pulitzer, but since I'm such a good citizen, I brought you this information *before* our broadcast."

"Make no mistake," Pritchard added. "We *are* going to air with this new development. But, as Kourtney said, we're willing to play ball. If, after you see what's inside this package, you have any special requests or want to tap the phones in my newsroom, we'll follow your instructions to the letter."

Jeffers slipped on gloves, then opened the clasp on the envelope. "If there's evidence in here, I hope to hell you didn't touch it."

Kourtney's face flushed. "I touched it when I made copies. And of course it was handled by mailroom personnel . . . but I'll know better next time . . . if there is a next time. I'm not stupid, I just didn't realize what this was until *after* I'd already handled it."

Kennedy looked at Spense, and Caitlin's chest tightened at the intimacy of her glance. She lifted her chin. Spense had rescued this woman from Lucy Lancaster only yesterday. So that sappy look in her eyes was to be expected. Hero worship is common after an individual saves your life. A wash of guilt swept through her. Someone was jealous, but this time, it wasn't Spense.

"You made fucking copies?" Martinez didn't bother to hide his contempt. "Do you realize you're *continually* comprising an ongoing serial-murder investigation? You keep saying you want to cooperate, but you keep pulling all kinds of stunts like showing up at Lancaster's place and handling evidence without gloves."

"So, you don't want to see?" Pritchard challenged Martinez, and he abruptly backed down, holding out a hand for his copy of the *new development.*

"Christ." The captain leaned back in his chair.

"I'll read aloud, and you can follow along, if you like," Kourtney offered.

The captain motioned for her to go ahead, then the news anchor struck a pose, as if she were reading for her television audience:

"*I would like to lay on the table before you as a point of information that I am the individual known in the press as the Fallen Angel Killer. I have been greatly misunderstood and misrepresented by the media. I move for a reconsideration of my circumstances before the police commit to an untenable position. For now, let us table any discussion as to my nefarious motives, for they are not nefarious at all.*

"*I would further like to amend the discussion to note that I am in fact the champion of these three fallen angels who have been so pitifully misused by those who hold the admiration of the public. How ironic that I have been held up as a villain, while those who truly deserve the name remain esteemed, nay, revered. Idolized men, such as Tom La Grande, have sorely used these angels.*

"I am here to hold the truly guilty accountable. To this end, I must use my point of privilege to demand justice. I have in my safe custody the escaped angel, Miss Gina Lola, whose words were heard by all, thanks to outstanding reporting by Kourtney Kennedy. Gina Lola's welfare is now in your hands. I demand that he who has used her for his pleasure while maintaining his esteemed place of celebrity in our society, come forward and admit his sin.

"Henceforth, he shall be known as Celebrity X.

"If Celebrity X confesses within forty-eight hours, if he admits his sordid relations with women such as Gina Lola, then I shall return her to you unharmed. If, however, Celebrity X continues to hide his sins, I shall transform our misused Gina into another fallen angel. You have forty-eight hours, beginning at 7 P.M. on October 10. Tick. Tock."

When Kourtney finished her reading, a collective breath released, yet no one spoke. Like Caitlin, Jeffers, Spense, and Martinez were probably churning through this information in their heads, trying to comprehend its meaning.

The wording in the letter seemed oddly reminiscent of . . . *something*. It was almost as though the writer was calling them to order in a board meeting and setting down the rules. "Does this phrasing seem off to you?" she asked Spense.

"Not really. It looks like the author is intentionally peppering his text with terms from Robert's Rules of Order: *lay on the table, move for reconsideration, point of order.* It's quite deliberate, in my opinion."

Leave it to Spense to instantly discern a pattern in a jumbled mess of a letter like this one.

"What does that mean?" Jeffers and Martinez asked in unison.

"No idea. But it means *something*." Spense opened his hands in an expansive gesture.

Kourtney leapt to her feet, eyes gleaming with excitement. "Maybe the killer is the chairman of a board or . . . maybe he's on the city council. Maybe he's the mayor!"

"I don't think we're going to swear out a warrant for the mayor or the city-council members based on a letter like this one." Martinez shot her an admonishing look.

"But you do think it's real? You believe this is from the Fallen Angel Killer?" An agitated Kennedy paced the room.

"The most important question at the moment," Caitlin spoke her thoughts aloud, "is not whether or not this letter is from the Fallen Angel Killer. The most important question is whether or not Gina Lola is safe. When was the last time you spoke with her?" Caitlin fixed her gaze on Kennedy. "And please don't tell us you haven't seen or heard from her since your initial meeting. You lied about not knowing where Lucy Lancaster was. Unless you want to be charged as an accessory to murder . . . and kidnapping . . . I suggest you tell us how to find Gina Lola."

"I didn't lie. I told you, I followed detective Martinez and Agent Spenser . . ." Her voice cracked. "You think he's really got her?" She sat down hard. "Oh my God."

"You need a minute?" Jeffers softened a bit toward Kennedy, who seemed genuinely distressed. Her hands shook, and her eyes had filled with tears.

Maybe Kennedy had suddenly realized that her selfish hoarding of information might cost a woman her life. Better late than never? Caitlin had been about to threaten her again but decided to back off for now. She took a moment, rereading the letter. They needed to make sense of this quickly if they were going to find Gina Lola before time ran out. The letter could be a fake, even a stunt from Kennedy, but they couldn't take that chance.

"The good news is," Caitlin said, "if this really is the Fallen Angel Killer, he's finally reaching out to us. And that means we have a much better chance of finding him. We need to analyze his message for clues from both its literal content and its subtext. The literal content is clear. He's kidnapped Gina Lola. He's challenged us to find Celebrity X, presumably one of Lancaster's johns, and compel him to come forward within forty-eight hours."

"That means we've been looking at victimology from a wrong angle," Spense put in. "This whole time, we've been proceeding as though the only victims were these women. But that's not right. If this letter is genuine, then the killer's real target may not be the escorts at all. Maybe he's really after Celebrity X, whoever that may be." Spense turned to Caitlin. "What do you think about the subtext? The letter is disorganized, hard to follow."

"Agreed, but perhaps that's also by design. The author wants us to believe he's lost his reason, that he's a crazed killer unable to think logically." She paused. "But if you look at the letter, it does flow. It has a beginning, a middle, and an end. An individual with a thought disorder, like a schizophrenic, for example, would display a flight of ideas, loose associations, tangential reasoning, etc. And I don't see any of that here. The killer wants us to believe he's crazy, but in reality, he's anything but."

If the letter was genuine, it would also seem to indicate Lucy wasn't the Fallen Angel Killer, and yet . . . it didn't fully rule her out. It could've been mailed before her arrest, or she might have an accomplice. But these were not matters to be discussed in front of Kennedy and Pritchard.

Caitlin paced the room, then came back to stand near Spense. "So we've got two critical problems. One, we need to find Gina Lola before it's too late, and two, we need to find Celebrity X, just in case we can't save her without him." Deciding Kennedy had had enough time to compose herself, Caitlin asked, "When was the last time you saw Gina? Where did you meet?"

Kennedy sniffled, then nodded at Caitlin. "I-I don't want anything bad to happen to Gina. I didn't think anyone would find her."

"We've got until Saturday at 7 P.M, Kourtney."

The reporter pressed her palms to her temples. "The last time I saw her she was at the Sogni D'Oro Motel in Brentwood. Room 183."

Martinez grabbed his jacket and sprang to his feet, nodding first at Spense, then at Caitlin. "You guys need a ride?"

The Hummer was parked outside, but Caitlin knew Spense wouldn't want to arrive second on the scene, and Martinez would no doubt use his siren to cut through traffic. Spense gritted his teeth and glanced down at his long legs. "Caity can ride shotgun. I'll take the back."

Chapter Twenty-Three

Thursday, October 10
11:00 A.M.
Brentwood, California

SPENSE HAD CALLED ahead, so when he arrived at the Sogni D'Oro Motel along with Caity and Martinez, the front desk clerk was ready and waiting to escort them to Room 183. As she led the way down a long, carpeted hallway that looked exactly like every other midpriced motor lodge in the Southwest, Spense couldn't help thinking that the only nongeneric thing about this place was its name. Although her hands shook, and she dropped the keycard at least twice, the clerk, whose name tag said KAREN, MANAGER IN TRAINING, managed to maintain a professional demeanor. She had to be curious as to why the police were interested in one of her guests, but she was discreet enough not to ask too many questions.

He made a mental note to send a letter to her boss, complimenting her on a job well done.

"You're doing great, Karen." He made his voice as reassuring as possible. He wasn't just being nice. The less nervous the clerk was, the better her recall would be. "When did you last see Miss Jones?" They'd already verified that the young woman who'd checked into the motel as Bridgette Jones, matched Gina Lola's description. It seemed this was a case of one fake name covering for another. They'd also learned she'd paid a week ahead—in cash. Leaving little doubt Kourtney Kennedy had told the truth . . . for once.

"Not since she checked in." Karen's eyes rounded, as if it had occurred to her for the first time that Bridgette Jones might have been the victim of foul play. She bit her lip, and he could see her struggling not to ask whatever question was on the tip of her tongue. Yep. He was definitely going to send her boss a complimentary letter.

"Will your housekeepers be available for interview?"

"Of course, but I'm afraid they won't be much use. Miss Jones explained on arrival that she wouldn't be utilizing maid service. And she kept her privacy card hanging outside the door at all times. She made it clear she wasn't to be disturbed."

Martinez made a disapproving noise in his throat. "And you just went along with that? She checked in under the name Bridgette Jones. She paid in cash. She hasn't left her room. Didn't it occur to you that something was fishy? Didn't it occur to you to call the police?"

Karen halted in her tracks and bravely met the lieutenant's gaze. "Of course I thought it was fishy. So I inquired after her well-being. She explained that her ex was stalking her, and she didn't dare show her face. I saw no reason to call the cops. Frankly, I've notified the police for much more substantial reasons and gotten no interest from the officers taking the call. I don't believe I've given you cause to treat me with disrespect, so I'll thank you to save your sarcasm if you don't mind."

Ha. Karen had put Martinez neatly in his place.

To his credit though, he seemed to know it. His cheeks turned a faint shade of pink, and he raked a hand through his short hair. "I apologize. I'm concerned for the young lady's safety."

"As am I."

They'd arrived at Room 183, where a DO NOT DISTURB sign hung from the knob. Spense pounded on the door. "Miss Jones, I'm Agent Spenser with the FBI. We have reason to believe you may be in danger. Let us in, please."

Without waiting for a response, he took the keycard from Karen and opened the door. They had plenty of probable cause and the consent of the manager. The door swung open, and he motioned for the clerk and Caity to wait outside. Pistol drawn, he entered the room, eyes and gun first, with Martinez giving cover. It only took a moment to clear the small room, closet, and bathroom. Though someone had obviously been there recently, the bed was unmade and there were used cups on the nightstands, there was no sign of a struggle, and no sign of Gina Lola . . . or Bridgette Jones either.

Returning to the hallway, he said, "It's all clear," using a complete sentence to convey this information for the first time ever. The terrified look on Karen's face when he'd drawn his pistol made him want to soften his words.

Caity touched her hand to the young woman's shoulder. "Do you feel comfortable coming inside and walking us through some things?"

Karen nodded.

Now that they knew there was no crime in progress, they all took the time to don gloves and paper booties in order to minimize interference with a potential crime scene before the techs swooped in.

In the process of clearing the room, Spense had opened the drapes to reveal a pair of arcadia doors exiting directly onto the parking lot. A metal slide, used as additional protection to keep the glass doors from being opened, lay in the middle of the floor as though it had been hastily tossed aside. Any fool could open those doors with a credit card, and Gina Lola had to have known that. "I don't see a young woman frightened enough to refuse maid service pulling out this slide and tossing it in the middle of the floor. Even if she removed the protective bar herself, I would think she'd prop it against the door, or somewhere out of the way."

It was possible, of course, that Gina Lola had fled the motel on her own, but he was getting a hinky vibe.

Martinez tugged on the door, and it slid right open.

Karen's hand flew to her mouth. "She was so worried about her ex. I can't believe she didn't lock her patio door."

"I can't believe it either," Martinez said. "Last time she ordered room service?"

Karen picked up the phone and hit the IN-ROOM-DINING button. A deep frown line appeared between her eyebrows, as she hung up. "She ordered pancakes yesterday morning at seven. Nothing since then."

Not good.

"Did she have any visitors?" Caity asked.

"Not officially. No one came to the front desk or asked for her room number. But . . ." Her face paled. "I'm so sorry. I should have mentioned this before. I-I don't know why I forgot. I guess I'm a little . . . scared."

Caity stepped closer to Karen. "You've been terrific. Isn't that so?" She glanced from Spense to Martinez.

"Oh yeah," Martinez jumped in, apparently eager to show Caity he'd remembered his manners. "If all our witnesses were like you, we'd have the best case-closed record in the division."

Karen looked up through her lashes and sent Martinez a shy smile. "One of the housekeepers told me that she saw Kourtney Kennedy in the hallway. She asked me if was she a guest and would it be okay if she asked for an autograph. I was sure it couldn't really have been Kourtney Kennedy. Anyway, I told Lydia, that's our housekeeper, that Kourtney wasn't staying here, but if she ever did, I thought it would be okay to get an autograph as long as she asked her politely. Then Lydia said something like it was definitely Kourtney Kennedy, and she must have been visiting the *weirdo* in 183 because she saw her lurking outside the door."

"And this happened when?" Spense asked.

"Yesterday, sometime in the early afternoon, I think."

This wasn't exactly new information. Kourtney had already told them she'd visited Gina at the motel. But this lent credibility to everything the clerk had said. They thanked Karen and sent her back to her desk with instructions to contact them if she remembered anything else.

As soon as she was out of earshot, Martinez said, "Kourtney Kennedy was the last person to see Gina Lola. Kourtney Kennedy is ass deep in every single aspect of this investigation. Kourtney Kennedy said she's looking to buy a Pulitzer. Those were *her* words."

"So what are you implying?" Caity chewed her lower lip, contemplating the spin Martinez had just put on the ball. "You think Kourtney's behind all of this? You think she's killing innocent young women in order to take credit for being an ace reporter? Merely to further her career?"

Caity seemed to find this incredible, but Spense knew that in Hollywood, furthering a career was a solid motive for murder.

"It's not as far-fetched as you make it sound." Martinez stripped off his gloves and shoved them in his pocket. "We've got a woman's DNA under Selena Turner's fingernails. SLY has gotten all kinds of publicity since the second body was found on their tour bus. Kennedy lied to us about not knowing how to contact both Lucy Lancaster and Gina Lola. The killer has been contacting Kennedy and only Kennedy, and even noted her *outstanding reporting* in his letter. Not to mention she's the only person to have had any contact with Gina Lola."

"Except Lucy. The same woman who resisted arrest, held a hostage at gunpoint, and threatened a federal agent. Not to mention Lucy's the one who had motive, means, and opportunity in all three of the other cases." Caity took the role of devil's advocate.

"Timeline doesn't work for the kidnapping," Martinez said. "We've had her in custody since yesterday afternoon."

"That doesn't necessarily exclude her . . . *or* Kennedy, I suppose. After all, we know Kennedy visited Gina at the motel and still had time to haul her butt down to Lucy's place in time to get in on all the excitement. The abduction, if there really has been an abduction, could've occurred in the hours before you and Spense arrived at Lucy's home. It's only a few minutes' drive from here to her Brentwood hacienda. And that letter was sent from a Brentwood FedEx . . . unfortunately the killer used a drop box, so we won't be able to pinpoint the exact time. Too bad our killer was also bright enough to charge the *recipient* for the FedEx, so we can't track a credit card."

Spense grinned. "IQ is 120. I'm putting ten dollars on it. You in Martinez?"

Caity wrinkled her nose. "Let's say, for the sake of argument, our Fallen Angel Killer note is the real deal, and Gina truly has been kidnapped. A frightened Gina wouldn't open the door for a stranger, but she *would* trust both Lucy and Kourtney. So I'm thinking Gina's holed up here, lonely, isolated, and scared. Either Lucy or Kourtney knocks on her door. She lets them inside, or maybe she steps outside to greet them. No one heard a struggle, so the kidnapper must have chemically subdued Gina, possibly with a tranquilizer."

Spense visualized the scene in his head. "It's more likely she'd use something fast acting and reliable—like chloroform. Why take a chance waiting around for a sedative to work? Especially if you don't know for a fact you can convince your victim to eat or drink." He shut his eyes, tuning in to his thoughts, "The kidnapper grabs Gina, presses a chloroformed rag to her face. Gina goes limp. She's unable to fight back, but she's not out cold. Our abductor tosses the sliding bar aside, opens the patio door, and walks a groggy Gina out to a getaway car." Spense opened his eyes and motioned for Caity and Martinez to follow him through the arcadia doors. "Which would be parked right there." He pointed to the parking space directly behind the room.

Martinez looked up. Spense followed his gaze and smiled. There was a surveillance camera in the parking lot, aimed at just the right angle. He had a feeling they were about to get lucky.

Thursday, October 10
12:30 P.M.
Hollywood, California

BACK AT HOLLYWOOD station, Spense, Martinez, and Caity settled in to the task of scrutinizing excruciatingly boring security footage. After about an hour, they spotted the kidnapping. Just as Spense had suspected, the surveillance camera caught the abductor, helping an obviously drugged Gina to a white van, parked outside her room. If he defined luck as confirmation of a terrible deed, then the team had indeed gotten lucky. As it turned out, although the surveillance tapes were usually erased nightly, the management hadn't yet purged them.

The unlucky part, aside from Gina's being taken, was that the medium-build abductor wore a Charlie Chaplin mask and wig. He or she must've known there were cameras in the parking lot. Even after repeated viewing, no one could tell if Charlie was a man or a woman. The van's tags had been covered with a plastic shield, the kind used to prevent photo radar cameras from grabbing a shot of the license number. So no luck there.

With a kidnap victim in danger, Spense knew the FBI couldn't remain in the background. He notified the NCAVC liaison, Jake Felton, at the Bureau's Los Angeles field office and every available agent was allocated as a potential resource for the Fallen Angel Killer case. Detectives and field agents canvassed the area, going door to door, searching for anyone who might have interacted with Gina or seen the white van. Others studied footage or combed through SID reports, and Felton helped Jeffers prepare for a joint press conference. A plan was set in motion to broadcast the killer's demands, and a media storm was certain to follow. Kourtney Kennedy was going to plead, on live television, for Celebrity X to come forward, admitting his relationships and sinful lifestyle. Meanwhile, Spense and Caity were tasked with interviewing both Lucy Lancaster and Tom La Grande in an attempt to obtain a list of possible johns—not to mention attempting to convince Lucy to give up Gina's location if she in fact had a hand in this.

First up: Lucy Lancaster.

AFTER INTRODUCING HIMSELF to Caitlin and greeting Spense like an old friend, Lucy's attorney, Sutton Benoit, began the session with a wave of his hand. "I want to be clear that Ms. Lancaster intends to cooperate with the authorities. She denies any culpability in the Fallen Angel case. You've stated you wish to question her regarding her relationship to one Gina Lola, an alleged prostitute who's gone missing. Please restrict your questions to that topic alone."

"I'll ask what I see fit." Spense shrugged. "Feel free to advise your client if you don't think she should answer."

"I wanna help find Gina." Lucy raised cuffed hands and wiped her dripping nose with the back of her arm. "I swear on my mother's grave that girl is like a sister to me. I had absolutely nothing to do with her disappearance. How could I? I've been in jail since yesterday afternoon."

"Gina was abducted yesterday around two o'clock. We have surveillance footage that confirms she was taken two hours prior to your arrest from a location just minutes from your home. So you're not in the clear for her abduction."

"Oh." Lucy looked to her attorney for help, but he avoided her gaze. "I-I thought it happened later." Her face brightened. "That proves I didn't do it, doesn't it? Since I didn't know the time."

"I'm afraid not," Caitlin said gently. She wanted Lucy to believe her a sympathetic ally even though her blood boiled at this woman's nerve. Lucy claimed to be a friend to this young woman, when all the while she'd used her for personal gain without a care for her safety. "But naturally, *I* don't believe for a minute you'd hurt Gina. And I've told Agent Spenser here as much. After all, you've been looking out for her, employing her for years. Without you, she'd probably have been on the streets, instead of living in that nice apartment out in Silver Lake."

Spense sent her an approving smile, and her chest expanded. Probably he hadn't believed her capable of manipulating a witness. Well, he'd been wrong.

"That's right. I'll do anything I can to help." Lucy's voice sounded relieved.

"Wonderful." Caitlin pushed a pen and paper in front of Lucy. "Agent Spenser is going to uncuff you."

After Lucy's cuffs were off, she continued. "Now then, all we need is for you to write down the names and the phone numbers, if you have them, of all the men who use your escort service."

Lucy's eyes rounded in disbelief. "I can't possibly remember all of them."

Caitlin shook her head. "Ah, of course not. I don't know what I was thinking. Forget that, I should've realized you couldn't recall off the top of your head. Just tell us where we can find your records instead."

"I keep them in my . . . wait, if I give you my books, you're going to charge me with pandering."

Spense reached over and tapped his fingers on the table in front of Benoit. "Please advise your client that producing any records that list the johns is in her best interest. You have my word she won't be charged with pandering if she does. If she doesn't, you have my word the DA will go for capital murder in the Turner case."

He seemed to be avoiding Caitlin's gaze. She knew he had no authority to promise any deals, and though Lucy *might* be facing murder charges in the Selena Turner case—*if* the DNA under the escort's nails turned out to match Lucy—they still probably wouldn't have enough to charge her with a capital crime. Depending on what evidence materialized, the DA might go with second-degree murder or even with voluntary manslaughter. The truth was that until the DNA came back, the only sure thing they had on Lucy was pandering, assault with a deadly weapon—on Kourtney Kennedy—and resisting arrest. Manipulating the suspect was one thing, outright lying about the charges was another.

Caitlin had never been able to stomach the latter—since a web of lies had been used to coerce her father into confessing to a crime he never committed. And yet . . . nothing seemed black-and-white anymore. If Spense's lie convinced Lucy to turn over her black book, and that black book led them to Celebrity X, and Celebrity X's televised confession saved Gina Lola's life . . . . Her throat clogged with emotion. It's difficult to admit when you've made a mistake, but she couldn't help thinking she'd been far too hard on Spense about his methods.

"Don't say a word." Benoit glared at Spense. "He's bluffing, Lucy."

"Maybe," Lucy answered. "Or maybe, Mr. Benoit, you're not really here to look after me. Maybe Tom La Grande sent you to look after his own interests." Leaning her head back she said, "I keep records going back five years in a black book in my safety-deposit box. If you think it might help catch the Fallen Angel

Killer, if you think it might help bring Gina home safe, you can have it."

Beneath the table, Caitlin touched her knee to Spense's, and her heart took up a more hopeful beat. The LAPD had been unable to get that ledger from Lucy, but Spense had gotten the job done. In this situation, even she couldn't argue with his tactics. Yes, he'd lied to a suspect, but Gina's life might depend on their finding Celebrity X.

One down. One to go.

Next up: Tom La Grande.

Fifteen minutes later, she and Spense found La Grande in a different interview room with Benoit already whispering in his ear. Caitlin hadn't seen La Grande since that day at Robb's Malibu mansion, and she was surprised by the deterioration in the actor's appearance. His face looked haggard, and his clothing was grimy and unkempt, making him seem more like a man who'd slept on the streets last night, than one who'd bedded down in a multimillion-dollar home. "Thanks for coming down, Mr. La Grande," she said, pulling a chair up to face him.

"Did I have a choice?"

"Legally, yes." She squared her gaze with his. "But morally, I'd have to say no."

"I think I passed the point of worrying about my morals a while ago." His lips turned down at the corners, and he brought raggedy nails that had been chewed to bloody stubs to his mouth. Maybe he really did have a remnant of conscience left. Why else would he look so guilt-stricken? *Good.* That would give them a fighting chance.

"With all the charges being dropped, you're a very lucky man, Mr. La Grande." Spense lifted one eyebrow in a way that conveyed he had no sympathy, regardless of what the actor had been through in the past few days.

"Lucky? My wife filed for divorce, and I'm stone-cold sober. How do you figure I'm lucky?"

"You're not going to jail for a crime you didn't commit, or for any that you did. At least not so far." Caitlin straightened her shoulders. "Under the circumstances, I'd say you're a most fortunate man."

"So what is it you want from me now? More blood samples? A list of my whereabouts for the past year? My firstborn child? Because I'm not so sure if I got a kid around somewhere or not." As argumentative as his words seemed, there was no fight left in his tone.

"Nothing so difficult as that. We'd simply like a list of names of all the prostitutes whom you siphoned off from Lucy Lancaster, along with the names of any amigos you might have *loaned* them to."

"Then this trip is a waste of all our time. Didn't Agent Spenser tell you the part about me not liking to share? I never give out the girls' names, and you already know the three girls I had on private . . . retainer."

"Only three? Not four?"

"Absolutely. Addie, Brenda   and Selena was going to be my new recruit. I'd just made her the proposition the morning she . . . fell." His lower lip protruded, and his eyes went glassy. Either he was genuinely upset about the death of these women, or he deserved the gold statues he had on his shelf and then some.

"Did you ever *retain* a woman who went by the name of Gina Lola?"

"No. I'd certainly remember a name like that. It's like Gina Lollobrigida . . . cute."

"And you never gave out any numbers to friends. Is there a chance someone could have gotten your numbers without your knowing, say from your cell-phone contacts list?"

"You mean like my wife? Hell no. I'm not that stupid. I had a separate cell I kept on me at all times. And I do mean *all* times. I've heard of that golfer, you know. And my wife is sweeter than your first fuck on a summer night in the hayloft. She wouldn't harm a fly, or a whore, or even a rat-bastard husband like me. If you're looking at *Anita* for these murders, you've just boarded the wrong bus."

Until this very moment, the thought had never crossed Caitlin's mind that La Grande's wife might be involved. From the corner of her eye, she saw Spense's shoulders rise to attention.

Benoit put his hand on La Grande's arm. "Nobody's crazy enough to accuse Anita." Then he rested his elbows on the table and steepled his fingers. "Dr. Cassidy is just fishing."

"For what? Has something else happened? Who is this Gina Lola person? If another girl's been killed, she's not on my head. I never even heard of her."

"We might as well tell you. Another of Lucy Lancaster's escorts, this one going by the name of Gina Lola, has been abducted. And the kicker is the kidnapper called *you* out in a letter to SLY. He specifically mentions you as a slimeball."

La Grande tore at his hair. "My life is over."

When pity for Tom La Grande tried to snake its way into Caitlin's heart, she chopped off its head like it was a venomous rattler. "No, Mr. La Grande. Your life is not over. Your marriage—perhaps. Your career—who knows? They say there's no such thing as bad publicity, after all. But no matter how far you've fallen from the heights, you're alive. You still have your freedom. You still have a chance to make your life count for something."

"Suck it up," Spense tossed in. "Only a moron throws every-thing away for kicks."

After La Grande exited, Caitlin asked Spense, "You believe him—that he doesn't know Gina?"

"Yeah. He's too beat down to work up a lie."

AN HOUR LATER, Lucy Lancaster's ledger was in their possession. Or rather, photographs of each page of the ledger. The book itself had been swept up by SID and was being checked for fingerprints, DNA, and other evidence. But Jeffers had insisted that even the photographic copies be treated as classified. Only a select group of detectives knew of the book's existence, and even fewer knew that it was currently being analyzed at Hollywood station. The reason for all this security: The pages of the ledger were littered with the names of foreign dignitaries, local politicians, minor celebrities, and the occasional Big Fish: an Oscar winner, a prominent direc-tor, a former governor of California. If the names in Lancaster's little black book got out, it could throw the whole city into chaos.

Though the authorities had once clamored to obtain the list of names with the idea that one of these johns might be the Fallen Angel Killer, Spense now believed the johns themselves—or at least the one they were currently calling Celebrity X, to be an in-tended victim. To him, and to Caity and Martinez as well, it ap-peared the killer was merely using the women to expose the false life of Celebrity X. And, if they couldn't find this mystery man in time, Gina Lola was destined to become the next *fallen angel*.

Huddled in an interview room with Spense were Caity, Marti-nez, and two of the lieutenant's most trusted detectives. Although cameras were recording the entire process, no one had been au-thorized to observe, and the curtains had been drawn over the window before they began poring through the pages of the ledger. Their mission: Find Celebrity X and get him to confess his *sin* on public television. Ironic that his *sin* consisted of enjoying Hollywood's abundant vices and putting on a false front. To Spense, it seemed you might as well accuse the entire city.

Down the hall, Jeffers had assigned a rotating team of detectives to question Lancaster. Since they couldn't rule her out as the kidnapper, they'd decided to keep continuous pressure on her to reveal Gina's whereabouts.

Though it was certainly possible Lucy had abducted the girl prior to her arrest, the timing would've been tight, and Spense's gut told him that Lucy had been telling the truth when she'd said she had nothing to do with the escort's disappearance. In fact, it seemed to him that Lucy's worry for Gina had been the deciding factor in her decision to release her black book of names.

Martinez had also put a tail on *his* favorite suspect, Kourtney Kennedy. But thus far, she hadn't traveled anywhere out of the ordinary. And so, without other leads, and with SLY going through with the broadcast with or without their blessing, they'd chosen to exactly follow the instructions set down in the Fallen Angel Killer letter.

It was 4:00 P. M. In just three hours, the forty-eight-hour clock would start ticking. With no time to waste, Spense handed around pens. "Let's break this big job down into easy pieces." Which was pretty much the only way he'd ever been able to accomplish anything. He had to screen out all irrelevant noise to get a clear picture in his head.

They had to work fast, and the last thing he wanted was to stress the team and cloud their reason. It was natural to try to leap to the end of any difficult task, but he knew the quickest way to the finish line was taking it step by step. So he started with a confidence-building task. One they couldn't possibly fail. "For the moment, don't even worry about who you think Celebrity X might be. All I want you to do, is circle any name you *recognize*. If you can't place the name exactly, circle it anyway—any name that rings a bell at all. If a name draws a blank, pass it over."

The letter had specified Celebrity X was a well-known member of the community. Though the ledger contained almost one thousand names, Spense reasoned that if not one of the five people in the room recognized it, that individual could safely be eliminated.

The tight expressions on the faces at the table told him everyone was taking the task seriously. It took an hour to go through the list, then another to enter the names on a spread sheet and eliminate those who'd been recognized only once, or who had likely returned home to a foreign country by now. They'd been quite fortunate in one regard: The majority of Lucy's clientele were foreign businessmen—with names not recognized by the team, or residences too far away to be included.

Spense now stood at the front of the room in front of a large map of Los Angeles. He marked a red X on the Sky Walk Hotel, the SLY tour-bus station, and Waxed. "Here we have the locations where the bodies were dumped." Pulling out a blue marker, he labeled Lucy Lancaster's home, the Sogni D'Oro Motel in Brentwood, and the residences of each victim. Next, with a green pen, he drew a circle that included all the marked locations. "We know from statistics that serials like to work within a geographic comfort zone."

"The killer likely lives somewhere within the green circle. And since this is where he or she finds his victims, most likely this is also where he's encountered our mystery man—Celebrity X," Caity chimed in.

It was a bit of a leap but not an unreasonable one. They had to narrow down this list if they were going to have any hope of beating the clock. People nodded, so Spense continued. "Now then, if we take our refined list of johns, and eliminate anyone who doesn't live or work within the green circle, *this,* is who we're left with."

Caity passed around a list. "Thanks to your hard work, we've culled Lucy Lancaster's roster of johns down to twenty-six candidates. If Celebrity X is in fact one of her clients, he'll likely be among these men."

Waving the list in his hand, Spense nodded at the crew. "Great work . . . now let's get out there and find our celebrity."

Chapter Twenty-Four

Thursday, October 10
7:00 P.M.
Forty-eight hours remaining
Beverly Hills, California

CAITLIN AND SPENSE had taken on five of the men from the list. The remaining names had been divided among special agents chosen by Felton and by Martinez's detectives. It was up to all of them to convince these individuals to come clean, not only with their wives and families, but with the public, via an SLY broadcast tomorrow morning. Given the self-centered nature of these beasts, the task seemed all but impossible. Caitlin and Spense had started with Councilman Bart Hawthorne, who had initially appeared cooperative, but then quickly changed his tune as they interviewed him in the study of his Beverly Hills home.

"You have no proof." Bart Hawthorne smoothed his silver hair back with a tanned hand, his diamond Rolex glittering as a ray of light struck its dial. "So what if my name's in your book? It was put there by a *criminal*. No jury would take the word of a pimp over mine."

He appeared more bewildered than nervous, Caitlin thought. He'd probably never been held accountable for his bad behaviors, and he couldn't seem to grasp the fact that his Teflon days were about to come to an abrupt end. "We're not planning on charging you with any crime, at least not at the moment. So it's not about convincing a jury."

"Oh, that's right. You only want me to go on national television and confess to frequenting prostitutes. An admission that's not only false, it's one that would destroy my family—and *ruin* me."

Caitlin tried to paste a sympathetic look on her face, but she doubted she'd succeeded. "*Ruin* is a strong word. Lots of careers have survived sex scandals. Plenty of politicians come to mind— even an ex-president. And in your case, a woman's life is at stake."

"I didn't know her."

Maybe he didn't. Nothing in the ledger listed which women the men had used. So it made their job even harder to convince those who might not have been with Gina to come forward. If the man didn't know her, he wouldn't feel for her. But Caitlin and Spense had no choice. They had to bring in all of the potential johns because it was impossible to rely on the men's statements about which women they'd encountered.

"This is a matter of life and death. Is Gina's life worth less to you because you never met her?"

He walked to a bar and poured himself a glass of bourbon, then turned his back to them. "Don't be ridiculous. I'm not a monster. But I'm not the man you're looking for. I can't be Celebrity X if I never went with that woman."

"No one knows the identity of Celebrity X, and the letter didn't specify which women he'd been with. That's the point. You *could* be him. And a woman might die if you don't come forward."

Spense cleared his throat. "If I were you, I'd get with my people and figure out how to spin this deal, because Kourtney Kennedy is going to read your name on the air in the morning. Surely you want to control the situation by making your own announcement."

Slowly, Hawthorne turned to face them again.

That was progress. "It says here the dates you requested escorts are December 25—" Caitlin paused and raised an eyebrow. The councilman was a married man with three young children. "January 10, and June 3 of last year." She forced gentleness into her smile. "This is going to be a blow to your wife. Isn't June 3 your anniversary? I wonder if we could somehow convince Kennedy to keep the dates out of it."

Hawthorne paled. "You said you have Madam Lucille in custody. Why not focus on her? Surely you can make some kind of deal to get her to tell you where the girl is."

"We're using every means at our disposal to get the madam to talk. But so far, she's denying any involvement in Gina's disappearance." Caitlin rose and walked over to the bar, leaned her elbows on it, getting close to the councilman. "If she's telling the truth, the Fallen Angel Killer is still out there."

"I can't do it." He brought his glass to his lips, and a bit of bourbon dribbled out of the corner of his mouth. His hand was trembling. They were beginning to get through to him, she could tell. "I'm too ashamed. It's not even losing my place on the council. It's my *wife*. Believe it or not, I'd be lost without her. I *love* her."

"Then talk to her; because if you don't, we will." Spense had no mercy in his voice.

"You can't do that!"

"We can, and we will. So you decide, Councilman." Caitlin met his watery gaze. "Do you want your wife to know that you made a terrible mistake, but when an innocent woman's life was at stake, you stepped up to take responsibility in what some might consider a heroic move? Or do you want us to explain to her that you're not only a liar and a cheat, but a coward as well? It's your life, so you make the call."

Chapter Twenty-Five

Friday, October 11
Hollywood, California
9:00 A.M.
Thirty-four hours remaining

EARLIER THIS MORNING, at 5:00 A.M., SLY had recorded the show of a lifetime, one Spense suspected they would never equal again. Kourtney Kennedy had read the Fallen Angel Killer letter and made an impassioned plea for Celebrity X to come forward. Then nineteen men—seven had not been persuaded to participate— lined up for their walk of shame, admitting to hiring the services of prostitutes and violating the trust of their families and the public. Spense could only hope that either Celebrity X was among the group, or that their good-faith effort would buy Gina more time. All the men apologized, many revealed plans to enter rehabilitation centers, and a few, Councilman Hawthorne included, announced retirement from public service. Tom La Grande wept openly as he begged for the safe release of Gina Lola, and inside the SLY newsroom, *quiet on the set* took on a whole new meaning.

In exchange for their cooperation, the men were provided safe escort to their homes after the taping, and extra patrols were placed in their neighborhoods. Later, before the show went to air, the newsroom was converted into a command center manned not only by members of Hollywood division and Robbery Homicide, but by FBI field agents. Among them, to Spense's consternation was Special Agent Alex "Dutch" Langhorne, visiting from Texas.

Just his damn luck he and Dutch were on assignment in LA the same week.

Back in his field-agent days, Spense had worked with Langhorne in Dallas. He'd found the man to be confident to the point of arrogance, and though Langhorne had his way of getting the job done, he was prone to taking unnecessary risks. Spense had called him out on it more than once, and when the two had parted ways, there'd been no tears shed, or false promises to keep in touch. While he was less than thrilled to see the agent burst into the newsroom, he didn't intend to let a grudge interfere with bringing Gina Lola home safely.

Clapping Dutch on the back, he tried to put any past unpleasantness between them out of his mind—and none too soon, because well before the broadcast ended, the tip lines started ringing. There was much work to be done, with everyone answering phones, taking notes, and looking for viable leads. Then Kourtney Kennedy's personal cell rang.

A twitch started up in her eye, and her bottom lip shivered, as she held the phone for Spense to see. According to the caller ID, the call was coming from *Gina*.

"Hello." Kourtney managed a measure of control in her tone though her hand trembled as she brought the cell to her ear.

Spense gave the signal for quiet, and all conversation ceased as he and Dutch quickly ushered Kourtney into an editorial office. Martinez and Caity followed, easing the door closed behind them.

"It's *him*," she mouthed.

Kourtney certainly appeared to be surprised, but Spense knew the fact that Kourtney was once again at the center of things would only fuel Martinez's suspicions about the anchorwoman. Sure enough, the detective folded his arms across his chest and shot Spense an *I-told-you-so* look.

Dutch nodded, and Kourtney said, "I'm in the newsroom, and I have the FBI with me. May I put you on speakerphone?"

Anticipating that the kidnapper would be contacting them at some point, Dutch had briefed the key players before the broadcast on some simple negotiation tactics, instructing them to tell the truth whenever it could be done without putting the hostage in danger, or whenever it was likely the killer would catch them if they lied. The more truth one told, the easier it would be to keep the story straight, and the greater chance of establishing trust with the individual on the other end of the line.

Kourtney put the caller on speaker, and a mechanically distorted voice, came over the cell. "Ah, the FBI. Then I assume you have Agent Spenser with you."

"I do."

"Pass me to him, then, will you?"

Kourtney handed Spense the phone.

"It's nice to see you again, Spense. I mean I can't actually see you, but you get my meaning."

"Not sure what you mean by *again*. Have we met?" Spense grimaced as he stared down at the phone.

"You never do seem to know me, even when I'm right in front of your face. But surely you remember Griffith Park. I was the one in the F-450. Sorry about your Prius, but I see you've traded it in for a Hummer."

"So I have you to thank for that."

Ask him his name, Dutch mouthed.

Spense shrugged. It couldn't hurt. "To whom shall I address the thank-you note?"

"Fallen Angel Killer works for me."

"Come on. Don't you want to take credit for all your accomplishments? What's the point in all this fanfare if no one knows who you really are."

"You didn't do what I asked." Despite the distortion on the phone, the unspoken threat in the caller's voice was clear. "Is Dr. Cassidy there? Let me speak to her."

Spense's jaw tightened, but he passed the phone to Caity. This guy was on a power kick, and Spense didn't enjoy being played.

"Caitlin Cassidy here. I want you to know we did our very best. We found the men who violated the angels, and we convinced them to confess on the air. I can tell you that wasn't easy."

"I'm sure it wasn't. But you should've been able to get Celebrity X. After all, you can charm the chrome off a trailer . . ." He paused, as if waiting for her to respond to his taunt. When she didn't, he said, "Pass me back to Spenser, please."

Keeping a neutral expression, she handed him the phone.

"Spense here." It took more self-discipline than he had to wipe his voice clean of fury.

"Oh, sorry . . . I forgot we were speaking of your lady. But you must agree she has a way with men."

His knuckles went white as he gripped the phone. He didn't intend to discuss Caity with this motherfucker. "Like I said, we did our part. You did a great job punishing these men. I'm sure they've learned their lessons. So now it's time for you to hold up your end of the bargain. Let Gina go. That's the only way to prove you're better than those losers."

"I wish I could, but you didn't bring me Celebrity X."

"That's everyone we could find. Tell us who X is, and I'll drag him down here myself to apologize."

"Tick Tock."

Spense raised a questioning eyebrow at Dutch.

Ask for more time, he mouthed.

"We'll get him, but we need more time. Give us another twenty-four hours."

"No can do. I'd get a move on if I were you."

"We're doing all we can. Why play games? If you really want to bring this bastard down, we'll help you, but we need his name, or even a clue. Just give me a little help."

"Oh my, Agent Spenser. And I thought you were so good at puzzles." The caller hung up.

Dutch tugged his chin. "If the killer's so keen on exposing this Celebrity X, why doesn't he just come out and tell us who he is?"

Made no sense to Spense either. Maybe he really wasn't after X. Maybe he was just looking for an excuse to kill his hostage, and this was all just another publicity stunt. But for now, the best option seemed to be to try to work with his demands. "We've got seven remaining men who couldn't be persuaded to do the right thing. You're the guy with the negotiation skills, Dutch. Maybe you should try to change their minds."

"I'll do better than try." Spense knew that look. Dutch would do whatever it took to bring the stragglers in. "You'll have those assholes here for an 8:00 A.M. broadcast tomorrow. Take that one to the bank."

Chapter Twenty-Six

Saturday, October 12
6:00 A.M.
Thirteen hours remaining
Hollywood, California

TRUE TO HIS word, Dutch Langhorne had the last holdouts lined up in the SLY newsroom at 6:00 A.M. Two hours later, a broadcast went out, and Spense was having a déjà vu moment. The phones jangled with new tips to be sorted, and agents and detectives charged in and out of the newsroom-turned-command center tracking down every remotely credible lead.

Numerous Gina Lola sightings came in, some of them miles apart at the same time. But nothing panned out. Some people might've questioned the value of all this fruitless activity, given the cost to the city of Los Angeles and the federal government, but Spense had seen the system work too many times to give up now.

There were no more dedicated men and women than those working the Fallen Angel case. If this team couldn't bring Gina Lola home safely . . . He wasn't even going to finish that thought. They would bring her home safely.

They *had* to.

Then Kourtney's phone rang, and like the day before, Dutch, Spense, Martinez, and Caity hustled her into a private office.

"May I put you on speaker?" Kourtney hit the button without waiting for the caller's reply. "Were you pleased with my broadcast?" she asked, going rogue in a flirtatious voice.

Martinez grunted. Caity flattened her lips. Spense and Dutch exchanged a glance, but they let her run with it. Spense was interested to see where she might go with the caller. After all, he hadn't had much luck yesterday.

"I was pleased with your legs," answered the creepy, electronic voice.

"Thank you." Kourtney's tone lost its confidence as she caught the unsubtle hint this killer might have more than a passing interest in her.

Of course, it might be an act. Martinez still thought she could be behind the whole shebang, maybe using an accomplice to call in to her phone, but Spense didn't see it.

With trembling hands, Kourtney tossed the phone to Spense like it was a ticking time bomb, which, in a way, it was.

Spense winked at Kourtney, hoping to put her at ease and let her know they'd take it from there. He had to admit she'd stepped up, following their instructions to a T. He placed the phone close to his lips. "Agent Spenser here. You got what you asked for."

"No. I'm *still* waiting for Celebrity X."

"There's no one left to confess. But if you just give us a name—"

"I gave you a clue, like you asked me to. A gift."

"It didn't arrive here. Did you send it to the hotel?" Spense waved at Martinez, who stepped to the back of the room and got on his cell. Probably calling the Sky Walk's concierge to find out if anything had been dropped off.

"I left it on the counter at the copy center two blocks from you. I wasn't going to just walk into SLY so you could arrest me. Besides, I knew nothing would get through to the SLY building. You'd probably have the bomb squad blow it up first."

"How was I supposed to know you left a clue at the copy center?"

"I just told you."

Dutch blasted out the door, no doubt on his way to retrieve the package.

"I'm tired of the games. Let Gina go. You say you're the good guy, the champion of fallen angels. Make me believe you." He kept his voice even, but he was wishing the whole time for this guy to come around the corner so he could rip that damn mask off and punch his lights out before hauling his ass to jail.

"Enjoy your gift, Agent Spenser. It should be easy enough to recognize. Oh, and . . . tick tock."

Dammit. He hung up.

Kourtney was shaking badly.

"Let's get you some java." Caity put an arm around her, then walked her out of the office and through to the lounge, with Spense and Martinez tagging along behind.

The burned-coffee odor in the break room reminded him of every cop shop he'd ever been in, and field office too. Apparently there was one in every bunch who forgot to turn off the coffee-maker. Martinez poured a cup of the black poison for Caity and Kourtney, and they all sat down at a laminated table.

"This is my fault," Kourtney said. "If I'd only told you where Lucy was to begin with. If I hadn't convinced her to stick around, so I could get a better story, none of this would've happened."

"You're doing the right thing now. So let's focus on that . . . and on getting Gina home," Caity said gently.

Kourtney nodded, then jumped to her feet—they all did.

Dutch was waving something in front of the break-room window and pointing. "It's your clue," he yelled loudly enough to be heard through the partially opened door. "A Rubik's cube— with one square missing."

Chapter Twenty-Seven

Saturday, October 12
12:00 P.M.
Seven hours remaining
Hollywood, California

I STROLL THROUGH the lobby of the Sky Walk hotel, and the woman at the front desk smiles at me. Since no one ever really sees me, I don't need my mask. If you ask her ten minutes from now to describe me, her mind will be blank.

She has no idea who she's looking at. I picture cutting her lips off with the fileting knife I use for fish and return her smile.

After taking the elevators to the second floor, I make my way to the rooms that look out over Hollywood Boulevard. I have a master key that I lifted from a maid's cart, but I pat my jacket, just to be sure, and feel the reassuring shape of the card in my pocket.

As I open the door to her room, I whistle, knowing this will make it seem as though I am doing something ordinary to anyone who might pass by. Of course, I'm not ordinary at all.

Not anymore.

Not since the killing began.

I step through the door, and my gaze travels around the neat room, past the pretentious, art-deco furniture, searching out the personal items she's brought with her. I walk to her bed and lift the blouse lying there. Pressing the soft fabric greedily to my cheek, I drink in her smell. It makes my head light and my blood sizzle. Next, I move to the dresser, run my hand through her silks. She wears a size four. So tiny—and yet she's a D cup. Perfect for whoring. She seems to like black lace.

So do I.

I open another drawer and find a small box. I turn it over, and pictures tumble out. Snapshots. One is of a little girl sitting on some porch steps with her father. In her hair, she wears a yellow ribbon. On the back of the photo it says *Caitlin age six with Tom on Valentine's Day.*

Looking down, I notice a room-service tray on the floor, with plates and utensils. I kneel and lift the silver lid, revealing the remnants of steak and eggs. A rather hearty meal for such a slight girl. The knife draws my interest. I pick it up and run my finger down its serrated blade.

Again.

And again.

Red drips into the runny yellow guts of the egg.

Swirling my finger in the bloody mess, I imagine the sound of her screams. I suck the blood and egg from my finger, but it doesn't satisfy my hunger. Then footsteps sound in the hall . . . and voices.

She's home early.

Rising to my feet, I slip the knife in my pocket, then hurry into the closet and pull the door shut behind me. Through the levers, I watch quietly and run my fingers across the blade.

IT WAS NOON. Only seven hours remained on the clock, and Caitlin and Spense had gone back to the Sky Walk to brainstorm. Horatio personally delivered a pot of coffee, along with a plate of cookies, possibly wrongly assuming they'd already had lunch— which was fine by her but not cool with Spense, who said he'd rather settle for black coffee than *poison himself with white sugar.*

As they poured over notes and scribbled ideas on a dry-erase board, she couldn't help wondering if Spense felt as helpless as she did. She knew, of course, that he had voluntarily given up the life of a field agent in exchange for his profiling work with the BAU, but he had to be even more frustrated than she was, knowing most of the other agents and officers were out on the streets following leads. Eventually, her frustration demanded a voice.

"I feel useless," she said, flopping onto the couch, nearly knocking over a half-empty cup of coffee in the process.

He frowned at her. "Then get over it because I need your help. This isn't about our egos. This is about bringing Gina Lola home safely."

"If she's even still alive." The words popped out before she could censor them, and Spense let out a breath and sat down on the couch beside her.

He picked up her hand, turning it over in his. "We're going to operate on the assumption that she is. And just because we're not out there playing shoot-'em-up doesn't mean we're useless. Far from it. No one else on the team has the luxury of analyzing what's happened over the past few days. They don't have time to look for patterns or ponder missing puzzle pieces. We do. We're here, doing what we're doing, because we can. We're lucky enough to have analytical minds, and if we do our jobs right, we can hand the rest of the team what they need to bring Gina back. Would I like to personally pull her out of that creep's clutches? Sure. That kind of action gives me a hard-on. But do I *need* that personal gratification? No. I'm not in it just for the rush."

He was right. Again. She munched a cookie and the poison—refined white sugar—made her feel better. In fact, the cookie was helping her think. "One thing is becoming clear to me."

"We can eliminate Lucy Lancaster as the Fallen Angel Killer."

"Exactly," she said. "While theoretically, it's possible she has an accomplice and is orchestrating all this from her jail cell, it's hardly parsimonious."

"Way too complicated, and Lucy never fit the profile to begin with. She's too private, and too successful at what she does. She's probably the highest-paid madam in the state, if not the country. She's achieved the things she's always aspired to, even though being a madam might not be what others would choose. Our killer is more likely someone who started at the top, and life has handed him a downward turn."

"And it's not Kennedy either."

"The whole idea that she'd do it to buy herself a Pulitzer doesn't fly. People have killed for less, but it would be *far easier* to simply fabricate a prizewinning story than commit murder. Kourtney's too smart to take the hard way when there's an easy way at the ready."

He climbed to his feet and began prowling the room. "It's absolutely key to consider all the pieces of the puzzle. We must be leaving something out." He pulled up short, and she figured his mind had turned to the gift the killer left him—the Rubik's cube with one square missing. "Let's assume that neither Lucy nor Kourtney is the Fallen Angel Killer. Now let's add in the forensics. The DNA under Selena Turner's nails belongs to a woman, and most likely that woman is Lucy Lancaster, who had motive, means, and opportunity to kill her. She was meeting her that very day for lunch."

"Agree." She pressed her palm to her forehead. "Lucy Lancaster probably killed Selena Turner. And Selena Turner's death is clearly connected to the other women's deaths, all of whom were blond prostitutes murdered in Hollywood. That's not a coincidence."

"But we just agreed that Lucy's *not* the Fallen Angel Killer." Spense took her hands and pulled her up to stand beside him, then looked deeply into her eyes, as if he could force her to come up with an answer. "What are we missing?"

Caitlin went to the board. "I don't know. Let's write our assumptions down in sequence, then try to connect them."

Lucy Lancaster killed Selena Turner.

The murders of Selena Turner, Adrianne Simpson, and Brenda Reggero are all connected.

Lucy Lancaster is not the Fallen Angel Killer.

Spense closed his eyes. "Therefore . . . the Fallen Angel Killer did not murder Selena Turner." His eyes popped open again.

Adrenaline flooded her system, making her skin flush hot. Oh, Lord. "I think I've got it!" She took a sip of water to soothe her dry throat. "Selena Turner was murdered by Lucy Lancaster, not our UNSUB."

"Our mistake has been in assuming Turner was our UNSUB's first victim." Spense seemed remarkably calm, whereas she could hardly contain her nervous energy.

"Turner wasn't his victim. Her murder was his *trigger*! I think we need a new profile."

Spense shook his head. "We'll have to throw out some of it, but the premise is solid. The well-developed fantasy life still fits."

"No. No. No." She leveled an insistent gaze at him. "The sexual fantasies don't fit at all. We're missing the most obvious piece of the puzzle. We're in *Hollywood*. Think about the killer's emphasis on Celebrity X. This whole case is steeped in local culture, and yet we haven't considered that culture's impact on our case at all."

Spense frowned and sent her a look that seemed to say he'd had enough of her baiting. He wanted her to cut to the chase.

Stepping close, she captured his gaze. "We forgot about the Zeitgeist."

He threw his hands up. "Explain yourself. And you can start by defining the term *Zeitgeist*."

She nodded, and tried to think how best to explain herself without sounding like either an egghead or a jackass. She knew Spense was self-conscious about her having more education than he did although she doubted he'd ever admit to such a thing.

"*Zeitgeist* means the spirit of the times—the prevailing way of thinking and being. And thinking just now about all those public figures parading in front of the camera to confess their sin, I had sort of an epiphany. Most of those men were *actors*. Don't you see?"

His jaw worked, and she could see him struggling to focus on her words. Then he took a deep breath, and his gaze shot to hers. He'd won the battle with his impulsivity and, at least for the moment, she had his full attention.

"We profiled someone we knew as the Fallen Angel Killer. An UNSUB who murders and abducts young women, then dumps them in public—make that *very* public places—and poses them salaciously in order to fulfill his elaborate fantasies."

"So whom do you suggest we should've profiled if not him?"

"Are you familiar with a psychologist by the name of George Kelly?"

"Am I supposed to be?"

She shook her head. Even if he'd had a doctorate in psychology he might not have heard of the man—Kelly's theories were that esoteric. "Not at all. But when I was watching the actors this morning, I couldn't help thinking about Kelly's fixed-role-therapy techniques."

Now Spense's face changed, as understanding dawned even before she'd truly explained. "Role therapy. As in, pretend you're someone you're not. Right?"

"Exactly. You see research has shown that behavior doesn't always follow feelings. Sometimes, feelings follow behavior."

"Don't muck up my brain again, sweetheart. Get to the point."

"If you behave as if you feel a certain way, eventually that feeling really takes hold. So let's say you're a shrinking violet, and you've never been able to get the girl."

Dropping into a chair, he smiled. "I can't relate to that, but for your sake, I'll play along."

"You're so shy you can't even speak to this girl you're interested in, much less ask her for a date. So you come to me, and say, 'Dr. Cassidy, please help me feel confident enough to ask Janie for a date.' Then I pull out my fixed-role-therapy playbook."

"Go on." His hand reached for a cookie but quickly pulled back. The man had willpower.

"And I write you out a character sketch—sort of like a screenplay. I write out a party scene, and I cast you in the role of Todd, the most popular, cocky guy in the room. Todd is the guy who gets all the chicks. So you go home and from then on, everywhere you go, you play the role of Todd. It may take a few days, or a few months, but eventually you start to believe you're confident and popular, just like Todd. You start to feel like you *are* him."

"Okay. I'm with you so far. You're saying that in a town full of actors, where playing a role is a way of life, our profile may need some adjusting."

She sighed. "My point is, we're profiling the wrong UNSUB."

He scribbled the words *role-play, actors, fallen angel* on a napkin. Then suddenly a eureka smile split his face. "Dammit. I hate when we have to throw out our main premise."

"Sorry about that." It was a good thing they were on the same page. They both had a clear idea of the killer's salient characteristics, but there was simply no time to develop a formal profile. They were going to have to wing it.

"But I love how smart you are." He grinned. "Jeffers is going to hate us when we tell him we cocked it up."

"Please, don't mind your manners around me, Spense."

"Don't worry, I won't." He stood up and pulled on his jacket. "Let's go break the news to the captain."

"WHAT THE FUCK do you mean we've got to scratch the profile?" The captain slammed a file onto his desktop.

With six hours remaining on the clock, Spense and Caity had come to Jeffers's office to break the news, and things were going pretty much as Spense had anticipated. "Not scratch it exactly, but amend it with regard to the posing of the bodies, the fantasy life . . . and so on. We did warn you from the beginning it might need revision. Our UNSUB isn't really the Fallen Angel Killer."

Jeffers screwed his mouth up as though he were about to spit in Spense's eye. "Either he is or he isn't." He sighed. "Isn't he? Please, just help me understand."

Caity dared a turn at explaining. "It's like those health-care commercials, where an actor holds up a medicine bottle and says *I'm not a doctor, but I play one on TV.* Even though the actor's *not* a doctor, the public has assigned him the same authority. That's how powerful role-play can be. Our UNSUB isn't really a serial killer. He's an actor, *playing the part* of the Fallen Angel Killer—a character scripted by the media. But in real life, his personality is entirely different from the personality of a sexual sadist."

"You mean he's a fucking method actor—like every other two-bit wannabe in this town."

She nodded.

"Well, that's fantastic news. Why didn't you just say so in the first place? I'm looking for a method actor in Hollywood. That really narrows things down. You two have been a big help."

Spense understood how the captain felt, since he'd been there himself just half an hour ago. "You're right. But our UNSUB's not just *any* method actor. He's someone who's compelled to compensate for his own failure by taking on an all-powerful role. He's regained the confidence he either lost or never had from the power the public assigns to the Fallen Angel Killer."

The captain grunted, then said, "If you got a new, improved profile, now's the time to lay it on me."

He and Caity hadn't formalized a new profile, but he felt confident in his assessment. And if Caity disagreed, she'd certainly jump in. "Here goes: Our killer is male, still five-foot-six to five-foot-nine and medium build. Still with an IQ of 120, and still someone who is underutilized in his job and desperately seeking attention."

"Doesn't seem so different to me."

And yet it was. "Initially, we believed the killer to be a sexual sadist with an elaborately developed fantasy life. The semen on Turner's body, and the sexual poses in the other murders seemed to support that. So our UNSUB should've shown some proclivity for hypersexuality. By the use of prostitutes or pornography, for example. But now we know that's not the case."

"So you're saying he's *not* one of Lancaster's johns."

"I highly doubt it. Not only does our UNSUB not have well-developed fantasies, he probably has no fantasies of any kind. At least not any of his own making. He posed the women salaciously because that's what he's seen serial killers do in the movies. Now he's behaving the way he *believes* a killer would behave, in order to feel powerful. He's taken on a different identify because he simply doesn't have one of his own."

"He has poor ego strength," Caity said.

Noting the confusion on the captain's face Spense translated. "Our UNSUB is a blank page. We need to go back and look at every individual with any connection to this case, and look for someone who fits this new profile. We've surely encountered him at some point. He's been on our screen, but we were busy watching the other players while he blended into the woodwork."

"What makes you so certain he's someone we've already been in contact with?"

"I think that's what he meant when he told me on the phone, *you never know me even when I'm right in front of you.* I think he came after Caity and me that night in Griffith Park at least partly because somewhere along the line, he got in our face, and we ignored him. Then there's the cube he sent to me personally. He's screaming at us to pay attention to him. He wants to be seen, but we keep refusing to look his way."

He heard a commotion outside, then Martinez burst through the captain's door. "He called again. Left a rambling message for Kourtney Kennedy. I've got the recording here."

"Then don't just stand there. Play the damn message." The captain came around and propped his hip against the desk, and the room went quiet, as Martinez hit the PLAYBACK button:

"My dear Kourtney, please do me the honor of passing on this message to Agent Spenser. I hope he enjoyed my gift, and I am sorry he won't have the opportunity to thank me in person. Despite the fact that he is the master puzzle solver, and considers it his private domain, I'm afraid you can't solve a puzzle when you don't have all the pieces. The world is my kingdom, not his. So file that in with all your other evidence.

"You see, I am in a class of my own. I am the first rank, the highest order. A genius like me is a master among our species. I have outplayed you all. Try to stop me if you will, but you shall surely be too late to save the maiden fair.

"Tick. Tock."

All eyes turned to Spense, but his mind was whirring, dropping, and sorting the paragraphs into lines, the lines into words and the words into categories.

After a couple of beats, Jeffers was the first to speak. "Fucked up. There's nothing of value here." He turned to Caity. "I like you, Cassidy, I really do, but I have to tell you the truth. Your profile isn't worth a hill of beans. It's constantly changing, and you don't seem to have a clue what's driving this killer. In my opinion, he's loony, plain and simple."

"We changed our profile to fit new evidence as it became available. There's no other way to get to the truth. You can't latch onto a suspect or a profile, then refuse to reevaluate. That's how murderers go free and innocents get hanged." Caity looked almost tall for a moment. "And we do know what drives him—a compulsive need for attention. A need to regain the power he's lost."

Martinez's gaze bounced from Caity to the captain. "I've missed something, haven't I?"

"I'll fill you in later. But know this, our suspect is a blank page," Caity said. "That's why he's taken on this role. Even this rambling message is an example of his acting the part of a crazy, irrational killer. It doesn't make him crazy, though. He's just a highly skilled actor. Look at how carefully he orchestrated the Simpson and Reggero murders. And he left no trace evidence at those crime scenes. An insane person couldn't pull that off."

"Play the tape again, please." Spense was still filtering, and he thought he might be onto something.

Rolling his eyes, the captain got a cup of water from a cooler against the wall. Then he rummaged in his desk until he found a bottle of aspirin and offered it around the room as though it were a pack of gum.

Meanwhile, Martinez played the tape again, then again.

"How many times do we have to listen to this asshole brag that he's a genius?" The captain grumbled, but he looked resigned to his fate.

Spense waved him off. "Play it again. But just the last part this time."

"*A genius like myself is a master among our species.*"
"Again!"

The captain buried his face in his hands, but Martinez hit PLAY anyway. Spense visualized the telling words, drew them in the air with his finger and smiled. "I've got it."

Caity reached her hand out toward him and pulled it back. Martinez leaned in, and the captain rubbed circles on his temple.

"I know who the Fallen Angel Killer is," Spense said.

"Enlighten the rest of us please." The captain looked up, as if half-interested.

Spense didn't bother with a dramatic pause. There simply wasn't time. "Jamie Robb."

The dead silence in the room told Spense the captain wasn't going to send a squad car out to pick up Jamie Robb—not yet. He was going to have to take the time to walk them through this, step by step.

"Are you familiar with the taxonomy system developed by Paul Linnaeus?"

Caity raised an eyebrow. "And this from the man who never heard the word *Zeitgeist*."

"I'm good with classification systems, okay? They're useful for puzzle solving." He pulled out a pad and scribbled the relevant words, then flipped it around. "These are all words contained in the killer's message." To him he could visualize them in red as the message was played, so maybe he had an unfair advantage, but he'd use anything he could to catch this guy. "*Domain, kingdom, phylum* . . . the killer said file, not phylum, but it's close enough. Then comes *class, order, genus* . . . he said genius, but again, it's a good enough fit, and finally, *species*."

"Oh my goodness."

Caity had it, he knew, but there were still two very important people who needed convincing.

"Think back to your high-school biology. This is the Linnaean system for classifying animals. That Rubik's cube the killer sent me had a missing square. I'm supposed to look for what's missing. The taxonomy goes like this—domain, kingdom, order, file, genus, family, species."

"He didn't say the word family." At last the captain unfolded his arms. He even gave Spense a halfhearted smile.

"So the missing piece we need to solve the puzzle is *family*. The word that was left out. We already had the rest of the clues. He gave them to us in his letter. Remember how it was peppered with those strange terms from Robert's Rules?"

Three heads bobbed up and down. Martinez's mouth hung slightly open.

"Now add our new profile—a method actor with no identity of his own. Fallen from his glory days. Suddenly, an angel falls from the sky, and he sees a way to recapture the power, the attention he craves. Now throw in the clues: Rules and family. *Family Rules.*"

Caity then turned to the captain. "You're still not convinced?"

Jeffers folded his arms across his chest.

Spense wasn't sure what she was up to, but he was sure she was onto something.

"I was observing carefully and taking notes the night we interviewed La Grande at Robb's house," Caity said. "Martinez asked both men to state their full names for the record. I'm absolutely certain Robb said his real name was James Robert Linnaeus. *Robert's Rules and the Linnaean Classification system.* I don't think you can get any clearer than that."

Jeffers's head snapped back. "This is too damn crazy to be wrong. It may not hold up in court, but if he's got that young woman held prisoner somewhere, we can't waste any more time.

Martinez, you and Spenser get out to Robb's place in Malibu. Take backup. I'll get on the horn and arrange the warrants."

"We should do a computer search for all his real-estate holdings," Martinez said.

"I'll handle that." Jeffers pumped his fist in the air. "What the hell are you two waiting for? Go get this bastard!"

CAITLIN SUDDENLY FOUND herself alone in the room with Jeffers. *Awkward.* Planting both hands on the desk, the captain pushed himself up and crossed the room to stand beside Caitlin. "Thank you," he said, offering her his hand.

His grasp was firm and warm as they shook, and she couldn't help thinking that this gruff man made a fine police captain. In truth, he was something of a rock—a stubborn, exasperating rock, but still.

"That was some damn fine police work for a shrink. You can be on my team any day." He paused and scratched the back of his neck. "If you want me to put in a word, we're bound to have some openings for a police psychiatrist in LA. If shrinking cop heads is something that interests you, that is."

"I'm flattered. But headshrinking's not really my thing. I'm more into consultation than therapy. I suppose I don't have the patience for it. And, apparently, I like catching the bad guys. It suits me more than I ever thought it would."

He held the door for her. "Well, aren't we a pair? Me and my administrative duties, and you and your consultative ones, hanging out and pushing paper while the others go off and get all the glory."

"A few hours ago, I might have agreed with you, but Spense

made me see that I don't have to be out in the field with a gun to add value. We both have our jobs to do. And the team needs us."

"Speaking of work to do, I better get on those warrants. Don't want to leave our boys standing out front holding their . . . hats . . . in their hands. What will you do today?"

"Since I fully expect Spense and the lieutenant to get their man, I want to be ready for the interrogation when they bring Robb back. I think I'll spend my time boning up on all things Jamie Robb. If I can get deep inside his psyche, I'll have a better chance of persuading him to tell us where he's holding Gina. Unless Spense and Martinez beat me to it." She held up crossed fingers.

"The minute we have him in hand, I'll ring you."

SINCE SPENSE HAD caught a ride with Martinez, Caitlin had to drive the Hummer back to the hotel. It must've been Spense's Y chromosome that made him choose a tank with a manual transmission. She wasn't used to a stick, but after a few clumsy efforts, she got it down. At the Sky Walk, she valeted the car, then hurried up to her room to settle in and hang out the DO NOT DISTURB sign. When she opened her door, she frowned. Something seemed . . . off. Unable to shake the feeling, she slipped her hand in her purse and clasped the butt of her pistol.

Then, casting a glance around the room, she released her breath. There was nothing out of place. She was letting the case get to her. Removing her hand from her purse and her purse from her shoulder, she entered her room, frowning at the mess. The housekeepers hadn't been there, and she'd left her room-service tray from breakfast, as well as the cookie plates on the floor.

Shrugging out of her sweater, she went to the closet to hang up her things. Slowly she opened the door.

Odd.

She didn't recall shoving her dresses to one side. But at least she could clearly see there was no bogeyman lurking in her closet. She stooped and picked a steak knife off the floor. She must've kicked it under the door with all her pacing earlier—and that pink smear. Then she remembered her steak had been so bloody rare she'd nearly sent it back.

Her shoulders dropped, and she suddenly felt the tension of the day drain from her body. She stepped out of her shoes, then sat on the bed and powered up her laptop. Spense and Martinez had their jobs to do, and she had hers. Time to immerse herself in Jamie Robb's world. After navigating to one of her favorite video streaming sites, she typed the words *Family Rules* into the search bar and held her breath. *Come on. Please be there.*

It was a long shot, she knew, but the site carried a lot of old movies and television series—which was why she'd bothered to pay for a membership. She closed her eyes, then popped them open.

Bingo.

The screen showed *Family Rules* seasons one through six, available for streaming. Begin at the beginning, she thought, and downloaded season one. Her heart contracted, at the sight of Jimmy Robb, as he was known back then, a lively, charming little boy, full of pep and personality. After a couple of episodes, she moved on to season two. Already, she could see subtle changes in Jimmy Robb. He'd grown a few inches, but that wasn't it. He played his role as Chester, the *momma's boy*, more convincingly than he had in season one. Ruth, his television mother, had him wrapped around her finger. Tom La Grande played the part of Billy—a character who, unlike Chester, never obeyed Ruth.

By season three, Robb's acting had improved to the point she could barely discern Jimmy Robb's real personality, which had often slipped through in earlier episodes. Of course that was an actor's goal—to become his character. But she couldn't help feeling a sense of loss, as from one episode to the next she watched Jimmy disappear bit by bit. She toggled to an Internet movie database, and noted that was the season Jimmy Robb had won an Emmy. How old was he when he first learned how to make his true self disappear?

Nine.

Her throat tightened, and she popped a lozenge to relieve the discomfort. An annoying burst of canned laughter sounded, as a young Tom La Grande came onto the screen. When she'd watched this show as a child, she'd always focused on Chester, the good brother, and had viewed his as the starring role. But now, watching through adult eyes, she realized her mistake. It was La Grande who'd had the starring role, as a flawed young man who always managed to redeem himself in the end. His character was far more interesting, and she realized for the first time that he got most of the good lines. Chester was merely the straight man for his hilarious big brother. Tom La Grande had been stealing Jimmy Robb's applause since childhood, and little had changed since then. La Grande had become a true star—Robb a barely recognizable has-been. She could see how he might feel invisible whenever the two men were together.

With a sigh, she hit the STOP button. She'd seen enough. The screen paused on an exterior view of the *Family Rules* home, and she tried to remember what she knew about the house. She thought it might be somewhere in the LA area. Through Google, she quickly learned that although the show had been filmed on a studio set, the old house was indeed real, and the exterior shots had been filmed on location in Encino. The house was still standing and still owned by the studio.

Jamie Robb was a method actor—maybe she was a bit of a method profiler. She believed in experiencing the killer's world. Encino was less than half an hour's drive from Hollywood.

Maybe she could take a tour.

A minute later, she found the address, called down to the front desk, and asked them to bring her Hummer around. She might as well enjoy an excursion to Encino while she waited to hear from Spense.

Before pulling out of the hotel, she texted Spense her plans, as well as the address of the *Family Rules* house. She sent the message to his private number rather than his BlackBerry, not wanting to interrupt his mission with Martinez. Minutes later, she found herself zooming down the Ventura Freeway. She rolled down the window, letting her hair blow in the wind, and even though the song, "Ventura Highway," was about a different road altogether, she sang the old tune by America at the top of her voice.

Chapter Twenty-Eight

Saturday, October 12
4:00 P.M.
Three hours remaining
Malibu, California

ON THE RIDE to Robb's Malibu mansion, Martinez and Spense agreed to go in easy. Since Robb had no idea they were onto him, the best way to secure entry into the house was simply to ask to come inside, then suggest he come back to the station for an interview. Spense and Martinez had met Robb's wife on their first visit and had no trouble convincing her to invite them into her living room.

No one believed he had Gina Lola on the premises of his family home, but they'd keep their eyes and ears open while there. Meanwhile, the captain was working on getting a search warrant for this house and all Robb's real-estate holdings. Once they had warrants in hand, a team of officers would swoop in. Unfortunately, with no forensics to implicate Robb, the warrants might not come through.

"I sure wish you'd called first. I could've saved you the trek out to Malibu." Deborah Robb smiled her apology, then narrowed her eyes at her son and pointed upstairs. "Don't you have homework to do?"

"Not really." The boy gawked at them, turning his head sideways as if checking for their guns.

Spense casually slipped his jacket off his hip to give the kid a peek at his pistol.

Mrs. Robb's eyes shifted nervously. "Well, then go clean your room."

"That's why we have maids." The kid seemed more puzzled than bratty. He'd probably never cleaned his room before, so naturally he'd be confused by his mother's sudden insistence he do so.

"One. Two . . ."

"Okay, Mom. I'm not a baby. You don't need to count." Bounding up the stairs two at a time, he reached the landing and glanced back over his shoulder.

Spense gave the boy a nod of acknowledgment. Then his hands balled into fists at his sides, as he thought of Caity, and how she'd watched her father being dragged away in cuffs by the cops. He hated knowing he was about to become the man who took this boy's father away from him. He exhaled a long breath. One big difference: Caity's father had been an innocent man. Jamie Robb was guilty.

With the boy safely tucked away upstairs, Spense returned his attention to Mrs. Robb and was struck by the normality of Jamie Robb's life. His wife was a little younger than he, and twice as attractive, but for a Malibu wife, her looks were nothing special. She had a nice smile that reminded him of his high-school sweetheart. Robb's son was prone to backtalking, but didn't seem spun out of control. Spoiled, sure, but Spense didn't see signs of psychological trauma—like the child of a serial killer might display. And yet, wasn't that expected from their new actor's profile?

Normal family man was just another one of Robb's roles. The good husband. The regular guy. And underneath it all: a big blob of nothing. Without a role to define him, he might as well not exist. Jamie Robb had become invisible, which is why they hadn't seen what was right in front of them the whole time.

"No worries. It's a beautiful area, so we didn't mind the trip. And frankly, it's our own fault for dropping in unannounced." They hadn't called ahead because they didn't want to give Jamie a heads-up, and it was best not to tip their hand to his wife, either. "We'll wait for your husband to come home if that's all right." He swept his hand toward the window. "That's a hell of a view you got there."

"Don't get me wrong, guys, you two are very good company, but somehow I don't think my husband would approve of my having gentlemen as overnight guests. Especially not such nice-looking ones." Her smile faded, and she wiped her hands on her slacks. Maybe she knew more than he'd initially thought.

"You don't expect him tonight?" Martinez asked.

"No. He's in New York City. He's been there since Tuesday."

The night someone had chased Caity and him through Griffith Park. And Wednesday morning, Gina Lola had been taken.

"You're certain he's in New York?" Spense asked. They could be wrong about the guy . . . but he doubted it. Most likely Robb had lied to his wife to cover up his absence while he was out killing, kidnapping, and running people off roads.

"I packed his bags and drove him to the airport myself."

That seemed odd. Wouldn't a driver normally take him? Maybe he'd needed to put on a show for his wife, so she wouldn't question him. "What's his business there?"

Perspiration beaded on her forehead, and she wiped it off with the back of her hand. "I'm not sure I understand what's going on here. What's Jamie's business in New York got to do with this killer you're trying to catch?"

"We just want to clarify a few points with him, and we need to know how to reach him. That's all. No need to worry, ma'am. When do you expect him? We'll come back then."

With a distressed look on her face, she shook her head. "He didn't say. And . . . that's not like him. But he's been so distracted lately."

"Distracted how?"

"Oh, I don't know. What exactly did you want to ask him? He already told you he was with Tom the night that poor Simpson girl was killed, and I thought you'd cleared Tom."

"We have. Just tying up loose ends. But if you don't answer our questions . . . fully . . . it looks like you're hiding something—I'm sure that's not your intention."

Tugging her lower lip between her teeth, she nodded.

"What did you mean when you said your husband's been distracted?"

Spense noted her throat working in a long swallow.

"He hasn't been his usual good-natured self. He's a very kind man, you know." Her eyes glistened. "But . . . he snapped at his own son the other day, and then he . . . he raised his hand like he was about to hit me." She rubbed her hand across her face and wiped away all trace of misery. Jamie wasn't the only one in the family who could act. "Of course, he didn't hit me. Jamie would *never* hurt a woman."

WHEN THEY ARRIVED back at the car, Martinez got on the horn directing men to LAX to interview airline personnel and review surveillance footage. And he gave Jeffers the name of the hotel where Robb was supposed to be staying in New York City. A call would be placed to their brothers in the Big Apple, and officers would be dispatched to his hotel, but Spense would be shocked if they found him there.

He checked his personal cell and frowned.

"Trouble with the little woman?" Hope crept into Martinez's tone.

Spense resisted the urge to snap at the lieutenant. Martinez's flirtation with Caity was irritating as hell, but he'd grown to like the guy. Trust him even. "Caity's gone off on a wild hair. She's on her way to Encino to check out the *Family Rules* house."

"I forgot about that place, but it seems like a harmless enough thing for her to be doing."

"Nothing Caity does is harmless. She has a knack for finding trouble." Maybe Martinez's interest in her would come in handy. "I'm thinking I wouldn't mind a side trip to Encino. It might be interesting to see the house for ourselves."

"Do I look like your chauffeur?" But Martinez hit the NAV button, and said, "Malibu to Encino driving directions." His jaw tensed, and Spense could tell he didn't like the idea of Caity out poking around on her own any more than he did—which was not a comfort in the least.

Chapter Twenty-Nine

Saturday, October 12
5:00 P.M.
Two hours remaining
Encino, California

CAITLIN ARRIVED AT Durango Road in Encino within twenty minutes of leaving the Sky Walk. Traffic had been miraculously light given the hour, and she counted herself lucky. She parked on the street, taking care not to block the drive, got out of the Hummer, and admired the house from the curb. The scent of roses from the garden mingled with her nostalgia, sweetening the evening air. This wasn't just a piece of Jamie Robb's childhood—it was a piece of hers, too.

Closing her eyes, she put herself in Jimmy Robb's shoes, coming to work every day before the sun was up. Memorizing lines. Getting her schooling in between scenes, and her only friend—a kid who upstaged her at every turn. Then it was home to bed, and up early to do it all over again the next day. Her body tensed with resentment.

Her life sucked.

Except, of course, for her handlers, feeding her bull about how great she was day after day. She let out a breath and smiled. No. It wasn't bull after all. She really was great—or at least the kid she played on television was. Why else would people point at her on the streets and beg for her autograph? Why else would they bring her whatever she asked for whenever she asked? Even in the middle of the night, if she wanted tacos, her mom would send for someone, and *poof,* there'd be tacos. And no one ever punished her. Once she'd slapped her teacher on the set, just to see if she could get away with it. And you know what happened? The teacher got fired. Because her mom said the teacher must've done something to provoke her.

She grabbed her stomach. Her belly ached as though she hadn't eaten for days even though she'd just filled up at the craft table. She had everything she wanted, but still there was a big empty pit inside her.

The sound of a car horn blasted nearby, and she jumped, jolting back to reality. But yeah, Caitlin could certainly see where Jamie Robb had gone wrong.

Up at the house, the curtains were drawn, and the drive was empty. She noted no signs of activity. Okay, so there was no tour this time of day.

But she'd come all this way. Might as well have a look around. She ambled up to the front porch. The spacious colonial was a quintessential all-American home, with tasteful pillars out front, yellow shingles, and redbrick accents. She pressed her face to the glass and peered between the gaps in the curtains into the living room. Inside, the house was empty. No furniture—and trash was scattered on the floor.

Her palms started to tingle.

Obviously, there were no tours here *any* time of day.

The house was unoccupied.

She hit Spense on speed dial, this time on his BlackBerry, but he didn't pick up. At the tone she left a message: "I'm at the *Family Rules* house, you've got the address already. The house is empty. Robb *may* have access to it, since it's owned by his old studio. I know it's a long shot, but I think there's a slim chance he brought Gina here. If there's a patrol car in the area, please ask Martinez to send it out. We don't have much time left. I'm going to take a closer look around."

She slipped her cell inside her purse, opting to leave the zipper open. She was glad she had her Ruger with her, just in case. And even gladder she hadn't rung the bell and loudly announced her presence. If Robb *was* on the premises somewhere, which she doubted, there was a good chance he hadn't seen her. After all, she certainly hadn't seen him, or anyone else for that matter.

She crept around to the back of the house. The chances Gina was actually here seemed small. It would be foolish to risk bringing her to a busy neighborhood like this one. But then again, this place meant something to Robb. If their profile was correct, he wasn't the type who'd have prepared an elaborate hideaway for his victims years in advance. He was only an actor playing at being a serial killer—a beginner, just learning the ropes. Her guess was that after he'd made the decision to kidnap Gina, he'd have prepared a place to keep her, but it would be one he could make ready fast.

Now that she thought about it, on the off chance Robb had

used *Kidnapping for Dummies* as his textbook, she'd rather have her gun ready than inside her purse. She pulled out her pistol, and with her hand firmly around the grip, tried to remember the way she'd seen Spense approach a potentially dangerous target. He always led with his pistol—that much she knew, so she stuck hers out in front, peering ahead of her before she let her body follow her gun. It didn't take long for her to develop a system of sectioning off one area to clear at a time, then creeping forward and clearing another. The studio had kept the place in good condition. The manicured yard blended well into the residential setting—but left her little cover, since there were only a few scattered shrubs and trees to hide behind if the need arose.

Focus.

Her ears pricked at a scratching noise. She tried to localize the sound, but it seemed to come from beneath the earth. She shivered as an image of a hand reaching up from the grave and pulling her into a tomb flashed across her mind.

No more horror movies for her. She heard panting—it was her. For goodness sake. It was still daylight. A patrol car was on its way. And this was nothing but a wild-goose chase anyway. But . . . maybe she ought to turn around. Yes. She'd wait for the patrol car out front. That was the sensible thing to do. But she heard that scratching sound again. Then . . . something more, a high-pitched noise.

A scream!

It was muffled, but . . . she recognized the cry for help.

No time to lose.

Gina might be inside that house, and with no sign of Robb, she had to act *now*. Spense might have him in cuffs *or* he could be headed here now.

Tick. Tock.

She slipped open the screen door and tried the doorknob.
Locked.

With one hand, she pulled out a credit card. With the other, she gripped her pistol—so hard her knuckles ached.

Yes!

She'd just opened the back door of the *Family Rules* house with her Macy's card. She tossed it back in her purse and snuck inside the doorway. Keeping her gun out front, she cleared the rooms one by one. By now, she was beginning to feel more comfortable with the process. Her heart rate, which had been giving her a fit, slowed down—a notch. Still no sign of Robb. To her right, a stairwell loomed. It had to lead to the basement.

She came to a sudden halt.

If Gina was in the basement, who was to say Robb wasn't down there with her? She should get the hell out of here and wait for backup.

"Help me!"

The voice sounded clear and close. Like hope had given its owner strength.

"Help me! I'm down here!"

And that's when her heart took over. Caitlin stuck her gun out front, ran down the stairs, and slipped through the basement door. This could be her one chance to free Gina. She had to take it.

Once inside, with only a small, high window to let daylight in, she could barely see. But after a minute, her eyes adjusted. As noiselessly as possible, she eased one foot in front of the other. But there was no hiding the creak of the old floorboards beneath her weight. Her eyes went to a long silver chute.

Her pulse thrummed in her ears, and her knees threatened to buckle. What the hell was that thing?

A cage.

He had Gina in a cage.

Chills rippled across her arms as she approached the back of the silver tube. She could hear the girl sobbing. Unable to bear the cries even one second longer, she raced around the cage, then clapped a hand over her mouth. There, huddled behind steel bars was a young blond woman. Wetness reflected light off the shiny floor. From the burning scent of ammonia assaulting her nostrils, Caitlin knew Gina lay curled in a pool of her own urine.

"Gina!" She whispered urgently. "I'm going to get you out of here. Do you know where he is?"

Rising on all fours, as if she really were an animal, Gina reached her fingers through the bars. "No, but I thought I heard him leave the house awhile ago."

Heart splitting in her chest, Caitlin reached out and touched her fingers to Gina's. A chain snaked through the bars, and a padlock secured it in place. *How* she was going to get Gina out was a question she hadn't yet asked herself. She bit her lower lip, tasting blood. The gate opened vertically, like the kind on a moving van; not side to side like the kind on a cell door. She could push the gate up—though it looked heavy, she had no doubt the adrenaline coursing through her veins would give her the strength she needed to raise the thing—but the lock . . . She tapped her Ruger on her thigh.

No way around it. She was going to have to shoot the damn padlock off.

"Get back and cover your ears," she ordered.

Gina crept to the back of the cage.

On a hard inhale, Caitlin stuck the barrel of her pistol inches from the lock. A split second later, she heard a noise behind her.

Before she could turn, a powerful hand grabbed her wrist, wrenching her gun up and away.

Boom!

Her arm jerked from the force of the blast, and her ears rang painfully as the shot ricocheted off the side of the cage. An elbow locked around her throat. Then a hand grabbed her by the hair. Her eyes rolled up, and she saw his face.

Jamie Robb slammed her head into the bars of the cage, over and over . . . and over . . .

SPENSE'S BLACKBERRY BUZZED with the sound of a voice mail dropping. He hadn't heard a call come through, but his reception had been spotty between here and Robb's house in Malibu. He grimaced and nearly tossed the thing out the window. He'd missed a call from Caity. Playing the voice mail back, he had to strain to hear the broken-up message above the outside noise. "Roll the damn window up," he told Martinez, then played it again.

Shit.

"What's up?"

"She's reached the *Family Rules* house, and she's poking around on her own. She says it's *deserted*. We need to get a patrol car out there now."

Martinez ordered a unit to assist, then keeping his eyes on the road and his foot on the gas, said, "Relax, we'll be there in less than five minutes."

Spense dialed Caity, but she didn't pick up. On the second try he left a message. "Do not enter that house. Just wait for the squad car. I repeat, do not enter that house."

Chapter Thirty

Saturday, October 12
6:00 P.M.
Sixty minutes remaining
Encino, California

A LIGHT TOUCH feathered across Caitlin's forehead, and an exquisite, throbbing pain accompanied each wave of motion as her head rocked back and forth. This must be some new form of brain-sloshing torture.

"Please don't die. Please don't die," an angelic voice pleaded.

More rocking.

Hell no, she wasn't going to die. But if the rocking didn't stop soon, she was definitely going to be sick. "I need to sit up." Her eyes flew open, and the hand that had been stroking her suddenly withdrew.

Gina Lola smiled down at her, then eased Caitlin's head off her lap, helping her slowly into a sitting position. "Thank God you're not dead."

She filled her lungs with a deep breath and nearly gagged on the smell of urine. But the odor also acted as a form of smelling salts. That assault on her nose, plus the sound of Gina's voice and the termination of that relentless rocking brought her back to herself just in the nick of time—her brain had been dangerously close to turning into a milkshake. Then her memory returned, along with a rush of emotion. Jamie Robb had pounded her already tender head against the steel cage until she'd passed out. Well, now she was awake again. She was sore, and scared, and . . . pissed off.

"How long was I out?" she asked.

"I'm not sure. It seemed like forever, but I don't think it's been more than a few minutes. I'm so happy you didn't die. He'll be back though. He always comes back."

"I'm glad, too." She took Gina's hand. "Do you know where he went?"

Gina pointed to the ceiling. "Up there. Sometimes he goes out. But he'll check on us again. He has a routine. When he's in the house, he comes down every hour or so. We probably have at least a half hour, maybe more until . . . until he comes back."

"Then we've got to get out of here, now."

Gina shook her head, making Caitlin want to brace her face in her palms to keep it from moving any more than necessary. "I'm afraid."

"If you're scared, that means you haven't given up. Fear can help us survive."

Gina's silent tears turned to earnest sobs.

Something Caitlin said must've triggered all of that emotion to burst through Gina's defenses. "It's okay. I didn't mean to upset you. I just mean fear's not a bad thing necessarily, as long as we control it rather than letting it control us."

Sitting cross-legged next to Caitlin, Gina threw her arms around her neck, then pressed her head against Caitlin's chest. The trust she felt as Gina clung to her, the vulnerability in Gina's embrace, made Caitlin's whole body tremble with the absolute need to make the right decisions and from the certainty that she had no idea what those right decisions might be.

So this is what it was like to be a parent. Until this very moment, she'd never imagined herself as a mother. Never tried to put herself in her mom's shoes, which seemed very strange since her job was to empathize with others. She'd always felt so keenly for her father. *Why* hadn't she worked harder to understand her mother? Her throat contracted to the point she couldn't get her words out.

Now is not the time.

She forced herself to breathe until the spasms in her chest and throat relaxed. "Gina . . ."

Another, louder sob, followed by a keening wail. "Please. I'm scared of dying, but that's not why I-I can't stop crying."

Caitlin tightened her arms around the girl. What could be more terrifying than death?

"I don't want to die pretending to be someone I'm not. And I'm *not* Gina Lola. If I'm going to die today, I want someone to know who I really am. I want *you* to know who I am." She pulled her head up. Her tears tracked lines through the grime on her face. "My name is Susan Smith."

"Susan Smith," Caitlin repeated. "That's a fine name. A name to be proud of."

Then a shaky smile broke across the girl's face. "You really think so?"

"I do," she said, her ears pricking at the sound of pacing above them. She sat up straight and took the young woman by the shoulders. "Susan, I want you to listen to me, and I want you to believe me when I tell you *he* doesn't have the power."

"But he has the *gun* . . . and the keys."

She shrugged. "True. And I'm not discounting those things. Those are two very good reasons for us to be frightened of him. But listen for a minute, then tell me what you hear."

"I hear him pacing, back and forth and back and forth. He does that all day long sometimes."

"Exactly." She waited for Susan to catch on. Susan was a smart woman, and Caitlin wanted to get her thinking on her own . . . just in case something happened to Caitlin.

"Oh my God. *He's* afraid, too." She raised her hands in the air, like a member of the church of Hallelujahs. "If he had all the power, he wouldn't be scared. Do you think he's afraid of the police, or of us?"

"Both, I'd say." If he wasn't worried, why keep checking on Susan every hour? "He can lock us up. He can even kill us. But he can't take away who we are. We're not going to wave a white flag just because he's got a pistol and the key. He's scared of two tiny little women like us. And he's the one with the gun! I don't think he's thinking straight at all—but we are. We're not going to let fear muddle our brains, and that means we've got a decent chance to escape."

"But how?"

"We can't run as long as we're locked in this cell, and we can't break out on our own, that's for sure. So we have to get *him* to open the door. And when he does, you run like hell. I'll grab his keys, shove him inside and lock him up. Your job will be to not look back. Your job will be to run."

"I will run."

"Promise me you won't look back." Then she saw something like guilt wash over Susan's features, and she added in her most severe tone, "I don't want to have to worry about you while I'm trying to get out of here."

"I won't look back. I promise." Susan nodded earnestly. "But . . . how are we going to get him to open the gate?"

"I haven't figured that out yet." She sat down and rested her back against the side of the cage. "Any ideas? You know a lot about men. If he were one of your clients, how would you get the upper hand?"

"With a different guy, I'd get him talking. A few of my johns are the all hat and no cattle type. Sometimes, the more you listen to a man, the longer he drones on, until eventually, he's satisfied, and you didn't have to open your legs or your mouth either." Her shoulders dropped, and she looked away. "But I don't think that's going to work with Charlie."

"You mean Charlie Chaplin." Caitlin's brain was firing at breakneck speed, and she realized right away, from the story Gina had told to Kourtney Kennedy, she was referring to the time she met Robb in the museum. The time when he'd disguised himself. "Getting him talking still might work. If he didn't say anything before, it's probably because he was playing the role of a silent film star. He's a *method actor*—that means he has to stay in character at all times."

As they plotted, the footsteps ceased crisscrossing the ceiling and began heading in one direction.

"He's coming! But it's too soon." Susan's pupils dilated with fear.

Tick tock.

Caitlin thought there was about an hour left on the clock, but maybe he'd realized he was the one who was running out of time. Maybe he thought he'd make good on his promise to turn Gina Lola into a fallen angel ahead of schedule.

Well, fuck that.

Caitlin's plan all along had been to get inside Robb's head and use it to her advantage. That's why she'd watched all those *Family Rules* episodes. Just because she was the one behind bars was no reason to abandon that strategy. Surely, she could come up with something. She dropped her face into her hands, visualizing the *Family Rules* scenes she'd watched one by one. With her fingers, she rubbed her pounding temples.

Concentrate.

She pictured the cast: Chester, Billy, Ruth . . .

Ruth!

She jerked her chin up and touched Gina on the shoulder. "I have an idea. Whatever I say, no matter how strange it seems, I want you to play along with me. Just follow my lead, and when he opens this cage . . ."

"Run like hell."

"Exactly! I want you to pretend my name is Ruth, and say my name as many times as you can. All you have to do is remember that I'm Ruth . . . and when you get the chance, run hard and fast as you can."

"Okay, *Ruth*." Susan sounded almost happy, and Caitlin knew she trusted her. Caitlin could only hope she'd made the right decision. Because if her trick made Robb angry . . .

The door creaked opened, and heavy steps thudded down the stairs. Then Jamie Robb ambled over to the cage and planted his hands on his hips. In one hand, he held her Ruger. In the other, a key. "Good to see you, Dr. Cassidy. Though since you're my guest, even though I didn't invite you, perhaps we ought to be on a first-name basis. You won't mind if I call you Caitlin."

"Her name is Ruth," Gina rushed in without prompting.

Caitlin shot Susan an approving look. Caitlin was about to take on the role of Ruth, the mother in *Family Rules*, putting her faith in her own theory.

His lips curled away in a snarl. "No. She's Caitlin. Dr. Caitlin Cassidy. And both of you may address me as the Fallen Angel Killer."

"But that's not who you really are," Caitlin said with all the authority she could muster.

"Of course, I'm him. You're in a cage, aren't you?"

"You may have done a good job pretending, and putting us in a cage was an Oscar-worthy touch, but you're no killer."

"I *am* the Fallen Angel Killer. When Tom didn't show up for my ceremony, I simply couldn't go on being that Caspar Milquetoast, Jamie Robb. Tom was supposed to be my best friend, but it was all an act. He never cared about me at all. And then I saw the angel fall from the sky—and I finally understood my destiny."

"You're wrong, Chester. Billy has to care about you. He's your brother."

He shook his head. "I'm not Chester! I'm the killer who has all of Hollywood running scared."

"Think what you're saying, darling. *Chester* is the one people adore. Chester is the one who got that star on the walk of fame. Chester is my loving son. My son who would never harm me or any of my friends."

His brow drew down, and he prowled the room. When he came back to the cage his eyes were glassy, disoriented.

"Not there, Chester." Caitlin pointed to a spot on the floor to his right. "You've missed your mark."

He sidestepped to where she'd pointed.

Her stomach knotted, and she had to clasp her hands together to stop them from shaking, but she couldn't stop now. This was *working*. "Chester, this lion's cage is filthy."

He tugged at his hair. "Shut up."

"Don't tell me to shut up, Chester. I'm your mother, and you need to let me out of this cage right now. Hurry, before Dad comes home."

"When will he be home, Ruth?" Susan asked.

She was so smart! She'd chimed in right on time.

Robb put his hands over his ears. "Shut up! I told you to shut up!"

Caitlin made a *tsk tsk* sound. "Chester, stop being disrespectful. Hurry, before your father gets home."

"My father?"

"Chester. Pay attention, please. It's *your* line. Did you forget?"

"My line?" His eyes took on a panicked glaze. "I-I suppose I might have."

"Don't worry, dear. I'll help you remember. You see, I say *let me out of this cage before your father gets home*, and then you say, *oh Mother. Billy put me up to it*."

"Oh, Mother. Billy put me up to it," Robb chanted.

"And then I say, *your brother is a scamp*. That's your cue. *Scamp* is your cue."

"To do what? I c-can't remember. I must've missed rehearsal."

"Your cue to take that key in your hand and let us out." She did her best to imitate Ruth's mannerisms and voice. "Hurry up, Chester. Dad will be so mad if he finds out you locked me in a cage. And you know *Billy* never gets in trouble."

He stumbled to the door, the key shaking in his hand.

"Hurry up, Chester!" The sound of the key tumbling in the lock made her heart leap to her throat, then her gaze fell on Susan.

Steel grated against steel as Robb pushed the gate up.

"Good boy!" She turned to Susan, and mouthed, *Run!*

Susan bolted out of the cage, and Caitlin followed. The moment Susan blasted past him, Robb's mouth contorted in anger. True to her word, Susan raced up the stairs.

She didn't look back.

Robb turned, but Caitlin wasn't going to fail now. Susan was not going to die in this basement. Caitlin pounced on Robb's back. He flipped her off of him and smacked her in the cheek with his fist. Her head flew back, and her knees cracked against the ground when she fell on all fours. Then she smiled. Those were Susan's footsteps she heard overhead. He'd never catch up to her now.

"You bitch!" He screamed, then grabbed her by the hair, dragging her toward the cage.

She wasn't going back in there.

She reached up, got hold of his wrists and yanked hard. He went flying onto the ground, then rolled on top of her. Straddling her chest, he balled his hands into fists and started flailing away.

"Chester, please, let me up."

"Ruth?"

The world was slipping away from her. She tried to speak, but couldn't.

His fist came down hard on her chest. "You're not Ruth. I'm not Chester."

She could barely breathe, but she managed to get her words out, "Tell me who you are. I *want* to understand." And she really did. Despite everything, she wished she could reach that part inside him that was real. But it was buried too deep. Or maybe it never existed at all.

"I'm *me*! Is it so much to ask for someone to see that?"

Wham!

He hit her again.

"I see you, Jamie. Please . . ." she gasped. "Think of your wife, and your boy. They love you, Jamie."

He leaned over her, buried his face in her hair, his knees squeezing her sides so hard she couldn't wriggle out from under him. She tried to get air beneath her shoulders to buck him off, but she was too weak.

His hands came around her throat.

She had to keep him talking. If she could just stay alive a little while longer, help would come. Her chest heaved, and something wet dribbled out of her mouth. It tasted tangy—like blood.

As he tightened his grip, his face blurred above her.

Keep him talking.

A fiery pain ignited in her throat, but she managed to whisper the only question she could think of, "Who is Celebrity X?"

Abruptly releasing her neck, he laughed. It was a sound of pure poisonous hate. But he'd stopped choking her . . . for now.

"There is no Celebrity X."

"I-I don't understand."

"And I thought you were so clever." He grabbed her throat and began squeezing again. "Let me enlighten you since you're too stupid to figure it out for yourself. Celebrity X is anyone and everyone who ever screwed me over in this town. Celebrity X is Tom La Grande. Celebrity X is the fucking Waxed museum that made a statue for every star *except* me. Celebrity X is every academy member who passed me over, year after year. Do you get it yet? Celebrity X is *Hollywood*."

SPENSE HAD BEEN dialing Caity nonstop, but she wasn't picking up. He and Martinez had beaten the two squad cars that were en route to Robb's place, and as he leapt out of the car, he tried to comfort himself with the thought that this was merely a matter of her cell phone not getting reception. Maybe her battery was dead. He could think of any number of reasons she hadn't answered her phone, but that didn't stop his jaw from grinding or his pulse from jumping. One good thing, though, the more adrenaline he had pumping through his body, the more his focus sharpened.

And right now, he was in the zone, on high alert, tuned in to every sound that didn't belong. As they rounded the corner of the house, heading for the back, he heard racing footsteps. Then suddenly, a blond woman burst around the corner. She smacked into Martinez with a loud thud.

Spense didn't stop to look after the blond or the lieutenant. Bringing his knees up, he hauled ass, reaching the open back door even before he exhaled. Pistol out front, he entered the home, charging through its rooms until he spotted a stairway leading to the basement. Without clearing the stairs, he barreled down them and crashed through the basement door. A figure leapt off a woman on the ground, and reached for something beside him. *Caity!*

Gun!

He pointed his pistol center mass.

"Police! Freeze!" He heard Martinez call out directly behind him.

Boom!

A muzzle flashed, and the stench of gunpowder filled the air. His head swiveled in time to see Martinez stumble backward, then crumple to the floor.

Caity moaned, and his heart vaulted to his throat. She was *alive.*

Just as Robb's hand jerked, Spense fired, aiming far enough to the side to give Caity a safety margin. Robb grabbed his arm. His gun clattered to the floor. Spense's eyes homed in on the pistol flying across the floor. Just when it skipped over the threshold of a large silver box, Spense recognized the object for what it was—a cage.

A fucking lion's cage.

A split second of surprise slowed Spense's reflexes enough to allow Robb to dash past him. Following Robb's gaze to the gun lying on the cage floor, Spense high-jumped, reaching for the bottom of the gate. At the same time, Robb dove for his weapon.

"*Noo!*" Caity screamed.

Spense's gaze locked on the gate as it crashed down on Jamie Robb's neck with a gruesome *pop.* Then Robb's body bucked twice . . . and went limp. His head lay at an unnatural angle from his body as blooded pooled around him. Sinew and muscle gaped from his neck wound. The fallen gate had all but decapitated him.

A single heartbeat of hesitation from Spense had proved fatal for Jamie Robb, but Spense had no regrets. Rushing to Caity's side, he pulled her to him in a tight embrace, then gathered her in his arms and lifted her off the ground, ready to carry her to safety even as tears streamed down his face. He'd almost been too late.

Suddenly, from across the room, he heard a loud, guttural moan.

"Shit." Martinez struggled to a sitting position and tapped his Kevlar vest with his fist. He made the sign of the cross, and muttered, "I think I busted a rib. Is somebody going to help me get up or what?"

"In just a second, buddy," Spense called back. Then he dipped his head to Caity's and pressed his lips to hers.

Chapter Thirty-One

Saturday, October 12
10:00 P.M.
Encino, California

CAITLIN POWERED OFF her cell and inhaled a deep breath. The pungent antiseptic odors in the Encino Community Hospital ER, where the medics had transported Martinez, Susan, and her might be aversive to some, but they reminded Caitlin of her days as an intern—a time in her life she'd found to be exhilarating. There was no question she had a bit of adrenaline junkie in her.

Then her throbbing head and aching chest reminded her she'd had enough excitement for the time being. The good news was it look liked everyone was going to survive their injuries—except of course for Robb. Terrible as it had been to watch that cage slam down on his neck, she couldn't deny she felt relieved he could never hurt anyone again.

She shifted from one position to the other, but that did little to dispel the discomfort of the cold metal exam table against her bare legs. Setting her cell down, she managed a smile for Spense, who'd just returned from checking in on Martinez down the hall.

He sat down beside her on the ER exam table. "He'll live."

Despite Spense's gruff declaration, she knew he'd been worried about the lieutenant by the way he kept checking for updates on his condition, and the *man hug* he'd given him in the waiting room.

As for Caitlin, her interaction with Susan Smith had made her realize how badly she wanted to work things out with her mother. "I hope you're happy," she said to Spense. "While you were gone I called my mother. I gave her a complete rundown on my condition and promised to check in at least once a week."

Turning his palms up, he said, "I'm happy if you're happy. You know me, I don't like to interfere."

"Is that so? I suppose you're not interested in interfering with Thanksgiving then. I told Mom we'd both be there. She's already planning a special tofu dish for you."

"I never turn down tofu."

Then she shivered, and Spense drew a blanket around her shoulders. "You still cold, babe?"

Her chattering teeth must've given her away. "Guess I'm still a little shocky." She was being admitted for overnight observation— again.

He swirled his hand in the air. "Open up, and I'll keep you warm until the doctor gets back."

She spread her arms, and Spense slid closer so they could share the warmth of the wool.

"How old do you think that kid is, anyway?"

Caitlin had been examined by an intern. "Probably around twenty-seven. Be nice. Everyone's a beginner at some point."

"Yeah, well, I don't know if I want you to be a learning experience for this guy. Are you sure he did the right thing using staples instead of stitches?"

"Staples are standard for scalp wounds. And I'm happy to pay it forward. I remember all the patients who were brave enough to act as guinea pigs for me."

Spense lifted her hand to his lips. "I hope you realize that you getting hurt is getting really old really fast. If it were up to me—"

"That's just it, Spense, it's *not* up to you." She let out a long breath. This wasn't exactly the perfect place to hash out their differences, but the truth was, there was never going to be a perfect time and place. They might as well get everything out in the open right here and now. Lord knew they could be waiting hours for a bed to free up for her upstairs.

She squeezed his hand. "Look, I get it. I understand that you feel protective of me. Because the truth is, I feel the same way about you. The thought of you getting hurt is . . . well, it's something I can't even bear to think about."

"That's different."

"It's not. And if we're going to both work together and *fraternize* outside of work, as you put it awhile back, I think we need to set some ground rules."

"Such as?"

"Such as you have to stop trying to save me from myself. If I screw things up with my mother, for example, that's on me."

He raised his right hand. "Scout's honor. I'll stay out of the middle of your family disputes . . . unless you invite me in, of course. But I'm still allowed to step in if you're being held prisoner by a serial killer."

She could tell he was trying hard to lighten the mood, but the look on his face was serious.

"Okay . . . life-and-death situations are an exception to the *no interference* rule. But you can't get your nose out of joint every time a man pays attention to me. Especially not when that man might be someone you'll need to have your back out in the field."

"You're a beautiful, incredible, sexy woman—I guess that's my cross to bear. What if I promise not to deck anybody for noticing? Would that be good enough?"

A smile tugged at the corners of her mouth. "I guess it's a start. Just keep things professional when we're on the job."

"I promise to try. And if you want ground rules, we can have ground rules." He shrugged. "But the thing is, whether you want to admit it or not, this is a done deal. What I feel for you is real, Caity. And keeping me at arm's length isn't going to stop me from making an ass of myself now and then. So you might as well accept the fact that I'm not giving up on us."

She didn't *want* him to give up on them. And sometimes she made an ass of herself, too. She knew that.

Turning her face up, she put her arms around his neck, letting the blanket slide to the table. His lips were parted, and she could feel his warm breath on her cheek. All she had to do was turn her face a quarter of an inch and open her mouth . . . With his finger, he lifted her chin higher, until his face was so close to hers it made her ache. He wet his lips, but didn't press his mouth to hers. He was waiting for her to come to him.

Be brave.

Bringing her palm to his cheek, she drew him to her. And then, finally, his lips were on hers. His tongue swept hers, so gently, but at the same time, she sensed something demanding. He was urging her to surrender, to trust him, not just sometimes, but always. Then a soft cry bubbled up in her throat—because she understood that this wasn't just a kiss.

It was a question.

And her answer was *yes*.

Chapter Thirty-Two

Tuesday, October 15
9:00 A.M.
Hollywood, California

CAITLIN GLANCED AROUND Jeffers's office, where she was gathered with the captain, Martinez, and Spense for a final debriefing, and realized that though her time here had been short, she was going to miss Hollywood.

"I have to give you credit, Dr. Cassidy. Anyone who can find the missing woman the whole force is out looking for, all on her own, then talk a serial killer into letting them both out of a lion's cage has got it going on." Jeffers gave her a mock salute.

Her cheeks grew warm. This had been a team effort, and she didn't deserve to be singled out for praise. "Thanks, but you give me too much credit. If it hadn't been for Lieutenant Martinez and

Agent Spenser and all the investigative legwork by the team, neither Susan Smith nor I would be alive."

"Well, at least let me say it's good to see you out of the hospital . . . *again*. But you and Martinez both need to take it easy for a
while." He turned to his lieutenant. "I hear you've been pushing
medical to release you for duty, but I'm not taking you back until
those ribs heal. Understood?"

"Yes, sir." Martinez walked to Caitlin's side, then rested his
hand on her shoulder. "Agent Spenser had better look after you,
Cassidy, because if he doesn't, you got my number."

She saw Spense's body stiffen, but he didn't say a word. Just
smiled and let the jab pass. Which was only right given the fact
Martinez had taken a bullet, albeit to a Kevlar vest, for both of
them. Besides, she knew Spense and Martinez had a bit of a bro
thing going on even though neither of them would admit it.

Spense clapped Martinez between his shoulders. "I appreciate
your having my back, buddy, but don't worry about a thing. *Cassidy* and I will be looking out for each other. Am I right, Caity?"

It must've been hard for him to acknowledge that protective-
ness needed to be a two-way street. All of those differences of
theirs seemed to be ironing themselves out—although she wasn't
exactly thrilled Spense had already arranged a Hummer for the
new case coming up in Dallas.

"I was glad to hear Lucy Lancaster pled guilty to second-degree
murder," she said, changing the subject not so subtly.

"That'll save the taxpayers a bundle." Jeffers swept his hand
across his eyebrows. "And we're looking the other way on Susan
Smith. Whatever she's done wrong in the past. Nobody here wants
to see her pay more than she already has."

"I heard she's been reunited with her family," Caitlin said. "Would you pass my number on to her, in case she ever feels like talking?"

"Will do."

Silence fell over the room. Saying good-bye was much harder than she'd expected it to be.

Finally, the captain broke the awkwardness. "I'm still amazed by the way you talked your way out of that cage. Would you say Robb had multiple personalities, and you managed to flip him out of one and into another?"

"Not at all. On the contrary, I don't believe Robb had *any* personality. He'd been acting since childhood, and over the years, he lost his sense of self. At least that's my theory. He was a true method actor, living and dwelling inside the heads of his characters. Even as Jamie Robb, he was playing the role of a hardworking, reliable family man. He played that role so perfectly his family never suspected that underneath the façade beat the heart of a desperate man. Imagine growing up with all that adulation from the public. Eventually, you'd come to rely upon it, need it to get you through life. Then one day, you're not a cute child star any longer, and *poof*, it all goes away."

Martinez shook his head. "Robb had every advantage. It's hard for me to look on either his life, or his death, as a tragedy."

"Not a tragedy, maybe, but he did lead a sad, lonely existence. He coped with the loss of his fame for a long time, but then when no one showed up for his star ceremony, not even his one true friend, it was the last straw. He felt invisible, and he just snapped."

The captain was quiet, attentive; and Spense took over for her. "We believe he murdered Addie Simpson first, because she was Tom's girl. Susan Smith, aka Gina Lola, was unknown to Robb, but he got Lucy Lancaster's number from Tom's cell on one of the many occasions his buddy was passed out drunk or stoned. Then he had a hoot calling Lancaster up pretending to be Ryan Winters and asking her to send a sweet blonde over to Waxed. But when Susan fought back, it caught Robb off guard. He didn't even chase after her, because he had no idea what to do when she went off script. After that, he went back to a girl he knew from Tom's list—Brenda Reggero—and stayed away from Lancaster."

"He stuck with the blondes to copy Turner's murder. Even I can see that," the captain said. "And it makes sense Robb got the numbers he needed because he was in a trusted position with La Grande and had access to his cell-phone contacts. I'm assuming the night he alibied La Grande, claiming they'd been talking all night at the Beverly Hilton, La Grande was actually passed out cold, giving Robb the opportunity to meet Reggero at Waxed. What I still don't understand, though, is how Robb tracked Susan Smith down at that motel. And where the hell did he get a lion's cage?"

"The cage matches one reported missing from a props warehouse at Robb's old studio—it must've been the closest he could come to a prison cell. As for tracking his prey, we think he must've followed Kourtney Kennedy to the motel, then waited for her to leave before nabbing Susan." Spense winked at Martinez. "Speaking of Kourtney, I hear she might be free for dinner. Maybe you should give her a call."

Caitlin knew Spense was teasing Martinez, referring to the fact that, even though Kourtney had obstructed the investigation, the ADA had decided not to press charges, given the fact she later proved invaluable in catching the killer.

"Me take *her* to dinner?" Martinez said, so forcefully Caitlin wondered if he protested a little too much. "No way. But what I am going to do with all this rotten medical leave is find myself a nice tropical island. I hear Tahiti's nice. Maybe I'll join the two of you on that trip you've been talking about."

Spense threw his leg out, as if blocking Martinez from approaching Caitlin. "We're not going to Tahiti. At least not right now. I'm afraid we've got urgent business in Dallas. You remember Dutch Langhorne?"

"The hostage negotiator?" Martinez looked puzzled, and well he might if he'd picked up on the strange vibes between Dutch and Spense. Those two had some kind of history that Caitlin wasn't privy to, but she figured she'd find out about it soon enough.

"Unfortunately, on Sunday night, the day after Dutch arrived home in Dallas, his wife was murdered. The BAU offered to send a team out to make sure the case is being handled properly, and to act as an advocate for Dutch. But for some reason I can't fathom, he requested Caitlin and me."

"I know you worked with the guy back in the day, but I'm surprised you'd use your leave to help solve his wife's murder. Especially after coming off back-to-back cases. The two of you must be very close."

"Not at all. But, he's FBI, and that means he's family." Spense pulled his shoulders back and stood a little taller in his boots, making Caitlin's chest swell with pride.

They might have a few bumps awaiting them on the road ahead, but one thing was certain, she could never regret throwing her lot in with a man like Spense. Their eyes met, and he put his hand on his heart. She did the same. From here on out, it seemed, they were in this together.

Acknowledgments

LENA, LEIGH, TESSA, Courtney, and Brenna, if I had just one of you in my life to advise and support me I would count myself blessed. To have all of you is a flat-out miracle—for which I am thankful every day.

Bill, Shannon, Erik, and Sarah. I know you make many sacrifices while I am writing, but you are my world.

Many thanks to my awesome beta reader, Carmen Pacheco, for her eagle eye and uplifting enthusiasm. Thank you to the FBI office of public affairs and the crime-scene writers' loop for technical advice.

Thank you to the wonderful women at K and T who share their wisdom and encourage me relentlessly: Lena, Rachel, Diana, Gwen, Manda, Sharon, Sarah, and Krista. I love you guys!

And finally, thank you to my fabulous editor, Chelsey Emmelhainz, who is not only both astute and kind, she makes me a better writer.

Want more Cassidy & Spenser?

Don't miss Carey Baldwin's heart-pounding thriller

JUDGMENT

Available now wherever ebooks are sold.

An Excerpt From
JUDGMENT

TODAY WAS CAITLIN Cassidy's eighteenth birthday, and in twenty-seven minutes, Thomas Cassidy was to be put to death by lethal injection for the murder of Gail Falconer: a crime so brutal, so sadistic only a monster could've committed it. Unable to bear the ticking off of the remaining seconds of her father's life, Caitlin squeezed her eyes shut, willing the merciless clock on the wall of the death-chamber viewing room to stop. Inside her chest, her heart slackened into a useless, gelatinous blob, its beat barely perceptible. With such an anemic pulse, she had no idea how oxygen still flowed to her brain. Yet vague as her heartbeat was, her thoughts were sharp and rapid-firing around a closed circuit.

Is he afraid?

He couldn't have done it!

Is he afraid?

A one-way mirror served as a window into the death chamber—

a stark white room, well prepared and patiently waiting for the prisoner. An intercom transmitted sound into the viewing area. From her front-row-center seat, she'd be able to see and hear all that transpired as her father's sentence was carried out. Gail's parents, she'd been told, would be watching from a separate location. Their daughter had been left naked and beaten, her body posed for the world in the most humiliating fashion. They would not be required to sit alongside Thomas Cassidy's daughter.

The room suddenly colder, she shivered.

He couldn't have done it.

When she was a little girl, her father would get low on one knee, allowing her to climb up his back and sit on his shoulders. Now she drew the memory around her like a warm cloak, and as the scent of his starched collar came back to her, she regained a temporary sense of well-being. Her body tilted forward, and she recalled bouncing rhythmically atop her perch while her father trotted her around the room faster and faster. She'd sway and squeal—delighted, but also queasy with fear. Then, sensing her terror, her father would grip her hands firmly.

I won't let you fall, Caity. Just hold on tight and trust me.

His low voice had soothed her. His word had been all she needed back then.

When her father had spoken, she'd believed him.

Absolutely.

But who was she to trust now?

Her eyelids flew open, and she saw that not quite a minute had passed. The sight of the long, padded table that awaited her father inside the chamber made her stomach roll and her teeth chatter. Clamping her jaw shut, she turned away from the terrible sight and found herself looking straight into the muted brown eyes of Mr. Harvey Baumgartner. Her father's attorney crumpled into the seat next to her and produced a wan smile. She hadn't seen him enter the room, and even if she had, she wouldn't have known how long he'd stood beside her with that pitying look on his face— time was too scrambled up in her mind. The clock on the wall was her only orienting anchor, and her eyes were both drawn to it and repelled by it. She kept her gaze on Baumgartner, refusing to look at that damn clock again.

Tick. Tick. Tick.

Her hands rose to cover her ears, but she quickly regained control and smoothed back her long, heavy hair instead.

"Caitlin, dear . . ." Baumgartner's voice was tighter and higher than usual. As his hand cruised up and down the length of his silk tie, light reflected off his fingernails, which had been buffed and coated in clear polish. His distress had apparently not affected his commitment to personal grooming. All of the Baumgartners liked to put on a good appearance, and Harvey was no exception. "I want you to understand I did all I could."

I know. She wanted to answer, to offer him the comfort he seemed to be seeking, but the words stuck in her throat. She didn't know. Not really. Oh, sure, he'd tried hard to get her father acquitted, but who knew if a more experienced attorney could've succeeded where he'd failed. Maybe a different lawyer could've gotten her father's coerced confession thrown out of court.

But Baumgartner and his firm weren't the only ones who'd failed her father. Maybe *she* could've done more. Both she and her mother had stood by her father, believed in him and loved him, but they'd left the matter of his defense to his legal team. A mistake she'd regret for the rest of her days. She should've *done* something. She should've *made* them see the truth—that her father didn't do it. He simply couldn't have.

"There's not going to be a reprieve, Caitlin, you know that, right?" Baumgartner's hand stopped cruising his tie and went to his sleek, coffee-colored hair.

The last-chance hearing had already been held, and clemency had been denied. Baumgartner had explained it to her twice already, but apparently he feared she was still praying for a last-minute miracle.

And he was right.

She nodded. Then her fists clenched, and pain cut through her, so sharp and real it seemed as though the shards of hope she clasped had suddenly been crushed into bits of broken glass.

There's not going to be a reprieve.

The days of holding executions in the dead of night to allow for last-minute maneuvering by the defense were gone. Arizona was one of a handful of states that had decided it wasn't practical for executions to be held at midnight. No phone was going to ring. No messenger was going to come crashing through the doors mere seconds before the clock struck the hour. That kind of thing only happened in the movies, and this wasn't a movie. This was real life.

Real death.

She should've *done* something to save her father, and now it was too late. Her hands twisted together in her lap. She'd never felt this helpless in her life. All she could do for her father now was to be present here today. Her mother, however, had chosen not to attend the execution. She'd begged Caitlin to stay home, too. *A child shouldn't have to watch her parent die,* she'd said.

But if death had come to her father while he lay in a hospital bed, wouldn't they both have been by his side?

Now Baumgartner leaned in close enough for his tobacco-stained breath to settle humidly on her cheek. "It's not too late for you to leave, dear. I'll take you home right now if you like."

Again, words failed her. Her throat clogged, and the desperate sob she refused to let out quaked down her body, rattling her knees and legs. Sucking in deep breaths, she jerked a glance around the room. It was a small space numbed by flat vanilla walls, rows of tan chairs, and gray floor tiles. It was a room purposely stripped of any sign of humanity, deliberately designed to quell emotion.

More people straggled in, claiming seats in the back row. One of the men was tall, with highlighted hair and eyes so blue she thought they must've been enhanced by tinted contacts. She recognized him as a local news anchor, but the others . . . she didn't know.

"The state requires a certain number of witnesses, and these were drawn from a pool of volunteers," Baumgartner whispered, seeming to read her mind.

Volunteers!

"Don't look at me like that, honey. The witnesses are here to make sure proper care is taken and that . . . this matter . . . is handled as humanely as possible."

Her mind tried to process that information. People who were in no way connected to the case had volunteered to come here today and watch her father be put to death. As yet another wave of nausea rolled through her, she heard the thunder of footsteps in the hallway and the sound of a door scraping open nearby. Its earlier vagueness obliterated, her heartbeat took up the ferocious rhythm of a fighter ready for battle. If her opponent were a man, she would punch him in the face—but her enemy was no mere mortal.

Injustice could not be defeated with a fist.

Through the mirror, she watched two men dressed in white medical garb enter the death chamber. Then, escorted by several prison guards, her father was led inside, his steps slowed by the short chain between his ankles. A thick belt cinched the waist of his baggy prison uniform, and his cuffed hands attached to it. But his chin was high, and his gaze active, as if he were looking to take in every last sight, no matter how ordinary—or maybe he was just showing her he would not be cowed. His face had thinned, and his hair had changed color—it was gray now, not blond, but he was still her father. Prison had not changed his essence. Thanks to the intercom, she heard his chains clanking, and like a clapped bell, her bones began to ring with fear. She wasn't as brave as he. Then a voice in her head shouted:

Do something!

She shot to her feet and took a step toward the window. Just as quickly, a guard who'd been leaning against the wall moved toward her, and Baumgartner threw a restraining arm across her quivering chest. Though she knew her father couldn't see her, she lifted her chin, not bothering to wipe away the tears that streamed down her cheeks. Her father's chin rose, too, and somehow, despite the one-way glass, their eyes met . . . and held.

The quivering in her body subsided.

Her father's low, soothing voice replaced the screaming in her head.

Hold on tight, Caity.

Trust me.

About the Author

CAREY BALDWIN IS a mild-mannered doctor by day and an award-winning author of edgy suspense by night. She holds two doctoral degrees, one in medicine and one in psychology. She loves reading and writing stories that keep you off-balance and on the edge of your seat. Carey lives in the Southwestern United States with her amazing family. In her spare time she enjoys hiking and chasing wildflowers. Carey loves to hear from readers so please visit her at www.CareyBaldwin.com, on Facebook https://www.facebook.com/CareyBaldwinAuthor, or Twitter https://twitter.com/CareyBaldwin.

Discover great authors, exclusive offers, and more at hc.com.